THE PRICE OF FREEDOM

C.F. FAIRTHORNE

the
PRICE
of
FREEDOM

Matador
9 Priory Business Park,
Wistow Road, Kibworth Beauchamp,
Leicestershire. LE8 0RX
Tel: 0116 279 2299
Email: books@troubador.co.uk
Web: www.troubador.co.uk/matador
Twitter: @matadorbooks

ISBN 978 1800465 442

British Library Cataloguing in Publication Data.
A catalogue record for this book is available from the British Library.

Printed and bound by CPI Group (UK) Ltd, Croydon, CR0 4YY
Typeset in 11pt Adobe Jenson Pro by Troubador Publishing Ltd, Leicester, UK

Matador is an imprint of Troubador Publishing Ltd

Dedicated to our daughter Joe.

If it had not been for her belief and encouragement, this novel would still be languishing on floppy disk.

ONE

JOSEPH WATCHED AS THE COAST OF FRANCE WAS slowly devoured by the murk of the sea mist. He strained his eyes as the last distant shadow that had been Calais was taken from his view. France was gone, Belgium was gone, but most important of all, Germany was gone. All of it now left behind them, swallowed by the mist. If only that same mist could swallow the nightmare of the last two years. Erase it from his mind as it had the coast from his eyes. But it could not. The horror of it all would torment him forever. Especially the memory of that night. He had told himself a thousand times that there was nothing he could have done. But still the guilt of inadequacy rested heavy on his shoulders. He had done what they had wanted him to do; he had got her out. But what of them? What hell were they living now? That is, if they were still living. There was no doubt in his mind that his dear brother was dead, beaten to death by the Nazi soldiers. He had seen it. But had the rest of them survived? His mind toiled yet again with the agony of his memories. It was the coldness of the morning that eventually encroached on the privacy of his

1

thoughts and made him think of the child. He squeezed the small hand that was nestled in his. There were just the three of them now. They had nothing but each other and their freedom, but it was enough. He looked down into the large brown eyes of his niece and smiled. She had not spoken since they had boarded the boat. It was as if somehow in her young mind she understood the significance of what was happening and with the obedience of a child had not questioned it. She had asked about her parents and brother and sister; every day she had asked. But not today.

'She will be cold,' he said, turning to his wife.

Elizabeth looked down at the child and then at him. It was some moments before she spoke.

'We will never go back, Joseph, will we?' she said softly.

'What is there to go back to?' he asked. 'We have no life there now, we have lost our family, the business, everything.' He put his arm around her and the three of them began to walk from the deck.

'No, we have no life there now.'

*

The ship was crowded but inside they managed to find two seats together and they sat. Elizabeth held the child on her lap, he held their one small case on his. Joseph reached inside his jacket pocket. They were still there, still safe, the precious papers that were to take them to their new life. It had taken nearly four months for the three of them to travel from Berlin to Calais. Moving from contact to contact, from house to house, always living with the fear of being discovered and returned to Germany. They had travelled on foot most of the way, cutting pieces of cardboard to fill the holes in their shoes, eating when they could and enduring the harshness of winter in Northern Europe. Eventually, they had crossed the border into France at a point just south of Strasbourg and then used the last of their money to travel by train from Metz to Lille. After spending the last two weeks waiting in Lille, it had finally happened: their new papers had arrived.

He was now Joseph Valsac, a German-speaking Swiss businessman travelling with his wife and daughter to England. He knew he would never be able to thank all the faceless men and women working throughout Europe to help the Jewish refugees, but he thanked God for them.

After Berlin, he had thought he would never trust anyone again. How could he? He had been betrayed by a man that he had loved as a brother. But others had helped them. One man had stolen trust from him, but others had restored it. As he took his hand from his pocket, he felt the cold metal of the pistol that had been his friend for so long and he told himself, *One day he would reap his revenge... their revenge.*

TWO

Herr Mannerheim brought his beloved Mercedes to a halt outside the Clinic de St Michel. The journey from Berlin to Mons in Belgium had been a long one and he was tired.

'Sit here and wait,' he told the small boy who had shared the journey with him. 'I won't be long,' he smiled as the child slid into the driver's seat and started to play with the steering wheel. 'Don't touch the brake!' he shouted back at him as he quickly climbed the steps that led to the large white double doors, which were the entrance to the clinic. Inside, the smell of disinfectant and medicants hung heavy in the air.

'Herr Mannerheim, I am so pleased to meet you.' The tall, thin redheaded man thrust out a hand in welcome. 'I'm Dr Meile, we spoke on the telephone, please take a seat.' The doctor waved his hand in the general direction of the chair across from his desk. 'Of course, I cannot be sure that she is the woman you are looking for, but the description fits.' Mannerheim took the cigarette offered and sat down on the rather hard straight-backed chair.

4

'How long has she been with you, doctor?' he asked, the urgency in his voice obvious.

'Since the spring of '45, she was brought to us by the US military, along with several others including a young woman called Rebecca Goshel.' The doctor removed his gold-rimmed glasses and sat back in his chair. 'It's rather an amazing story really; it would appear, from what Rebecca has told us, that this woman was arrested sometime in the winter of 1938. She was separated from her husband almost immediately; apparently there was some trouble when they were arrested. God knows what happened to him. But she did manage to keep her children with her.'

Mannerheim watched as the doctor pulled a handkerchief from his pocket and slowly started to polish his glasses. 'It would appear that her good looks were the main thing that helped her survive. She was sent to a transit camp just outside Heidelberg where she quickly became a favourite of the camp commandant.' The doctor leant forward in his chair. 'I am afraid, Herr Mannerheim, this man was not the best humanity had to offer. Apparently, he had several sexual perversions, and the woman was forced to suffer the indignity of these. But she was determined she and her children would survive, so she did what she had to. For his part he kept her at the camp for nearly three years and allowed the children to stay with her. But believe me, she paid the price.' The doctor frowned, 'I tell you this, Herr Mannerheim, only so you will realise what this woman has been through. In 1942 the man was posted to another camp and that was nearly the end of her and the children. She was put on a train to one of the extermination camps along with her children but yet again fate took a hand in her life. The officer in charge of the train recognised her

5

from a previous, shall we say, "meeting" he had enjoyed at the transit camp. She managed to persuade him to get her and her children off the train at another transit camp near Stuttgart. It would seem that they stayed there for almost two years; God knows how she managed it, but she did.' Again, the doctor sat forward, this time he put his glasses down on the desk. 'She's one hell of a woman,' he said, a smile coming to his face. 'You have to admire her.' Mannerheim did not reply.

'It was in this camp that she met Rebecca Goshel. The two women became firm friends with Rebecca often helping to provide for the children. Again, the women's good looks led to them working to survive. In 1944, however, their luck finally ran out; both women and the children were sent to Dachau. There it was to be their end but incredibly, yet again, luck was with them. Rebecca knew a sergeant who was stationed there. It seemed that they were at school together and had been good friends. But for him, we would not be sitting here today having this conversation. He had them both sent to what they called the "relaxation hut", where both women then worked, keeping the enlisted men happy. The German soldier likes his women with some flesh on them, it would seem, so the extra food they got went to Mary's two children. Is this disturbing you, Herr Mannerheim?' The Belgium doctor was sparing him nothing; after all his own country had been under the grip of Nazi Germany. To him, Herr Mannerheim appeared to be a caring man, but he could not be sure.

'I said, is this disturbing you, Herr Mannerheim?'

Mannerheim's reply was curt, 'Doctor, there is little now that can disturb me.'

'Then I shall continue. Rebecca told us that, as the news of the Allied advance reached the camp, the Germans' work was increased. There was a sense of urgency, an urgency to murder as many as they could and destroy any evidence that the camps even existed. Mass graves were hurriedly dug, and people were marched into them in their hundreds. They would then machine-gun as many as they could and bulldoze in the earth; many were buried alive.' The doctor shook another cigarette from the packet of Camel that still carried the 'US ISSUE' tab and lit it with a Zippo lighter.

'The women could hear the Allied gunfire in the distance the afternoon they were marched to what was to be the last of the mass graves of Dachau. It was late in the day, almost evening on the 23rd April 1945, when they were ordered along with nearly 200 others to climb down into their own grave.' The doctor paused as Mannerheim looked up at him. 'Ironic, Herr Mannerheim, do you not think? After over six years of surviving oppression and depravity at the hands of the Nazis, she and her children were to die the day before Dachau was overrun by the Americans.'

The doctor did not wait for Mannerheim's reply. 'The two women tried desperately to shield the children from the hail of bullets as the guards opened fire. It was a brave but futile effort. Apparently, both children died almost instantly but by some miracle the women did not. The children's mother took a bullet to the face. It entered her right cheek, shattering her jawbone and removing four teeth before exiting just below her left eye.' The doctor stood up from his chair and walked around his desk, sitting himself on the edge of it close to Mannerheim.

'Rebecca was more seriously injured. A bullet hit her in the back, severing her spinal cord and piercing a lung before it lodged against her breastbone. All four of them lay for hours among the bodies; both women were still alive but only just, both children dead. The next day, the Allies overran the camp, the Germans having left in the night. It would appear that in their hurry to leave, this last grave was not filled in. The Americans found the two women still alive amongst the bodies the next day. Rebecca was barely alive; she was hanging on to life by a thread. The other woman, well, she was hanging on to the bodies of her dead children.'

The doctor turned to Mannerheim. 'It seems that the death of the children was just too much for her; with everything she had suffered, it was the final straw that pushed her over the edge. From that day, she has not uttered a word. Her mind has shut out everything. If Rebecca had died, no one would ever have known her story. But despite their friendship she never did know the woman's surname, so you see, Herr Mannerheim, we cannot be sure that she is the woman you are looking for.'

*

When Dr Meile opened the door to the small room, she was sitting on the floor, her knees pulled up in front of her. She rocked slowly backwards and forwards, but her eyes remained fixed on one spot on the wall. Mannerheim could clearly see the huge star-like scar that covered most of her right cheek; he had seen some sights in his search but the frailty of her shocked him. She was skeleton-like, with only in the barest covering of flesh. He looked at the doctor and the man must have read his thoughts.

'She can't eat much yet; it will take a long time.'

Mannerheim moved slowly towards her. She appeared oblivious to him. He did not stop until he stood beside her, then slowly, very slowly, he crouched down next to the woman and looked closely at her. As he did so she turned, and their eyes met. Dr Meile could not be certain but for a moment he thought he detected something in the woman's eyes, in her expression, showing that she may have recognised him.

'Well, Herr Mannerheim, do you know her? Is she the woman you are looking for?'

THREE

THE LOUD METALLIC TICK OF THE OLD SMITHS clock echoed around the room and was somehow amplified by the surrounding silence. Its hands indicated 5.30pm and the last of the day's light had long since slipped away taking with it whatever warmth the bleak November day had mustered. Glowing manfully on the far side of the room the small Belling electric fire was doing its best to hold back the cold chill of another winter's night, but Ruth was cold and she knew the others were too. She had contemplated asking him again but then decided against it. What was the point? He would only refuse. They all knew that no amount of argument would ever persuade Mr Stone to switch on the other bar of the fire. Hell would freeze over first. She closed the ledger and pushing it to the edge of her desk took thanks in the completion of her task. It was all done, all checked and corrected, she was confident. At the last count she had found a total of seventeen mistakes, nothing on a grand scale, all quite minor in fact, but mistakes just the same. They were all now clearly marked and corrected, and both the bought and sales ledgers carried evidence of her pencil workings in the margins. The clock had ticked slowly on, the hands now resting at a 5.45pm. Ruth slipped off her shoes and rubbed her feet together in the hope that the friction may generate a little welcome warmth. The manoeuvre could not be deemed a success.

Stone pulled his watch from his waistcoat pocket and let it swing back and forth on its gold chain for a few second before catching it between his fat fingers and prising open the case to reveal a finely decorated face. Stone was a man well into his fifties, overweight and full of self-importance. He was, however, fair, extremely loyal and, despite the few mistakes that he was now known to make, good at his job. The company held him in high regard and so they should as he had come to them as a boy apprentice and spent his entire working life slowly climbing the ladder of Brooks and Son until he held the coveted position of head of department, third floor! An accolade indeed as the third floor dealt primarily with the company's top customers. He had reached the pinnacle of his career.

'Miss Valsac,' Stone's voice broke the silence and Ruth was conscious of all heads turning in her direction, 'come here a moment will you please?'

Ruth's feet started a desperate search for the discarded shoes, chasing them around under the desk until both were securely back in place.

'Yes sir,' she replied and sliding out from the desk made her way to the front of the office. Ruth had not done too badly herself on the Brooks' ladder of promotion. At the age of twenty-seven she was the highest-ranking woman in the company. With the exception of Jennifer Dawson, of course, and well, she didn't count. Ruth was Stone's number two, his right-hand woman, so to speak, and everyone knew how heavily he relied on her these days, everyone on the third floor anyway.

'The Bingham accounts, Miss Valsac, are they finalised?' Stone took a handkerchief from his top pocket and wiped his forehead as he spoke. Ruth could not help but notice the beads of perspiration on the man's face and wondered how on earth anyone could sweat so in such a low temperature.

'Yes, Mr Stone,' she replied, 'everything is completed, and all my workings are detailed as you requested.' He looked relieved. This was a big new account, and it was important.

'Excellent, Ruth, I knew I could count on you.' Stone seldom used her first name; it was praise indeed! 'Now everything must go smoothly tomorrow; you know how important this account is to the company. Mr Brooks has arranged for a taxicab to pick us up at 9.30am prompt, so I would like you in work at, say, 8.45am just to do a final check with me. Oh, and make sure you are well presented for the day, my dear, you know what I mean.'

Well presented for the day. His words stuck in her head and irritated her, but by the time she had returned to her desk, he was forgiven. She knew how important this account was to him and, after all, he had called her by her Christian name! Anyway, he must be worried to sweat like that on such a cold evening.

The clock had finally dragged its tired hands to the vertical position of 6.00pm and the long ring of the bell in the hall signalled the end of another day. Joan, who for the last ten minutes had been sharpening her pencils, swept the shavings into the bin with her hand and got up from her desk almost before the clatter of the bell had left their ears. She would be the first to the cloakroom, the first to the door and probably the first to the bus stop. Ruth watched her as she hurried to get her coat. She liked Joan, she was honest and outspoken, a little older than the others and married with two sons. In less than thirty minutes she would be cooking their tea. Despite her rush to get home Joan was a good worker; she had spent the last ten years working with Stone in the various departments of Brooks and Son and many thought she should have been rewarded with the number two position. Joan to her credit did not agree; she was not a career woman and knew her limitations. She worked to help support her family; it was a means to an end and that was all. It would be wrong to say she did not enjoy her work, she did, she liked the people, well most of them anyway, and she found the majority of the work interesting. She was, however, quite happy for Ruth to take on the role of second-in-command and admired her for doing so. Joan took down her coat from one of the pegs just inside the main door and removed the gloves from the pocket. Ruth watched her as she prepared to meet the cold night. Joan was tall, Ruth estimated about five foot nine, slim with quite long fair hair and she was attractive. She looked younger than her thirty-six years.

'If you don't hurry up, Ruth, you will get locked in.' What Mary, the office junior, really meant as she swept past her was, 'For God's sake hurry up, Ruth, you know Stone won't let us out until we are all ready.'

Ruth smiled. 'You will just have to wait, Mary, and so will that young man of yours.'

'I don't know what you mean, Ruth,' Mary said grinning, her bright eyes unable to hide her excitement at the thought of the evening ahead, 'I'm sure I don't.'

Mary's new boyfriend had been on the scene some three weeks now and was, in her eyes, God's gift to women. She had driven them mad describing the mental torment she was enduring, for despite being a virtuous young thing, she was sorely tempted by the desires of the flesh. Everyone knew that in the end she would of course succumb, and Ruth was convinced that it would be sooner rather than later. Mary was one of life's romantics. She fell in and out of love with, what had become to the others, boring regularity. But she was really a sweet girl who wore her heart on her sleeve. Ruth often smiled at Mary's naivety and wondered how any woman could allow men to have such a controlling influence on their life!

'Are you ready, Ruth?' The voice belonged to Ann, another one of Brooks' long-standing employees and the last member of Stone's team.

'The rest will be waiting for us; you know how Joan likes to get away quick or she will miss her bus.' Ruth picked up her bag and the pair of them walked together to the door to put on their coats.

'It's foggy again,' Ruth said looking out of the window. 'The traffic will be bad.'

Mr Stone stood by the back door, the bunch of Chubb keys in his hand.

'All present and correct, ladies?'

He said the same thing every night, come rain or shine, and always they would reply, 'Yes, Mr Stone, good night, Mr Stone.' Tonight, was no exception.

'One day he'll say something different,' Mary mumbled.

'What was that, Miss Jacobs?' Stone asked in a tired voice.

'I said, weather's no different, Mr Stone. You mind how you go in this fog, sir.'

Outside, the night was cold and the fog appeared even denser in the darkness of the alley.

'What a bloody stupid way to carry on.' Mary's cockney accent reverberated through the yellow air as the back door slammed shut.

'Listen, Mary,' Ruth tried hard to sound annoyed, 'I've told you before, keep your voice down, you will get into trouble again if he hears you.'

'Well!' Mary replied, in an attempt to redeem herself. 'Why can't we all go out the front door like the managers? We're only going to bump into them when we turn into the main street and then we all say goodnight again; this way we have to say goodnight to the old sod twice! It's bloody silly; this is 1960, you know.'

Ruth's look was enough to convince Mary not to pursue the point, but she had to agree, it was an archaic way of doing things!

The alley ran along the rear of the offices between Savile Row and Regent Street and every night the employees of Brooks and Son, excluded from using the front door of the building, would have to tread its winding course. Tonight, they had to travel more than three-quarters of its length before the lights of Regent Street infiltrated the murk and allowed them the dimmest of illuminations. Their arrival at the end of the alley coincided as usual with Stone's as he turned the corner of Conduit Street.

'Good night, ladies,' he mumbled as he hurried by.

'Good night, Mr Stone,' was the chorus.

'There I told you, Ruth, it's bloody silly.' But Mary was gone, swallowed up in the fog, before Ruth could reply.

Ruth did not dislike the fog, it was not pleasant of course, but as with all extremes of the British weather it seemed to have the effect of uniting its fellow sufferers. It was the comradely atmosphere that she found pleasant, and the way people just got on with things. It amazed her how life would carry on, shrouded as it was in such a peasouper. It reminded her of children playing under a blanket with all the activity and hustle and bustle of life going on but shrouded from view. Somewhere in the distance a paper boy shouted. 'Evening Standard! Read all about it! Judge sums up on Lady Chatterley!' His voice came from out of the murk to her right, above the steady drone of the slowly moving buses. Ruth had already crossed Regent Street at the traffic lights and was well on her way to the bus stop. The street was busy with people trying to make their way home, many with scarfs wrapped around their mouths and collars turned up to protect them from the elements. Suddenly, the entrance to the Underground loomed up, opening like a crevasse in front of her with its large sign and steep stairway. People were rushing headlong into its dimly lit depths. Ruth had come further than she realised; she stopped amid the throng and was pushed several times as people tried but failed to avoid her. Eventually she made her way to the side of the pavement and looking around her could just make out the red glow of Jim's chestnut stand. She was on course again.

'Evenin', miss.' Jim's cheeky grin welcomed her as she appeared out of the fog. 'Stinker of a night, innit?' He offered her a bag of chestnuts with one hand the other already in the large pocket on the front of his apron where he kept the change.

'One of the worst this week, Jim.' Ruth took the small hot bag and gave him a threepenny piece. The smell was delicious. She took one out and, despite having to juggle it between her fingers to prevent it burning, she peeled it and put it into her mouth. 'We must stop meeting like this, Jim,' she laughed, throwing her head back and brushing the long dark hair away from her face.

'Orr, I dunno miss, I look forward to our dinner dates.' Jim was shaking the pan of chestnuts, but his eyes were firmly fixed on what he considered to be one of the best-looking women to frequent his mobile restaurant. He had enjoyed the brief encounters that had taken place since October, when he had set up his stand for the winter season. Three nights a week she would stop and buy a small portion of chestnuts and they would pass the time of day. She was slim, dark and had the most amazing eyes. What man wouldn't enjoy the chance to talk to such a woman?

'You mind 'ow you go tonight, miss,' Jim said with genuine concern, 'this fog is real thick, you mind them roads, I don't wanna lose one of me best customers.'

'I'll be careful, Jim, don't you worry.' Ruth smiled at him. It was one of those lovely warm smiles that she kept for those she really liked.

'Cor, you could melt stone, you could, miss,' Jim said, as she turned and walked away into the fog.

'I'll see you Thursday,' Ruth replied, looking back over her shoulder, but before Jim could answer she had disappeared into the fog.

'Room on top!' the conductor shouted as Ruth climbed on to the crowded bus. She followed his instructions and climbed the tight turning staircase, stumbling at the top as the bus lurched into movement. The air was thick with smoke and at first it appeared to her that all seats were taken. Slowly, she moved along the rows and had almost reached the front of the bus before she spotted an empty place. She squeezed onto the end of a seat next to a rather large man who was engrossed in his paper. He moved ever so slightly. As the bus trundled its way slowly through the evening traffic Ruth looked around her but recognised none of her fellow travellers. The combination of the fog and the reflection from the small bright lights inside the bus turned every window into a mirror, and Ruth soon became bored at the sight of her own face looking back at her. The temptation to peer at the paper over the shoulder of the man next to her became overwhelming.

'Do all your packaged products stand up to the eye appeal test?' She read the large print of the Jackson Glass advert first and then looked more carefully at the article next to it. 'MORE EAST GERMAN REFUGEES. 21,000 IN OCTOBER.'

The rest of the print was too small for her to read, so she gave up and closed her eyes.

*

The BOAC stewardess smiled politely.

'Are you all right sir? It shouldn't be too long now.'

That's what she had said twenty minutes ago when they had first started to circle the airfield and the strain was now beginning to show on her pretty young face. Friedrich returned the smile.

'It is your English weather as usual, I expect.'

'There is some fog, sir, but it's not too bad.' She turned to the middle-aged woman sitting next to him. 'Captain Whitelock is a very experienced pilot, madam, he flew Lancaster bombers in the war and is used to all kinds of weather. There's no need for concern.'

The woman had been nervous when she boarded the plane in Berlin; now she was petrified. Both her hands were firmly fixed to the arms of the seat and her knuckles showed white beneath the skin. Friedrich smiled at her but said nothing; he had already tried several times to reassure her but had now given up. He closed his eyes and let his mind wander. How ironic, he thought, that here he sat, confident in the knowledge that his life was safe in the hands of Captain Whitelock, the experienced ex-RAF bomber pilot. The man that had flown countless missions over Germany in the war, some probably had been over his own city of Berlin. It may well have been that Whitelock had flown in one or more of the notorious thousand bomber raids; he may even have flown to Berlin on the night of 15th November 1944. Friedrich stopped his thoughts there. No purpose was to be gained in letting them continue.

The voice of the captain crackled over the intercom. Friedrich could just make out the words, 'We shall be landing shortly.' The rest was lost to the steady rumble of the Britannia's engines as the pilot opened the throttles to correct the height. The majestic structure of Harrow School, shrouded in fog and steeped in tradition, slipped away silently beneath them as the captain started a turn that brought them in line with the Harrow gasometer. The aircraft began to shudder and then dropped violently as it passed through the cloud layer at 4,000 feet. Friedrich's stomach turned and the middle-aged woman grabbed his arm.

'I don't like flying,' she said in a frightened voice.

The large N painted in white on the side of the gasometer was the normal landmark that pilots used on their approach to Northolt Airport but tonight it was only the red lights fixed to its summit that could be seen from the fight deck. The rest of the structure was lost in the fog. The captain had been waiting for the lights, they were his marker and the Britannia passed over them at just under 3,000 feet leaving South Harrow Station away to its left. By the time the plane flew over South Ruislip and Victoria Road it was at a height of less than 1,500 feet and had entered the layer of ground fog. The buffeting had become intense but the beam from the outer marker of runway twenty-nine indicated that their course was true. The landing was heavy but welcome, the reverse pitch roar of the engines filling the cabin as people lurched forward against their seat belts. In seconds the aircraft speed had reduced to little more than a crawl. It took the pilot several minutes of skilful taxiing before the Britannia finally came to a halt in front of the arrivals building on the commercial side of the airfield. Through the window Friedrich could just make out the small single-storey buildings and the boiler house chimney, their silhouettes highlighted in the fog by the amber glow of floodlights. The noise from giant engines began to wane and throughout the cabin the click of seat belts could be heard as the passengers, anxious to disembark, started to leave their seats. The middle-aged woman had staged an amazing recovery. Having now decided that death was no longer imminent, she had rapidly come to terms with the fact that she had to again face life, and not wishing to do so poorly presented, was busily applying her lipstick.

'I'm sorry to have made such a silly fuss,' she said smiling at Friedrich. 'It's just that I hate flying, I know it's stupid but there you are.'

Friedrich undid his seat belt and stood up. 'I understand the fear of aircraft,' he replied as he lifted down a large bag from the luggage rack and handed it to her.

'Well yes I'm sure you do.' She thanked him and took the bag.

The small arrivals lounge was busy with people, most of whom were milling around in an effort to retrieve their luggage. Friedrich was happy to let Edward undertake that task for him and watched as he and a porter loaded his two cases onto a barrow.

'Have you had a pleasant flight, sir? I was worried about the fog.'

They followed the porter as he pushed open the large swing doors with the heavy metal barrow carving yet another groove into the wood.

'Not too bad thank you, Edward.'

'I've been running the engine now and again, sir, so she's nice and warm inside.'

Edward opened the rear door of the Bentley for him.

'And your case is on the seat, sir.'

Friedrich climbed in and sank back into the rich soft leather of the seat. The car was one of his favourites. He opened the leather briefcase that Edward had left there for him. It contained two files; the top one was yellow and had 'Mannerheim UK' printed on the cover. He removed it and laid it on the seat without further examination. The second file was blue; on its cover was printed the name 'Bingham Ltd'. This too was removed and from beneath it, Friedrich took the bottle of Royal Lochnagar Special Reserve. Another of his favourites. He opened the cocktail bar in the rear of the seat in front of him and, taking out a tumbler, poured a drink.

'It may take a little longer tonight, sir,' Edward said as he climbed into the driver's seat. 'The fog's really quite thick in London and the Western Avenue is bad.'

'Take your time, Edward,' Friedrich replied as he savoured the malt.

Edward was right: the journey did take longer. A lot longer. For most of it he was hard pushed to find the white lines and cat's eyes that marked the centre of the road. The Western Avenue was poorly lit, and it was not until they reached the White City Stadium and followed the road round into Shepherds Bush that things started to improve. It was a 7.15pm when the car finally turned off the Bayswater Road and came to a stop outside the Grange Hotel. The manager greeted him almost before he had managed to step clear of the heavy oak revolving doors.

'Mr Mannerheim, sir! How pleasant to have you back with us again. I have taken the liberty of reserving you a table in the restaurant for 9.00pm, I trust that is in order and I have made sure you are in Room 109.' The manager took the register from the receptionist. 'If you would just sign here, sir. Thank you.'

Room 109 had not changed since his last visit a month ago. It was as immaculate as ever. The heavy deep red velvet curtains had already been drawn and the bed turned down. There were other rooms in the hotel, of course there were, some twenty or so. But this was his room. He always booked it and he loved it. The walls were richly panelled in oak with several beautiful watercolours hung about it. The lighting was soft and a wonderful open fire, which had been well tended, sent a warming glow around the room. There was a large leather armchair by the fire and next to that a small oak table with a silver tray and four cut-glass tumblers. A decanter of malt sparkled in the fire's glow. The hotel epitomised everything he had come to love about England and its heritage. This room was his own little part of it.

*

Joseph was reading his book; it was good but not terrific. He had long since discarded his tie and collar both of which now lay on the small table beside him as did both collar studs and a half empty glass of stout. He was trying to relax but was not finding it easy. She was late and it bothered him. He had guessed that she would be, what with the weather being so bad, but he was worried. Elizabeth often told him that he worried too much and of course she was right. He just couldn't help it. It was the way he was.

It was 7.20pm when he finally heard the garden gate swing open. He had been meaning to oil its hinges for months. Quickly he put down the book and heaved himself up out of the chair. If he wasn't quick, she would be up the stairs and then he would have to chase after her.

'Ruth!' he shouted as he scurried along the passage to the front door. Shouting served little purpose really and he knew it; she would not hear him from there.

'Ruth!' he shouted again as he threw open the front door, 'I've been waiting for you! I want to talk to you.'

He had been in time; she was still returning the front door key to her purse and as yet had not made the stairs.

'Hello, Uncle,' she said kissing him on the cheek, 'what a filthy night.'

He did not bother to confirm the obvious. 'Ruth, you must eat with us tonight. Your aunt has been cooking all afternoon and the salt beef is wonderful. She says to tell you eight o'clock.'

Ruth could not help but smile at him as he stood there, a look of anticipation fixed firmly on his tired face. If not in name, in every other way, he had been a father to her, and she loved him. She knew that he had most probably been sitting waiting for her for ages. The fog would have worried him. He was just sixty years old, but Ruth had always thought he looked older than his years. Probably this could be attributed to his lack of hair, and what he had managed to keep of it being painfully white. He was also overweight and his trousers stretched around a liberal corporation and as usual were supported by braces and belt.

'Such an invitation, Uncle, how could I refuse?'

'Good! I shall tell your aunt.' He turned and started to make his way back into the flat. 'Eight o'clock. Don't be late,' he said closing the front door behind him. Again, she smiled.

The house was one of those large Victorian places that were so common in Hampstead. It had been rather grand in its time but many years since had been converted into flats by the landlord and now provided him with four separate sources of income, little of which had been reinvested in the property. Inside, the property was rather dismal and in places in the hall the wallpaper had peeled away in several large patches. It was cold and draughty in the winter and prone to damp but nevertheless it was home and Ruth loved it. The ground floor flat belonged to Ruth's uncle and aunt. It consisted of two small bedrooms, a kitchen, a living room, and a bathroom and toilet. It had been their home since 1940 and despite limited funds they kept it nice inside. It had been Ruth's home too up until three years ago when the man who lived in the attic flat decided that England had little left to offer and emigrated to Australia. She had pounced on it almost before the poor man and his cases had descended the stairs. The Isaac family had the first and second floor; there were five of them and they needed the three bedrooms. Old man Isaac and his wife shared the place with their son, his wife and daughter. It had been old man Isaac that had got Uncle the flat in the first place.

Mrs Widdowson occupied the basement; she had lived there longer than anybody and took great delight in making everybody aware of it. She, like Ruth and her family, had been born a German Jew. She had lived most of her younger life in Munich before marrying an Englishman and moving to London. Sadly, he had died quite young, and she had been devastated by his loss. She had never remarried. It had been her that had first taught Ruth English. Hours and hours they had sat together working on Ruth's pronunciation. She had been a good teacher and they had become great friends. Ruth's flat was small, but it was her castle in the air. She had to climb four flights of stairs to reach it but from her window you could look out over the rooftops and see all the way to Whitestone Pond. Uncle had been against her getting it, but she had stuck to her guns and with her Aunt Elizabeth's support had got her own way. It was more than a flat, it was her independence.

*

Ruth was on time and dinner was excellent. Her aunt fussed about her in her normal manner making sure everything was just so.

'Ruthy.' She always called her Ruthy; she spoke with a heavy accent. 'You want a little more bread or gravy, you just say.' For as long as Ruth could remember, Elizabeth had struggled with the English language. After more than twenty years of speaking it she had resigned herself to the fact that the virtues of English grammar were always going to elude her, so she no longer bothered with its refineries.

'If she wants a little more she will say so, that's the third time you have asked her!' Uncle snapped as he poured the last of the wine into Ruth's glass.

'That was delicious,' Ruth told her aunt as she sat back in her chair.

'Ruthy, now you tell me all about work, you tell me all about your day and how you run the office for that silly Mr Stone.'

A broad smile lit her aunt's face as she waited expectantly. It was her favourite pastime, listening to her niece's achievements, and talking about them. Ruth knew that whatever she told her tonight would be faithfully relayed tomorrow, over coffee, to Mrs Widdowson. Her career development had proven to be a constant source of enjoyment to both of them.

'Well,' Ruth lingered over the word to enhance the moment. The wine had relaxed her and if the truth was known she enjoyed telling as much as they enjoyed listening. Their attention was fixed. 'Mr Stone and I are going to a business meeting tomorrow. He wants me to be particularly well presented.' Ruth brushed back her hair and tugged at her blouse in a mocking gesture.

'Hm! What does he mean "particularly well presented"? You tell him you are always well presented!'

'Elizabeth, be quiet, Ruth is telling us!' Uncle was eager to hear more and her interruption irritated him.

'It's a very important meeting,' Ruth continued, 'Mr Brooks himself has booked a taxicab to take us to Bingham's.' Ruth sat back and waited for the news to take effect.

'Oh, my goodness!' Elizabeth exclaimed, 'See Joseph, see how important our Ruthy is?' But Joseph did not bother to reply; he had got up from the table and was in the act of pouring himself a small whisky from the bottle he kept in the Welsh dresser. He said nothing until his return.

'Why is this Bingham's so important, Ruth?' he asked, sitting himself back down.

'Well,' Ruth replied, again lingering, 'you know we have all been working on their accounts for weeks now? Well, we've finally finished them.'

'You see, Joseph? Our Ruthy, she has finally finished them!' Elizabeth just had to say it, she couldn't help it, she had to say it.

Ruth continued before Joseph could. 'It seems that Bingham's has been bought out lock, stock and barrel by a very large company and tomorrow we are to meet one of the directors for his approval of the accounts. It would appear that they have also asked Mr Stone to provide an independent appraisal of their financial position.' Elizabeth looked blank; this was just too much for her. All this high finance. She just hoped she could remember all the details to tell her friend.

'That's unusual, isn't it?' Joseph asked. 'First they buy the company, then they find out if it's making any money.' He scratched his head. 'Very strange.'

'Listen to him, Ruthy, here he goes, Mr High Finance.' The mischief sparkled in her eyes at the serving of his rebuke.

'Yes, it is unusual, Uncle, but it happens.' Ruth hoped her reply would be good enough for him, but it was not.

'Well, what company would do such a thing?' he asked. 'Who are they?'

'I've no idea, Uncle, they don't tell me things like that.'

That was a lie and Ruth knew it.

*

Dinner, as usual, had been a particularly enjoyable experience and only now, as he sat relaxing by the fire in the lounge, did Friedrich begin to feel the tiredness brought on by what had been a long day. The malt was excellent and as he savoured it his tired mind pondered over his liking of England and how events had first brought him to the country. Strange really, he thought, as a child he had hated the English. Well, everybody hated the English. It was the way of things; they were the enemy. The most vivid memory of his childhood days had been those spent in the war-torn streets of Berlin. They had played soldiers shooting the English Tommy while all around them the destruction had been unbelievable. The stench of death everywhere. And yet they played, children actually played. On those rat-infested death-strewn streets, they had played, he had played. And now, some fifteen or so years later, he was in London and not only that, he liked it. England, of all of Germany's enemies in the war, had been the most hostile, the most aggressive and yet now after its cessation it was the readiest to forgive. It would trade freely and without prejudice with most West German-based companies and spoke with one of the loudest voices to protect the rights of the West Berlin population, shunning Herr Ulbricht's demands. That was one of the reasons his father had first asked him to look for an English-based company. It was to be a toehold on acceptability in Europe. Business within the confines of West Germany was limited and the rest of Europe would feel easier trading with the respectable Bingham's. Anyway, his English was good. They had considered one of the Scandinavian countries, but language would have been a problem. So, it was England, and where else but London? He finished his drink, contemplated having another, decided it was not wise and went to his room.

*

The small boy sat gripping his mother's hand, a mop of tangled blond hair hanging untidily about his eyes. Large tears ran down his young face, carving clean rivers into the dirty cheeks. He was crying but he made no sound. Fear gripped him, an uncontrollable overpowering fear that seemed to lock him into a motionless pose. It was the same fear that was controlling most others around him as people sat in silence, huddled together. It was a pitiful mass of humanity that was enduring the ravages of war. They were starved of food, deprived of water, cold and humiliated. Their country had followed the ranting of a madman and now they were suffering the consequences. The scream of the bombs was coming ever closer as wave after wave of enemy bombers passed overhead in the unprotected Berlin sky. It was another thousand bomber raid. A baby cried; the mother, desperately trying to bring comfort to its young life, held it to her breast. An old man in the far corner of the shelter lit a cigarette and looked upwards as if his eyes could see through the three feet of concrete that was to protect them from the ever-nearing thunder of explosions. The boy's mother looked around her at the hundred or so people in the vain hope that she might see her husband, but she did not. She cuddled her daughter and pulled the boy closer to her.

'We will be all right,' she said brushing the hair from his face.

But almost before she had spoken her words the last of the shelter lights flickered and went out. They were in darkness, complete and utter darkness. An explosion and then another; people screamed as the high-pitched whine of the bomb grew louder and louder; he felt his mother push him to the floor as she fell on top of him. Where was his sister? He could remember his sister. Remember? His mind was in turmoil, was it present or past? Was this happening? Suddenly there was a light, a blinding light that carved away the blackness in an instant, leaving horrific images to linger in his mind. All around concrete fell, showering down in huge great lumps that bounced around them with terrifying crashes. The screaming went on and on in a horrific mayhem of noise. Then it was gone, as quickly as it had come, it had gone. Now there was just the darkness, the pain and, almost as terrible as the noise of destruction, there was silence. He lay still in the darkness; the weight of his mother's body pushed against him. He could feel the softness of her flesh, smell her perfume. There was the taste of blood in his mouth and the pain in his twisted leg was unlike any pain he had ever felt before. He struggled to move an arm and, in the darkness, pulled at his mother's dress.

'Mummy,' he whispered, 'Mummy.' She did not reply.

The eternity of entombment closed in on him. In the darkness he strained to free himself, he fought to breathe. His body was soaked with sweat. As young as he was, he knew life was leaving him. Then, quietly and in the darkness, he gave up, he resigned himself to his death. Then he heard the voices, the noise of moving masonry. He felt the hands around him pulling him. The light made his eyes sting as its fingers suddenly reached between the rocks.

'Don't let him see her,' he heard a voice say. But she was there, she was next to him. His mother was there; he could feel her, he could touch her, he could see her in the light. It was all right, she was all right.

'Mummy,' he cried, 'Mum.'

There was blood, lots of blood. But he could see her now, he could move his arms. Then her face, he could see her face and the young eyes stretched wide with horror at the mutilation.

Friedrich sat up in bed, his eyes wide open, his body drenched in sweat. He was instantly awake; the nightmare had returned again, as it had so often done. It would not leave him, it would go for a while, only to return, to return as vivid and as horrid as it had ever been. Even now, although he was awake, he could taste blood, her blood. He got out of bed, lit a cigarette and pulled back the curtain. It was 2.10am. The light from the streetlamp reached out through the fog and spread a yellow glow across the room. He stood in the shadow of the curtain as he stared out into the murk; he cursed the night for returning his nightmare.

*

Less than fifteen miles away in Ealing, two other men cursed the night. They cursed as they tried desperately to make their way through the fog to number 67 Elimont Avenue. But the headlights of the ambulance were no match for the fog and by the time they arrived at the small semi-detached house, the middle-aged man was dead. He lay in the hall cradled in the arms of his wife. It was the untimely death of a man as yet still young to meet his maker. Well short of his three score and ten. But it was a death that would shape the destiny of two people. Two people from different worlds and different cultures.

FOUR

THE MEETING

IN ALL OF HIS LIFE ERNEST BROOKS HAD NEVER BEEN in work at such an ungodly hour. He looked at his watch again. He had already looked at it a dozen times; it was 8.20am. He peered up and down the street in a vain attempt to spot her among the early morning commuters. He was out of luck. She would be there soon, that was a fact, but he was finding the waiting intolerable. He was growing more agitated by the minute; he had made up his mind that if she had not arrived by 8.30am he would make his displeasure painfully obvious to her. Deciding it was rather undignified for a man in his position to be seen loitering in such a manner on his own front steps, he went inside to watch from the front office window.

As a girl she had always enjoyed swinging from the plastic-clad centre bar that bisected the platform of the Routemaster buses. She had been scolded for it several times in her youth, but the enjoyment had followed her into adulthood. Today, however, she resisted the temptation and remained standing well inside the bus. It would not do for her to arrive at work in a windswept condition. After all, today she had to be particularly well presented. Ruth waited until the bus had come to a complete stop before stepping off to join the throng of pedestrians. She was early and there was no need to rush. It was going to be a day to enjoy, a different day, an important day. She could not help but be excited by the thought of her first ever business meeting. Mr Stone would be in charge of course but he would need her help. If they asked questions on the figures, he would turn to her and that made her feel important. Ruth had some trouble trying to cross Regent Street; last night's fog had cleared, and it appeared every driver was trying today to make up for yesterday's slow going, but eventually she reached the corner of Conduit Street safely.

The realisation that all was not normal hit her when she was just a few steps along Conduit Street. The front door of the office was open. A sudden panic seized her as for a moment she thought that she may be late. She checked her watch; it was only 8.25am. The front door was never opened until 9.00am on the dot. It puzzled her. When the gaunt figure of Mr Brooks appeared in the doorway waving frantically at her, the puzzlement turned to sheer astonishment, which prompted her to wave back. As Brooks continued to wave his arms about like a man floundering at sea, she realised that this was no mere gesture of welcome and so quickened her step. She regretted waving.

'Good morning, sir,' Ruth said, somewhat out of breath from the exertion over the last thirty or so yards.

'Come in, girl, come in!'

Brooks ushered Ruth through the door without acknowledging her greeting. It was the first time in all her eleven years with the firm that she had ever entered through the front door. The day had started well and she smiled to herself. Brooks was halfway up the stairs before he spoke again, and his tone was brisk.

'Come along, Miss Valsac, come along, my office, straight away.'

She thought today would be different, but she had never expected it to start like this. Brooks did not speak again until they were in his office on the fourth floor. He shut the door behind them and made his way to his desk; sitting down behind it, he waved his hand in the general direction of one of the chairs facing him across the vast expanse of oak and leather desktop.

'Thank goodness you're early, Miss Valsac, very commendable.'

Ruth smiled. She had not often had the opportunity to talk to him; in fact she had seldom ever seen him. They all knew he existed all right, but normally an encounter with Mr Brooks would only occur every Christmas.

'Miss Valsac, I have some, err…' he hesitated for a moment and she noticed for the first time that the man was really in quite a state. He was sweating and his face was as white as any she had ever seen.

'Miss Valsac,' he began again, 'I'm afraid I have some rather bad news for you. I received a telephone call very early this morning from Mrs Stone. It would appear that poor Mr Stone suffered a heart attack last night and by the time the ambulance managed to fight its way through the fog, well, err, I'm afraid he was dead.'

Ruth was still smiling when the impact of the word 'dead' struck home. The cold shock of it numbed her brain and removed her smile.

She felt the handbag slip from her lap but was only able to make a half-hearted attempt at catching it before it met the floor with a thud, its contents spilling out onto the polished woodblock flooring.

'I'm sorry, sir,' she heard herself say, 'there must be some mistake, I mean, Mr Stone…' She did not finish the sentence but looked down at her lipstick as it rolled beneath Brooks' desk.

'I'm afraid there is no mistake, Miss Valsac.'

Ruth, gripped by a compulsion to retrieve her bag and its contents, dropped to her knees without waiting for him to continue. She found the lipstick first. It was as if the rational side of her mind had taken control, going about things as if they were the norm while the part of her mind that dealt with emotion struggled in turmoil in a secluded corner of her head. She was really quite amazed when a tear splashed off the back of her hand and she realised it was hers. Brooks knelt down beside her and picked up the bag; he also gave her his handkerchief.

'Come along now, get these things together, we have a crisis on our hands.' His words were now clipped by an air of authority.

Ruth could only stare at him in bewilderment and had to dig deep within herself before she could manage a response.

'A crisis?' she replied feebly.

'Yes, the meeting, we must decide what we are going to do about the meeting.'

'Meeting?'

'For goodness' sake, stop repeating everything I say, pull yourself together, Miss Valsac. The Bingham meeting, it's today. Can you handle it?'

'The Bingham meet…' she stopped herself from yet another repeat.

Brooks was looking at her expectantly, his cold grey eyes fixed wide with anticipation. The meeting, of course. What did he say? Could she handle it?

The realisation of what he was asking swept like a new broom through her emotions pushing before it the numbness of grief and shock and replacing those with inadequacy and self-doubt. Her mentor was gone, could she now pick up his banner?

'Well, Miss Valsac?' Brooks sounded agitated.

'Yes, sir, I can handle it, I've done all the figures, I've checked all the work, I know the job inside out.' The words just seemed to spill out of her before she could stop them.

'Good!' He sounded more relaxed. 'This meeting is very important, Miss Valsac, Bingham's could be a big account especially now they have been purchased by Mannerheim International. They will be our first European customer and a very wealthy one. Make it work, Miss Valsac, do whatever you have to do but make it work.'

'I will, sir, don't worry I am sure I can.'

Ruth wiped her eyes again and blew her nose.

'I'm sorry, I didn't mean to cry, sir, it was a shock that's all, poor Mr Stone.'

She straightened her skirt and brushed her jacket down with her hand.

'Yes, it was a shock to us all.' He walked back around his desk and sat back down in the large leather chair. 'And it couldn't have happened at a worse time for the company.'

For a moment Ruth questioned that she had heard him correctly but when she realised that she had, she felt contempt for the man's attitude and anger at his obvious lack of emotion. She had to struggle hard to contain her temper. *I bet Mrs Stone wasn't too happy about it either*, she thought to herself. All the years he had given the company and he threw it all away by not bothering to die at a convenient time! Brooks didn't give a damn about Stone; all he was really worried about was the Bingham's meeting and Mannerheim International.

'I will of course make you acting head of department, Miss Valsac, with immediate effect. I can't of course say whether or not the board will make it a permanent position, that may well depend on the outcome of your meeting.' He forced a smile. 'It's an ill wind, Miss Valsac.'

Ruth would have dearly loved to tell him what to do with his acting head of department. But she did not. She did not like herself for it, but she had to admit the opportunity excited her. The thought of Stone, as yet probably not even at the Pearly Gates, did temper the excitement with the feeling of guilt, but somebody had to do the job.

'Yes, we can't have young Mannerheim thinking he's dealing with anyone lower than a head of department.'

Brooks' comment brought her down to earth again. It was all calculated, of course, all for the good of the company, but if she made it work, if she did a good job, they would have to consider her as Stone's permanent replacement. They would have no other option.

'There's just one thing, Miss Valsac.' Brooks leant forward in his chair and rested his elbows on his desk. 'This company, Mannerheim International, you have no problem working with them, do you?'

Ruth knew straight away what Brooks was hinting at but chose not to make things easy for him. It was a chance for her, in her own way, to seek some recompense for the man's remarks about Stone's untimely death.

'Problem, sir? Why should I have a problem?'

Brooks looked awkward.

'Well, I realise it might not be easy for you.'

'Why's that, sir?' She was enjoying it.

'Well, you know, Miss Valsac, err, with your religion.'

'Oh, you mean because I'm Jewish, sir? Well, it doesn't worry me if it doesn't worry them.' She stood up to leave. 'I must get the office organised if I'm to be away all day, sir, and I will need to break the news of poor Mr Stone to the others. Shall I report back to you today, sir, or if I'm late will tomorrow do?'

*

Ruth's mind was in turmoil as she hurried down the stairs from the fourth floor. There was so much to do, and she had to do it! There was no time now to ponder on Stone's demise, she just had to get on with things. There was the office to get sorted and she had to tell the others about Stone. She looked at her watch. It was not quite 9.00am, they would be arriving soon. She would have to be firm, take control from the very start. She was no longer the number two; she was in charge now and knew that all eyes would be on her. There were those that would love her to make a mess of it, especially Robert Brooks. He wouldn't be happy about her new position.

The office was cold; it was always cold in winter. For as long as she could remember the outdated heating system had struggled come November. The Belling would be needed as usual. Stone's Dickensian attitude about the heating had always irritated her. She made her way between the empty desks and crouched down in front of the fire. The two small silver toggle switches shone out at her from the front of the heater, one for each bar of the fire. She hesitated for a moment before making her first management decision, then reached out and turned on both switches. Slowly, the elements began to glow, dimly at first but then brighter; she began to feel the warmth on her legs as she enjoyed the moment. It was her first move forward; she was going to do things her way now. No more cold feet! Suddenly there was a pop and she jumped back; smoke rose from the plug and the fire's glow died. It was as if Stone had taken a hand in things, even from the beyond. Now there would be no heat. The door of the office opened and Ann walked in. She looked across at Ruth standing staring at the fire.

'Good morning, Ruth, where's Stone?'

*

The taxi came to a halt outside the main entrance of the large whitewashed buildings that was Bingham's. Ruth gathered up her briefcase and the files that she had brought with her.

'That'll be nine shillings and sixpence please, miss,' the driver said as he reached out of his window and turned around the 'For Hire' sign. Her Jewish nature made her, if only to herself, question the value. That was a lot of money for a twenty-minute ride, but she had not the time nor the inclination to argue the point. She gave him a ten-shilling note and without waiting for the change hurried up the steps into the building. Once inside Ruth stopped for a moment to get her bearings. It was a large entrance hall with great slabs of polished marble forming the floor and a high painted ceiling that supported a massive chandelier. In front of her at the far end of the hall was the reception counter behind which a woman busied herself with some papers. Ruth felt her stomach churn. She had not felt this nervous since she had sat her exams. She took a deep breath.

'Can I help you, miss?' the woman behind the counter asked as Ruth approached. She seemed a nice lady and had a pleasant smile.

'I have an appointment to see Mr Mannerheim. My name is Valsac, Ruth Valsac, from Brooks and Son.'

She had spoken slowly and with as much authority as she could muster, anxious that her nervousness should not show in her voice. The woman looked down at a large red appointment book that lay already open in front of her; she turned the page and ran her finger down the list of entries.

'Oh yes, Miss Valsac, it's you and a Mr Stone, is that correct?'

Ruth was taken aback for a second; she knew she would have to bluff round Stone not being there but had not expected it to begin so soon.

'Mr Stone is unable to attend I'm afraid, it's just myself.'

It had been easy. The woman had not questioned her, she just smiled and directed her to the lift. Ruth's confidence began to grow.

Herr Mannerheim's office was on the third floor and Ruth, after taking the lift, did as instructed and made her way along the corridor until she reached the large double doors at the end. She stopped for a moment and putting down the box files and briefcase brushed down her skirt and straightened her jacket.

'Well, Ruth, here we go.' The words rang in her head as if spoken by another. She was at the edge of the precipice and had to jump. She knew only too well how much depended on her; she wanted to succeed, she wanted to be head of department, this was her chance. She swallowed hard, knocked twice, picked up her things, opened the door and walked in. The tranquillity of the room in which she found herself was a surprise to her: far from being a hive of commerce with people rushing hither and dither as she had expected, there was just one person in occupancy. She was a woman in her thirties, and she was sitting at a large desk positioned in front of the window at the far end of the room. She had been typing when Ruth came in but now sat looking at her, waiting for some communication, the Olivetti typewriter dormant in front of her.

'Good morning,' Ruth's voice echoed around the quiet room, 'Miss Valsac to see Herr Mannerheim.'

Her words seemed to have the desired effect and, as if in a bad play where actors dwell waiting for their cue, the woman suddenly spoke her lines.

'Mr Stone, it's you and Mr Stone from Brooks and Sons isn't it? 10.15am appointment, Herr Mannerheim is expecting you.'

The woman had made no attempt to return Ruth's greeting and her manner was frosty. She gazed past Ruth as if waiting for Stone to appear at the door.

'Mr Stone is unable to attend today, I'm afraid it is just myself.'

Ruth's reply seemed to throw the woman for a moment, she was obviously not used to coping with the unexpected.

'I'll tell Herr Mannerheim you are here then. Are you sure Mr Stone is not coming?'

'Unlikely,' Ruth replied.

The woman got up from the desk and made her way across the office towards the double doors that Ruth assumed led into Herr Mannerheim's office.

'Please take a seat, Miss Valsac, I am sure Herr Mannerheim will see you shortly.' She disappeared through the doors.

Ruth hoped that the woman would not be long. Dealing with her nervousness was difficult enough; the waiting would only add to the ordeal. She looked around the room in a vain attempt to occupy her mind. It was large room with little or no character. Apart from some framed certificates behind the woman's desk, the walls were bare. At one time they may well have been painted a brighter colour, but it had long since faded to a grimy cream. There was one redeeming feature, however, and that was a rather nice tiled fireplace with a bright brass fender. It was obviously never used, as a pot plant was living in the empty grate.

'Herr Mannerheim will see you now, miss.' The slightest trace of a smile appeared at her lips as she beckoned Ruth towards the door. She gathered her files and stood up. The sight of the large door standing open in front of her almost produced panic but somehow, she managed to contain it. The temptation to turn and run was almost overwhelming. But she did not. She smiled at the woman and walked through into the room.

The contrast between the two rooms was drastic and took Ruth by surprise. If the secretary's office was plain then this room was positively palatial, and she had to work hard to keep her concentration from wandering as her eyes surveyed the room's magnificence. There was no grimy-cream paint to be seen here. Instead, the walls were oak-panelled with several oil paintings hung about them, each illuminated by a small brass wall lamp. To her left there was a huge oak glass-fronted cabinet, the shelves of which were heavy with silver cups and shields and to her right a large immaculately polished table set with twelve chairs and obviously used for important meetings. Amid the opulence of the room sat a fair-haired man, his head bent over his desk, his hand moving quickly over the open page in front of him. He was engrossed in his writing and seemed oblivious to her presence.

So quiet was the room that Ruth could clearly hear the scratch of nib on paper as she moved tentatively forward. She stopped just a few feet from him and waited. He continued to write. She realised that he was aware of her presence and was confident that in a few seconds he would put down the pen and greet her. He did not. She stood silently shifting her weight from one foot to another as her arms began to ache under the weight of the files and her briefcase. His arrogance and bad manners began to irritate her and she could not help but feel intimidated; he was making her wait as a schoolgirl waits outside the headmistress's door. She was unable to see his face properly, looking down as he was, but he was younger than she had expected and that made the intimidation all the harder to take. Realising that she could not allow this to continue or her destruction would be complete before she had even begun, there was no alternative other than to grasp the nettle.

'Good morning, Herr Mannerheim, Ruth Valsac from Brooks and Son.'

Ruth smiled and waited for the head to lift; it did not.

'I am aware of who you are, Miss Valsac, and of your company.' He continued to write, not once looking at her. 'Stone. I was expecting Stone as well as yourself.'

Ruth took some satisfaction in provoking a response; she was starting to fight back.

'I'm afraid Mr Stone is unable to attend, sir, but I am fully briefed and have checked all of your books myself.'

As she spoke it crossed her mind that the man must have a serious neck complaint as he still made no attempt to raise his head.

'Why?'

The simplicity of the question took Ruth back.

'Why what, sir?'

He sighed heavily.

'Why is Stone unable to attend?' He remained looking at the page, but Ruth noticed he had stopped writing.

'He's dead, sir, he dropped dead from a heart attack late last night.'

The words had just come out, she could not lie about the truth. She had suddenly not wanted to lie about the truth, she had wanted to shock this arrogant pig of a man into acknowledgment. It worked; for the first time he looked up at her. It had taken shock tactics but Ruth now felt it was fifteen–all.

'I am sorry to hear that, Miss Valsac, I had only spoken to Mr Stone once on the telephone. I did not really know him; it must have been a shock for you all.'

She was surprised; compassion from this hard-nosed young German, this man who had chosen to ignore her and make life difficult right from the start.

He stood up and walked around the desk holding out his hand.

Ruth shook it firmly. Thirty–fifteen to her.

'I am sure we can get things done quickly, Miss Valsac, you said you had worked on the books?'

He hesitated for a moment and Ruth felt conscious that for the first time he seemed to be looking at her, really looking at her.

'Of course! RV, the initials on the corrections in the margins, that's you?'

Ruth smiled.

'Yes, sir, that's me.'

'You have done a great deal of work on the books, Miss Valsac; it would appear that you were responsible for finding a good many mistakes.' He raised an eyebrow. 'It's a pity that others in your company are not so vigilant.'

His praise had a sting in the tail and Ruth had felt it.

'Please take a seat, Miss Valsac,' he motioned to the chair closest to his desk and returned to his own. Ruth sat and put the files on the floor at her feet.

He was tall, she had to look up at him when she shook his hand, and unreasonably handsome for one so arrogant. The fair hair was a little too long, she thought, but it was tidy, and the eyes were typically blue.

There was one blemish to his good looks and that was the faintest of scars that ran down the left of his face from just above his eye to halfway down his cheek. She guessed that he was about twenty-six. Having gained the initiative, she was determined to keep it. She smiled again and opened her briefcase.

'Where would you like to start, sir?'

'With Stone's report,' he said coldly, opening his desk drawer and pulling out a blue file. Ruth could clearly see the words 'Brooks and Sons' in black print on the cover. The smile faded from her face. She was lost; she had fallen at the first hurdle. Stone had not told her he had sent the final report yet and there had been no copy on file. She could only guess at its contents.

'Were you involved in the writing of this, Miss Valsac?'

She hesitated; she could not say yes because she hadn't the faintest idea what was in the thing, and if she said no, he would think Stone had not thought enough of her to consult her on it. She cursed Stone for not telling her of its completion.

'I was not involved directly, sir, but I am sure Mr Stone based his report in line with our general discussions on your company.' It was the best she could do and she hoped it was good enough.

'You were aware that I had asked Stone for an independent financial report?'

It had not been good enough; he was on to her, there was no alternative but to come clean.

'Yes, I was aware that we were to submit such a report along with the final accounts and audit, sir, however, I was not aware we had already done so.' Ruth looked down at her feet, she felt humiliated. She had not known the contents of the report nor that it had already been sent and he had very soon realised it.

'Good, very good, then we can start again.' He smiled. 'I am glad you were not aware of the contents of the report, it gives me an opportunity to hear your opinion.'

Ruth breathed again; she was still in with a chance to impress.

'Tell me, Miss Valsac, with all the work you have done on our accounts and, how did you put it just a moment ago, oh yes, the general discussions that you had with Mr Stone,' he opened the report and slowly turned the pages as if to taunt her with his knowledge of its contents, 'what would you have said in this report should it have been you that had written it?'

She was puzzled. Why ask her for her views? Why did he want to 'start again', as he had put it? Her mind raced. He had put down the report now and had sat back in his chair. Ruth could detect the slightest hint of a smile on his lips. He was enjoying this; of that, at least, she could be sure.

'Well, sir, if you want the truth, I was a little surprised.' Honesty had been the best policy before; perhaps it would work again. She waited for a response but there was none. His eyes were fixed on her and he was listening with interest. She kept on, 'Increase in gross turnover over the last five years has been negligible, less than three per cent.' She again waited for some reaction but still there was none. She was going down the hill now, she had no option but to gain momentum, there was no going back.

'You see, sir, I would have expected a greater investment in the company itself, new equipment, more advertising, general modernisation. But this has not been the case. The company is a long and well-established one with a wide customer base but little or nothing has been done to expand that base. Turnover has increased slightly but only in line with inflation and in fact profits have been declining steadily for some time.' She was in full flow now; the words just came tumbling out. 'When you look carefully at the pattern of things over the past five years, sir, you can see that the company has stagnated. Certain assets have been sold, for example, the warehouse in Perivale, some of the larger pieces of equipment have also gone. At first, I thought this was to make way for modernisation but when you look at new equipment purchase it is practically non-existent. I would admit there has been a general tightening up on expenditure and a trimming of the labour force but at director level, little change.'

He leant forward, putting both elbows on the desk, his eyes still focused on her in what was for her becoming an uncomfortable stare.

'"At director level, little change"; what do you mean by that, Miss Valsac?'

She realised that she may have gone too far in her eagerness to impress and hesitated for a moment wondering if she should backtrack, but she did not.

'Dividends have remained high sir and so have salaries.'

'Are you suggesting, Miss Valsac, that there has been mismanagement at director level?' The question was direct and betrayed nothing of the man's feelings.

'No, sir, I am just stating the facts as I would have put them in the report. I am assuming that as you are to pay good money for our services you expect us to be factual and to the point. It is for you to draw your own opinion from the facts presented. I would only say, sir, that in my report I would be bound to point out that growth has been negligible, investment minimal and profit pitiful!' She sat back and waited, wishing her last statement had not come out quite so bluntly and aware that if Stone had had the good fortune to have made this meeting today, the shock of her comments would probably have killed him anyway!

'You are very clear and to the point, Miss Valsac, perhaps now we may spend some time going through the books, during which time we may be able to substantiates some of your comments.' He picked up the telephone and asked his secretary to bring in some additional files.

'Now we start work!' He motioned towards the large table.

They spent the rest of the day going over the books and files that made up the last complete year's trading figures. When this was done, they were checked against the previous five years and the profit and loss reports in the audited accounts. Ruth discussed the accounts and suggested changes to simplify the system and to minimise mistakes. She was completely absorbed in the work and had become more relaxed, and although he was forever questioning and probing, she was enjoying the challenge.

At lunchtime they did not stop; he ordered coffee and sandwiches and they worked straight through. It was late in the afternoon when he finally sat back in his chair and tossed his pencil onto the table in a gesture of surrender.

'Well, Miss Valsac, I think we have covered everything; you have been very patient with me.'

'It's my pleasure, sir, I hope you have found the day worthwhile.' Ruth smiled; she was pleased with her work and she was reasonably confident that he was pleased too. He looked at his watch.

'It is 4.30pm and normally at this time I visit the print rooms to see how things are going.'

Ruth stood up and started to gather her things. 'Then I must not keep you, sir, I will be on my way.'

'On the contrary, Miss Valsac, I was rather hoping you would accompany me on my walk around, it will give you an opportunity to see how we work.'

Ruth did not hesitate; the idea of walking around the factory appealed to her. It would, as he said, give her the chance to see how things worked. Not only that, but she was also enjoying herself. She had suffered all the strain at the beginning of the day so why not enjoy it now? The tour took longer than Ruth imagined, and it was 5.30pm before they returned to his office. He had spoken to many people on their walk and had introduced her only as Miss Valsac, never once mentioning what company she was from or why she was there. He had taken a great deal of time explaining what things were and his

49

ideas for the future. Ruth had watched him and listened with interest. He had become almost like a child in a toy shop, the moment he had walked onto the factory floor. If there had been any restraint left in him it had fallen away then, and he had spoken freely of his plans for the future.

'I am sorry to have kept you so late, Miss Valsac,' he said walking over to the cabinet near his desk. 'Perhaps you would join me in a drink?'

Ruth agreed to a sherry and watched as he also poured himself a whisky. The pair of them sat down, each in one of the large leather chairs that were positioned in front of his desk. He raised his glass.

'Your very good health, Miss Valsac.'

The drink was good, and Ruth sat back in the chair and crossed her legs. She was relaxed, the day was over it was just the niceties left.

'Why do you think Mannerheim International would invest such a large amount of money in a company that has, as you would say, stagnated?'

The question had come out of the blue just when Ruth had been silly enough to think work was over; it was not. He was staring questioningly at her again, glass in hand. It was a leading question, and she was again on the spot.

'I had wondered that myself at first, sir, but the more I thought about it, the clearer it became.' She took another sip of her sherry and smiled at him. 'This is very good sherry, sir.' She wanted him to wait for his reply. 'The answer, I think, sir, is clear if you ask what Bingham's can do for Mannerheim International?' She was off on that downhill run again and she knew she would not stop until she had reached the bottom. 'Mannerheim's is a large progressive company, it has done well since the end of the war and has expanded throughout Germany. However, there are larger and more lucrative markets elsewhere and Bingham's could well open the door to those markets.'

He got up, took her empty glass and without asking refilled it along with his own and returned it to her. He sat back down.

'Please continue, Miss Valsac.'

'There are many countries in Europe into which Mannerheim International would no doubt love to expand, however, this is difficult for you. There is still resentment and I dare say discrimination against German companies and this is stopping your expansion. Bingham's on the other hand is a well-established British company, which with the right amount of investment and modernisation could easily move into the European market. It also owns a small subsidiary company in France which has done little since the end of the war, but nevertheless it is there, and who knows with the right management could be a ready-made stepping stone into that market.' Ruth had done her homework and her desire to impress would not let her stop. 'Then of course, sir, there is Mannerheim Inc., a subsidiary of your own company, which specialises in the manufacture of print machinery. I am sure they would follow along behind with the sale of that machinery. I believe, sir, Mannerheim International had done its homework well before it purchased Bingham's; that is, you knew exactly what you were doing and the only reason you have asked us for an independent report, after purchase, is to use it as a stick to wield against your board.' She had reached the bottom of the hill and having done so sat back to reflect on her trip.

'You too have done your homework, Miss Valsac.' He leant forward in his chair, his eyes fixed on hers. 'It had been my intention this morning to thank you for your work on our accounts and to inform your Mr Stone that we no longer require the services of your company. His report was inadequate. I must admit your accountancy could not be faulted, however, sadly he failed to identify the problems that we have inherited here.' He paused as if to ponder his options.

'Are you prepared to rewrite that report, Miss Valsac? Are you prepared to give me the stick to wield?' For the first time the urgency in his voice betrayed the man's need and she grasped it. She had been right: he needed the report to spare no quarter, he needed it to supply the stick.

Ruth's feeling of self-satisfaction was gratifying; for the first time she felt the match had swung in her favour. She put the score at forty–thirty. Deliberately, she took her time in replying, finishing the last of her sherry before getting to her feet.

'Herr Mannerheim, I have worked long and hard on your accounts and I am confident that I have a good insight into the way things are, and I am prepared to say so in my final report.'

He smiled; she had given him his stick. Standing up he walked round to the other side of the desk.

'Then here you are, Miss Valsac.' He tossed Stone's report across the desk to her. 'You no doubt can have your report with me by Friday?'

She confirmed that it would be no problem and, putting down the empty glass, began to collect her things.

'I am sorry to have kept you so late, Miss Valsac, but I am sure you will agree that it has been a very successful and interesting day. You must allow me to drive you back into London, I know an excellent restaurant, perhaps we could have dinner together?'

FIVE

SALLY FROM THE TYPING POOL HAD BEEN ADAMANT when questioned about the report on Bingham's.

'There were just three typed,' she had told Ruth. 'One to be bound for the client, and two for Mr Stone as requested.'

He had insisted that there was no need for a file copy. This puzzled Ruth. Mrs Stone had sent in the contents of her husband's briefcase amongst which Ruth had found one copy of the report. But as for the third copy, she had no idea why Stone had it typed, or where it was now. There was no doubt about it, though, the report was toothless, more of a twig than a stick. There was something else that she could not understand: Stone had glossed over most of the facts, painting a picture of a company that was well established with modest but acceptable growth. It was not like him to have been so charitable. It had all seemed rather strange to her, but she had put it to the back of her mind when she rewrote the report. It now spared no quarter; it was hard-hitting and factual, stopping short only of direct criticism of the directors, but the implications were obvious.

'I have just the final report to deliver now, Mr Brooks, I think Herr Mannerheim will be pleased with it.'

'Good, good,' the old man's face beamed. 'You have done very well, Miss Valsac.' He waved away the copy of her report. 'I am sure it is very good, Miss Valsac; I have every confidence in you. Just get it to him and keep him happy.'

The meeting had been brief, but satisfying, and what's more Robert Brooks had said nothing. He had sat quietly with a fixed smile on his face while his father had spoken. Ruth knew that he must have hated every minute of it. There was no love lost between her and Brooks' son and she knew that would always be an obstacle to overcome if she were to gain promotion. His rather ham-fisted advances when she was the office junior had got him nowhere, and she had slapped his face very hard when he tried to grope her in his office one day. Robert Brooks was not the kind of man to forgive and forget and he had told her so!

She had told no one about her dinner date with Herr Mannerheim. It had been pleasant but businesslike and there was no way she wanted people to think she was attempting to use anything other than her business talents to win the man over. The arrogance he had shown when they first met had soon disappeared and he had proved himself to be a perfect gentleman throughout the whole of their evening together. She had thought a lot about him since then and could not help but admire him for his grasp of business and his vision, but there was a ruthless side to him too. She had very soon realised that and had no desire to sample it first-hand. The report had to be good, it had to be what he wanted. But she was confident and when she put the blue-bound copy into her briefcase that night she did so with a feeling of nervous anticipation and excitement about the meeting the following day.

Her journey home seemed to take forever despite the fact that the fog of the previous few days had finally cleared. The night sky was now wonderfully clear and played host to a countless number of stars, but it had a chill the likes of which Ruth had not felt for some time, and already a frost was beginning to form. When her bus finally did stop at the top of Malden Street, she did not relish the idea of again stepping into the frozen air. It was on her walk home from the bus stop that she decided that tonight she would tell them. It was silly trying to hide it; there was no point. She would tell them at dinner. They would be bound to want to know how she had got on with her visit and why she had been so late last night. Oh, he would huff and puff, there was no doubt of that, but it wasn't her fault, she was just doing her job. And when they heard of her promotion, well that would make them happy!

*

Inside, the warmth of the house felt wonderful. She did not bother with her coat but went straight to their door and knocked. Her aunt opened it. She was wearing her normal black dress with her apron tied loosely at her waist. She was pleased to see 'her Ruthy' and, wiping her hands on her apron, gave her the usual hug.

'Where have you been, Ruth? Why you so late home last night? Is it you avoid your old aunt and keep her guessing on how things go at work?'

All the questions came one after the other and before Ruth had even reached the kitchen. Uncle looked up as she came in. He had known it would be her; he looked over the top of his *Evening Standard* and smiled. Ruth thought he looked tired.

'Not working late tonight then, Ruth?'

She smiled but did not reply. Aunt Elizabeth put a large mug of steaming coffee in front of her and Ruth held it with both hands, letting its warmth defrost her fingers.

'Now then, Ruthy, you tell me all about everything.'

Ruth smiled. 'Well, it's a long story.'

Ruth's story lasted all through dinner and both of them listened intently to her. Aunt Elizabeth butted in now and again in her normal way.

'So poor Mr Stone he die, his poor wife.' She wiped the corner of one eye with her apron. 'But you do a good job anyway. I always say you do good job!'

Joseph said nothing. He was content to listen and absorb. It was not until Ruth had finished and he had shared out the last of the red wine that he spoke.

'So, you are now in charge of the office.' It was a statement, not a question. 'And you handle all this big account on your own.'

Ruth cringed, as she guessed where he was leading.

'So, tell me, Ruth, what is the name of this company that has bought up Bingham's? Who are they?'

Ruth knew that the time had come: she had to tell him. She prepared herself for the huff and puff.

'It's a company from Germany, Uncle.' She waited.

'It's from where?'

Before Ruth could answer, Elizabeth, knowing what was about to happen, instinctively sprang to her defence.

'Is it Ruthy's fault that they are German? Can she help it? She just do her job, Joseph.'

The old man did not respond; he was just staring at her. Slowly, he took off his spectacles and pulling his handkerchief from his trousers pocket started to polish the lenses. Still he said nothing.

'They're quite a well-respected company, Uncle.' Ruth bit her tongue; she knew she had said the wrong thing.

'Well respected!' The old man's voice was soft; his concentration fixed on his spectacles as he turned them gently in his hands. 'Well respected!' he repeated, only this time he spoke louder as he returned the spectacles to his nose and looked at her. 'So was Adolph Hitler when he first started!' His voice, even louder, carried a new harshness. 'So was Himmler when he first started! So was the SS!' He slammed his fist on the table sending the empty glasses every which way. 'They were all respectable. All respectable, while they murdered and tortured millions of us, men, women and children, your own mother and father, your brother and your sister, you of all people, Ruth, must know how respectable they were.'

Ruth's temper, fanned by his words, suddenly flared as she struck back. 'Yes, I know, Uncle, and I will never forget, I don't need you to remind me! I don't need you to tell me, every time someone mentions anything German. I live with it every day, every day I look at their picture, every day I say a prayer for them. The scars are cut deep into my heart and will always remain.' Ruth felt the tears fill her eyes; she was angry and the emotion showed in her voice, but she was not going to let herself cry. 'We can't live in the past, Uncle; the war is over. We must not forget but we can't keep harbouring such hatred. If we do it will destroy us. We too are German, born in Germany, lived in Germany.'

Joseph stood up, pushing back his chair with such force that it fell over.

'I am Jewish, I was born Jewish, I will die Jewish. I had the misfortune to be born in Germany, but I am Jewish!' Again, he banged his fist on the table but this time he retrieved his glass with his other hand and turning from the table went to the cabinet to pour himself a whisky. Elizabeth, seeing a chance to defuse the situation, took it. She stood up and started to clear the dinner plates, righting the chair as she did so.

'Why you two always have to argue about these things, I will never know. What is the point?' She took Ruth's plate and scraped the few scraps that remained onto her own.

'I tell you the point! I tell you the point!' he replied as he turned back to face them both, the half empty bottle of Scotch in one hand, his glass in the other.

'In some of us the hatred, the pain and the fear can never be lost; it is with us always, it remains in our hearts and in our very souls.'

He wobbled a little as he took a step back towards them.

'You tell me, you tell me how those of us that have lost so much will ever forget?' He sat back down at the table and with words now spent, stared silently down at the glass in his hand. Ruth felt her anger ebb away; she could not help but feel compassion. She knew the hurt he felt inside, she knew his pain.

'I am sorry this has upset you, Uncle; I did not want it to.' Leaning towards him she reached out and took his hand. 'You asked me, I had to tell you. It's just a job, another client. I can't pick and choose who I work for, they tell me and I do it, that's all it is.'

'There you are, Joseph, I tell you, our Ruthy, she just do her job that's all, she just do her job.' Elizabeth continued to clear the plates.

When Joseph did look up again and into the large brown eyes of his niece, he smiled. He could not help it.

'I too am sorry, Ruth; I am a foolish old man.' He squeezed her hand. 'I know it is just your job and I am proud of you; now come, tell me more about this company.'

Elizabeth returned to the table wiping her hands on her apron as she did so.

'Now tell me the name of this company, Ruth.' Joseph emptied his glass and waited for her reply.

'Mannerheim International,' Ruth replied, happy that his anger had gone and that he was interested.

Joseph looked at his wife; a cold chill ran through them both but neither spoke. It was a nightmare returning.

*

Friedrich Mannerheim finished reading the report and closed the folder. It was good, in fact it was excellent, but he had found it hard to concentrate. Several times his eyes had wandered and he had found himself looking at the pair of long slender legs that remained frustratingly close together at the knees. It was not businesslike to allow one's mind to be distracted so, and he was disappointed with himself for letting it happen. But they were nice legs! It had been an uphill struggle for him from the start. He had fought against it but eventually had to admit that he had been fascinated by her from the first moment they had met. She had somehow possessed a kind of magic, a magic that had been working on him ever since. Slowly the thought of her had penetrated every corner of his mind and now, like all good magic, he was left wondering how it had happened. What was making it even more difficult was that she looked much more beautiful than he had remembered her to be. The long dark hair was softly curled and fell gently about her shoulders, the dark eyes full of sparkle and life, soft white skin complemented with only the slightest hint of make-up. Oh yes, she was beautiful, he had to admit it and for a minute he gave way to temptation allowing his eyes to search her body. She was wearing a blue suit that, although smart and businesslike, did little to disguise the curve of her figure. Her blouse, open at the top button, revealed the merest hint of an elegant soft neck above the crisp whiteness of the material disappearing beneath the jacket, which remained buttoned, denying him further pleasure. He shook his mind free.

'This is good, Miss Valsac, very good.' He looked back at the report. 'Much more like what I had in mind, thank you.'

She smiled at him, and again he found his mind wandering.

'I'm glad you're pleased with the report, sir, I've left nothing out.'

Her words forced him to concentrate, and he went on to discuss the report and its contents for some while before looking at his watch. It had been a deliberate move on his part to request that they should meet at 4.30pm that Friday afternoon. He knew it would be late in the day before their meeting ended and that he could then offer her a lift back to town and perhaps dinner again. It was crafty and he knew it, but he could not feel guilty.

'I'm glad you are satisfied with our work, sir,' she said. 'If we can do anything for you in the future, please do not hesitate to contact us.'

He watched as she started to gather her things. She was getting ready to leave and the urgency of the situation struck him. He had to offer the lift, but if she declined his invitation, what would he do then? She got to her feet, offering him her hand; instinctively he took it and thanked her.

'I am sure we can do business again in the future, Miss Valsac, thank you, thank you very much.' He heard himself say the words and cursed himself for the inadequacy of them.

She smiled at him. 'I'm sure we can, sir.'

With that, she turned and started to make her way to the door. He stood watching her walk away from him; she was so slim, her figure so perfect. He watched, fascinated, unable to speak. Suddenly she was at the door, if he did not act now, she would be gone.

'Oh, Miss Valsac, you must forgive me, it is nearly 5.45pm and I am about to leave myself; perhaps I can offer you a lift back to town?'

She turned. 'That's very kind of you, sir.'

'Perhaps you would tell me more about London and the wonderful sights that it has.' He put the report into his briefcase and followed her to the door. 'I know it would be twice in one week, Miss Valsac, and I hope you do not think I am being forward, but perhaps you would like to join me again for dinner?'

*

Frederick made his way straight to the hotel bar and ordered himself a large malt. He had not known what to say when she had declined his invitation for a meal and now, he felt foolish. He had heard her mention something about cooking dinner for her uncle and aunt every Friday, but he had only been half listening. His mind had been racing trying desperately to find another reason to see her again, but he had only been able to manage 'Perhaps some other time then.' He had stood motionless, like some dumb idiot as Edward had driven her away. Now he cursed himself. He had known few women in his life and now that he had met one, one that he really liked, he had just stood there and watched her being driven away. Not only that, he had actually supplied the car and the driver! He finished his drink and ordered another.

*

Ruth had watched him walk up the hotel steps and was disappointed that he did not look back. She watched him until the car turned into the Bayswater Road and he was lost from sight. Now, as she sat back in the soft leather seat, thankful for the lift home, she could not help but think about him. She was sorry that she could not accept his dinner invitation but knew that to do so was impossible. Every Friday since she had moved into the flat, she had cooked dinner for them; tonight as usual they would be at her door at 8.00pm sharp. Both of them would have taken the trouble to wash and change and Uncle, hair combed, tie and jacket on, would have a bottle of her favourite red wine. She could not disappoint them and besides, they knew that she had a meeting with him. She dared not be late again; after all, she had told them it was just a job and they had accepted that. If they thought that she was having dinner with him, if they thought that she was attracted to him, a German, well that would be just too much. She thought about it. Was she attracted to him? If she was then why should she allow their fears to inhibit her feelings? She was allowing them both to control her; two old people, both of whom had a deep fear of Germany and anything associated with it, were imposing that fear on her. That was just not fair, she told herself.

As Edward struggled to negotiate the traffic around Marble Arch, Ruth was also struggling, but for her it was an inward struggle, a struggle with her emotions. She had come to like the man, to deny that would be foolish, and he was good-looking, but he was also good at his job and she admired the way he went about it. It must be difficult for him alone as he was in England and she felt desperately guilty for declining his invitation, but perhaps it was for the best. It was just business, after all; it would be stupid to think otherwise. But why had she been so looking forward to meeting him again? Why had she been so disappointed when she thought he was not going to offer her a lift back to town? The realisation of how she did feel about him frightened her. Not a German, she could never fall in love with a German!

For the rest of the journey home, Ruth sat looking out of the window. She made no attempt to talk to Edward nor he to her. Her thoughts were of the man she had just left and of how dangerous it would be for her to see him again. They had nearly reached Hampstead before Ruth spoke.

'Would you mind dropping me in the High Street, Edward? There's a deli there where I shop.'

Edward told her that he would be pleased to and that if she wished he would wait and take her the rest of the way home.

'That's very kind of you, Edward, but you must be eager to get home yourself.'

'Who me, miss? I've got nothing to rush home for.' He pulled the car to a halt outside the deli. 'And the traffic back across town will be bad for a while yet.'

As Ruth queued at the counter, she could not help but think about what Edward had said. *The traffic back across town.*

She was not long in the shop and as they drove the short distance to her home, she turned an idea over in her mind. The car stopped outside the house and Edward started to get out. Ruth knew it was now or not at all.

'Edward, before you get out…'

He turned in his seat and looked at her.

'Do you go back across town then?'

'Yes, miss, I've got a small flat in Hammersmith.' He looked a little puzzled.

Ruth hesitated, 'Then, err, you must go almost back past Herr Mannerheim's hotel.'

Edward smiled, 'I go right past it, miss.'

Ruth opened her briefcase and, taking out a piece of paper and her pen, she quickly wrote:

Dear Herr Mannerheim,

I am sorry about dinner; I hope you do not think me rude. I am in town tomorrow to do some Christmas shopping, perhaps we could meet when I have finished and I will show you some of London. Say 11.00am at Speakers' Corner, it is not far from your hotel. I will understand if you have other arrangements.

Regards,

Ruth

'Would you mind dropping this note in for him on the way back, Edward?' she said, putting it in an envelope and sealing it down.

'It's something I forgot to tell him, and he might think it important.'

Edward took the letter and smiled. 'I'm sure it must be very important, miss; I will make sure he gets it tonight.'

So, tell me Ruth, was your meeting a success?' Uncle was opening a rather nice-looking bottle of Bordeaux Claret as he spoke, his face red as he strained at the stubborn cork. They had arrived early, and he had been under her feet ever since.

'Uncle, this kitchen is just not big enough for the both of us. Go and put the wine on the table and stop stealing the cheese, there'll be none left.' She threw a tea towel at him as he disappeared through the door.

'You never answered my question!' he shouted back.

'And I'm not going to, I'm far too busy at the moment.'

Ruth had been busy ever since Edward had dropped her back at the house. Cooking was not one of her favourite pastimes. She could do it and do it well, but after work she found it hard to get motivated for the task. Tonight, it was lamb chops, one of her uncle's favourites, and on her tiny stove they had taken longer than she had expected. It didn't help them being early. Uncle appeared at the door, a glass of red wine in his hand.

'For the cook!'

*

'They were by far the best lamb chops I have ever eaten.' Uncle pushed the plate away, the two naked bones now being its only contents.

'They can't always be the best lamb chops, Uncle; you say that every time I cook them.'

'I swear, Ruth, they just get better and better.'

Elizabeth laughed, 'He just making sure he can come again.'

Ruth cleared the plates and returned from the kitchen with the coffee pot and cups.

'Well, are you going to tell us now?' he asked.

'Tell you what?'

'Was the meeting a success?' They were both waiting.

'Yes, thank you, it went very well,' she smiled. 'He said my report was just what he wanted.'

'And who is he?' Elizabeth asked.

'He is the new managing director. I told you they had a new director.'

She paused, hoping that her next words would not provoke her uncle.

'He is over here from Germany.'

There was a silence as the old couple both looked at each other, the concern on their faces obvious.

'Oh, come on now, he's not the SS, he is just a businessman. Well, actually he is not just a businessman, he is Herr Mannerheim himself.'

The glass slipped from Elizabeth's fingers, spilling what was left of its contents over the tablecloth.

'Herr who?' Joseph asked, ignoring the spilt wine.

'Herr Mannerheim,' Ruth replied, somewhat taken aback by their lack of concern for her cloth.

'You have met the man?' His agitation was clear.

'Well of course I've met him!' Ruth prepared herself for another lecture on the horrors of Germany and its people.

'What did he look like? How old is he?'

She was taken aback by her uncle's sudden hostility.

'What do you mean?'

'Well, was he my age?'

'No, he's nearer my age. Why is his age so important? Or is it just that he is German?'

'Perhaps,' his reply was still aggressive. 'Did he say why he was here?'

Ruth did not like this sudden cross-examination but, determined not to have another argument tonight, she remained calm.

'Uncle, he is here to sort out Bingham's, it's as simple as that.'

Elizabeth picked up the glass, but she kept her eyes fixed on her husband and said nothing.

'Has he asked any questions about you or your family?'

'Uncle, don't be so ridiculous, he is not interested in me or my family. I've told you it's just business, it's my work!' She had allowed her voice to rise a little and now regretted it.

'And have you finished your work? Will you need to see him again?'

The urgency in Joseph's voice was growing and this prompted her to turn to her aunt.

'What is this, Elizabeth? Why is he getting so excited?'

She had expected her aunt to come to her defence, to tell her he was just being silly, but it was as if she had not even heard her question. She remained silent, her stare still fixed on her husband.

'Answer me, Ruth! Do you need to see him again?'

'Of course I will need to see him again. I'm handling his account for heaven's sake. What do you expect?'

'You're head of department, get someone else to do it.'

The indignation Ruth felt at his last words spilled over into anger.

'I shall do no such thing! If you think I'm going to jeopardise this account and my promotion just because you fear all Germans, then I'm sorry, you're going to be disappointed.'

There was a silence. When Joseph spoke again it in a quieter, calmer fashion.

'Ruth listen to me. Has this man mentioned his father, is the man still alive?'

'No, he hasn't mentioned his father and no I don't know if the man is alive.'

She dwelt on her words for a second. Of course his father was alive; she remembered now, he had mentioned him when they had dinner.

Joseph was quick to read the doubt that showed on her face.

'Are you sure?'

She hesitated. 'Well perhaps he is alive! I can't be sure. For goodness' sake I'm not interested in his father!' She got up from the table and started to remove the cups. 'You don't think I cross-examined him about his family, do you?'

'No, we don't think that, Ruth. But you must be careful.' Joseph's voice remained calm. 'We left a past behind all those years ago when we left Germany. There may still be people there that wish us harm.'

She looked at him. 'What people? Who would want to harm us now? We were the persecuted ones, Uncle. They've done us wrong. We should have no fear of the past.'

'Things are not always that simple, Ruth, believe me.' He reached across the table and took hold of Elizabeth's hand. 'It is for the best that we have nothing to do with Germany or its people. We have our life here now.'

Ruth had been busy fielding his questions, her mind moving from one to another. It was only now that the significance of her uncle's words struck her. 'Just a minute,' she said sitting back down at the small table, 'what do you mean, did he mention his father? Why did you ask me that?'

Joseph did not reply.

'Oh, come on, Uncle, what's going on?' She waited.

Elizabeth spoke for the first time. 'We once knew a man named Mannerheim. We can't be sure, but your Herr Mannerheim may be his son.'

Ruth banged her hand on the table in a gesture of disbelief. 'Why didn't you just tell me you knew him, for God's sake, why all the secrecy?' She got to her feet again. 'You mean all this concern, all these questions because you once knew a man, and this might be his son. There must be more to it than that!'

'There is no more.' There was a finality in Joseph's tone that stopped Elizabeth from continuing.

'So that's it?' Ruth replied. 'You once knew a man call Mannerheim. Well, there must be hundreds, perhaps thousands of people in Germany with that name.'

Joseph was annoyed with himself; he had gone too far, and she had already found out more than he had wanted her to know. If this went on there was a danger she would realise there was more, much more.

'We are being silly. We just don't want to dig up the past, that's all. Anyway, he will probably be going back to Germany soon and that will be the end of it. Just do your job, Ruth.' He took her hand. 'But please, don't tell him more than you have to, and don't get involved.'

SIX

CHRISTMAS SHOPPING

I T WAS A WINTERY SCENE THAT GREETED RUTH WHEN she peered out of her bedroom window the following morning. Snow had fallen during the night, not a lot, but just enough to turn the rooftops white and cover the pavement. In fact, the odd flake could still be spotted now and again as it drifted in the wind and the sky remained an ominous grey. She wasted no time in seeking the sanctuary of warm clothing but even as she dressed, the struggle with her conscience continued. Since dinner last night it had been on her mind. It had even entered her dreams and troubled her there and had returned from the minute she had opened her eyes. She had not told them. She had dared not tell them. But it wasn't her fault. That's what she had told herself time and time again, but still it troubled her. She was going to meet him. No matter what they said. *Why*, she asked herself, *should she let their silly fears enter her life?* It was not rational. So, they once knew a man called Mannerheim, so what? Even if it was the same family, and it probably wasn't, what would they care? They probably wouldn't even remember and if they did, what did it matter

70

anyway! Well, she was going Christmas shopping, and that was a fact. She had told them that. It was not a lie. It was what she had not told them that tugged at her conscience.

Breakfast was two slices of hurriedly eaten toast and a cup of sugarless coffee. She had a lot to do and little time to do it. She always brought them a Christmas present despite their religion. Joseph would probably huff and puff as usual, saying it was not proper, but Ruth knew that secretly he enjoyed it. And as for Elizabeth, well she would make no attempt to hide her pleasure. The snow crunched under her feet as she stepped out into the cold of the morning and great clouds of mist issued instantly from her mouth as the severity of the weather caused her to shiver and involuntarily blow the breath from her lungs. It was 8.30am and she would have to be quick if she was to catch the 9.00am bus. An hour later she was making her way along Oxford Street, her scarf wrapped around her ears to protect them from the stinging cold.

It was difficult for her to concentrate on shopping. She could not help but feel like a naughty schoolgirl who was about to embark on some forbidden adventure. But she had to confess, the feeling of nervous anticipation was not unpleasant. She had never gone out with a man before. Well, not like this anyway. There had been a couple of boys in the past. But that was it really, they were boys, not men, and there had never been a romance. The nearest she had ever come to a man, if you could call him that, was when Robert Brooks made a ham-fisted lunge for her breasts that time in his office. But this was not to be a proper date, she told herself as she walked into yet another shop, this was just business.

The rather overweight woman in the department store was very helpful, showing her several handbags before Ruth finally committed herself and bought one for Elizabeth. It was black,

71

all leather and cost her a fortune but she knew her aunt would love it. She also bought her a dark blue head scarf. Uncle was a little easier: it was slippers, size eight, and gloves. By the time she had completed her shopping and stepped once again onto the frozen pavement of Oxford Street it was almost 10.45am. How could she have done such a thing, she asked herself? Sending him silly schoolgirl notes. The thought of it alone was now causing her acute embarrassment and it was an embarrassment that seemed to grow with every step she took as she made her way towards Marble Arch. He would probably be laughing at her right now, that is, if Edward had even bothered to deliver her letter. How stupid she had been to act on an impulse like that, what must he think of her? She quickened her step as she crossed North Audley Street. It was nearly 10.50am, and, well, if he had decided to meet her it would not do to keep him waiting. All at once she found herself hoping desperately that he would be there. She felt stupid enough about the note; if he chose to ignore it, well that would be devastating! The thought of that brought an almost instant panic. What would she say to him when they did meet again? How would she ever be able to dismiss it as a casual thing that did not matter? Of course it mattered. That was obvious and as she made her way along the crowded pavement, half frozen from the cold, it suddenly became clear to her just how much it mattered.

*

By the time she had reached the corner of Park Lane she was short of breath and could hear her heart pounding against her chest. She had almost run the last two hundred or so yards, anxious as she was to see if he was there. She stopped a little way back from the kerb and looked across the busy street towards the corner of Hyde Park. It was the corner which, over the years, had become a safe haven for those with an overpowering ambition to address the world and all those in it. From where she stood it was impossible to make out if he was there or not. The pavement was busy with passers-by and with the constant flow of traffic she just could not tell. She checked her watch; it was exactly 11.00am. Her fingers were cold and she was suddenly conscious of the fact that her nose was running. Taking out her handkerchief, she quickly remedied the situation, and also took a few minutes to check her appearance with the aid of her compact mirror. She felt now how she had felt when they had first met, nervous and uncertain of herself. She knew she had no option other than to cross the road and see if he was there but, as she stood there, she had an overwhelming urge to turn on her heels and run. Then all at once, and unbelievably, the traffic cleared, the road was empty. As Moses had been presented with a path through the waters, Ruth was now presented with a clear way across Park Lane. Without further thought she took it and before she knew it, was mingling with the people on and around Speakers' Corner, being bumped and pushed as she made her way through the crowds who were braving the cold to either listen to or barrack the speakers. She looked at her watch again; it was 11.05am. There were people everywhere and even if he had decided to come, she despaired at ever being able to find him. It started to snow again, this time larger flakes that persistently landed on her nose or fluttered into her eyes. It was impossible and she knew it. The whole thing had been stupid and ill-contrived. Her embarrassment would be complete and absolute. Why the hell had she written that stupid note!

'Good morning, Miss Valsac.' The voice came from close behind her, making her jump. She turned, but even before she did so, she knew it was him.

'You came!' she cried without thinking and straight away wished she had not said something so obvious.

'Of course, I could not refuse such a kind invitation.'

Ruth felt strangely awkward and more than a little embarrassed as they both stood looking at each other, each waiting for the other to speak.

'I'm afraid it's rather a cold day for your first tour of London,' she said smiling. 'Perhaps we should find a warm museum somewhere.'

'I am in your hands entirely, Miss Valsac, and I like the cold; the snow reminds me of Christmas. Come, where do we begin?'

Ruth laughed. 'Well, if you don't mind the cold, how about Buckingham Palace?'

'We must get a taxi?' he asked.

'No, we must get a bus!' She took his arm and pointed to the bus stop. 'Come on, let's go. Oh, and my name is Ruth, you can't keep calling me Miss Valsac all day, it will drive me mad.'

'And my name is Friedrich, and I think we are both a little mad to catch a London bus, from what I have heard about them.' It was his turn to laugh.

*

Friedrich insisted that they ride on the top deck of the number 16 bus that finally arrived at the bus stop on Park Lane.

'If I am going to ride on a London bus then I must ride on the top,' he said, taking Ruth's arm and pulling her up the stairs behind him.

When they got off at Buckingham Palace Road the snow flurries had stopped but it remained as cold as ever. As they walked together, they chatted happily. The awkwardness that they had both felt when they had met again that morning had evaporated and now it was as it had been before, when they had first met and had dinner together. Despite the cold there was a fair-sized crowd at the Palace. People were milling around, some with cameras and many with small children. The pair of them slowly made their way through the crowd and after a few minutes they stood side by side against the large black railings.

'It is very impressive,' Friedrich said, peering between the railings. 'So, this is where your Queen lives.'

'Not always,' Ruth replied. 'Sometimes she lives at Windsor, sometimes at Balmoral and sometimes at Sandringham. It depends.'

'It depends on what?' he asked turning to look at her.

'I don't know,' she replied. 'It just depends.'

He smiled.

The day just seemed to fly by. After Buckingham Palace they visited Parliament Square and Westminster Abbey followed by a walk down Whitehall to Downing Street where Ruth pointed out the famous door of Number Ten. They stopped for lunch in a small cafe just off Birdcage Walk. It was busy but warm, and although it was not the Ritz, it was pleasant enough. There were several small tables spread with neat gingham cloths, and each had a small vase of flowers as the *pièce de résistance*. There was a definite Italian flavour to the place with empty Chianti bottles adorning tables and shelves. Ruth loved it.

As they ate lunch together their compatibility became unquestionable. Like two well-crafted pieces of a jigsaw puzzle their minds just seemed to click together, each one firing the zest for life into the other. And they laughed and they laughed. Even at the least funny of things they laughed, as if the troubles of the world were for others and dare not touch them. To him, she was full of life and beauty, with the darkest of eyes that flashed with enthusiasm and sparkled with joy. And her smile held a magic that bewitched him and left him longing for its return. To her, he was handsome and intelligent, full of drive and determination, but prepared to listen, to listen to her. She liked his love of London and watching as his blue eyes stared in amazement at the city's great landmarks. Locked within the man remained the enthusiasm of the boy, and that she found the most appealing.

It was a hectic day as they rushed from place to place. From Downing Street to St James's, from Whitehall to the Strand, the pair of them marched on, unperturbed by the cold and the odd snowflake. They were together and they were having fun. So involved were they both that neither realised that afternoon was slipping into early evening, and that the last of the day's light was fading fast. As they returned down the Strand the lights of Theatreland blazed out at them through the gloom, and by the time they had reached Trafalgar Square the lights of the huge Christmas tree sparkled in the darkness of the cold night air. They stopped beneath Nelson's Column and stared at the tree. It had started to snow again, only this time the flakes were larger, and it was starting to settle. A Salvation Army band was battling bravely on against the elements and their rendition of 'Once in Royal David's City' echoed out across the crowded square.

'This is my most favourite place in all of London,' Ruth said, 'and Christmas is the best time to see it.' She took a few steps away from him and turned; looking at him and smiling, she lifted her arms. 'It's all this!' she said, her breath turning to small clouds of mist in the wintery air. 'Everything, the hustle and bustle of the crowds, the tree, the carols and even the snow, I love it!'

She laughed as she shook the fresh snowflakes from her hair. 'What do you think, Friedrich? What do you think of it all?'

He walked towards her. Inside, he knew what he thought of it all, he knew he had never in his life felt happier, and he had to tell her so. He reached out taking both of her hands. 'I think, too, that this is my most favourite part of London.' He gently pulled her closer to him. 'And I think that the snow on your hair makes you look more beautiful than I could have ever imagined.'

His words took her by surprise, and she lowered her head to hide the blush. The warmth of his soft leather glove touched her chin, pushing her face gently up until she was looking into his eyes. 'I do not wish to sound foolish, Ruth, but ever since I first met you, I have not been able to get you out of my mind. Last night when you left me at the hotel, I thought I may never see you again. I couldn't let that happen. I know we have not known each other long, but I am falling in love with you.'

As the reality of his words reached into her mind, it spread a panic that seemed to run through the whole of her body. Just a few short seconds ago she had felt so confident, so happy. Now, his last few words had, in an instant, reduced her stature to that of a lovesick schoolgirl. She started to tremble and her heart began pounding inside her. It was as if a key had turned in a lock, and a door inside her had opened, allowing her feelings for him to flood out. They were feelings she could not remember ever experiencing before and the intensity of them scared her. It was now clear, clearer than it had ever

77

been before, she loved him too. She could not help it, it was uncontrollable. He was holding her close, too close. Her whole body was pushing against his. It was wrong to let him hold her so, but she had not the desire nor the will to pull from him. They were in the middle of Trafalgar Square, and surrounded by hundreds of people, yet they were alone. It was the first time any man had held her like this and she did not want it to end. Not yet. Then, as she looked at him, he kissed her. It was the most wonderful kiss, and she unashamedly enjoyed the feel of his warm lips on hers, the softness of them, the intimacy. It was a kiss that lingered, a kiss that awakened desires within them both.

When it did end and her mind returned again to normality, Ruth felt embarrassed and found it difficult to look at him. She had made no attempt to hold back; she had made her desires obvious. Anyone of those around them could have told from that kiss that she wanted him, and of the passion she had felt. The thought of facing the Salvation Army Band made her blood run cold!

'I am sorry, Ruth; I did not mean to be so forward.' He was concerned.

'It's all right,' she whispered, still not wanting him to let her go. 'It's all right.'

They stood holding each other for a long while, neither of them wanting the closeness to end.

'If we don't move soon, we will be arrested,' she said finally, trying to bring them both gently back to earth.

'I do not believe your English policemen would be so hard on two people in love, would they?'

His voice betrayed the need for her to answer.

'You don't know our policemen.'

It was not a reply with which he was content.

'Are we two people in love, Ruth?' he persisted.

For a moment she was silent.

'I've never really been in love with anyone before, Friedrich,' she paused. 'But nothing else could make me feel like this.'

He moved to kiss her again.

'No, not again, not here,' and then she laughed. 'You will get a good Jewish girl a bad reputation!'

SEVEN

O TTO MANNERHEIM SLIPPED HIS ARMS INTO THE
heavy overcoat, wrapped his scarf around his neck, and
walked out into the cold winter air. It had snowed heavily again
during the night and the wind had whipped up drifts against
the wall of the house and the huge stone steps that led down to
the drive. Even the stone lions that guarded the foot of the steps
were now half buried beneath a white covering. All around him
he could see the bent shapes of men as they dug and scraped to
clear the road that led to the gatehouse, and the world beyond.
Carl would have had them out before first light to clear the
road, and no doubt the frozen figures were cursing heaven as
they worked for bestowing on them this latest delivery.

At the top of the steps he stopped, taking time to look
about him as he slipped on a pair of soft leather gloves, retrieved
from his coat pocket. The sky was grey and threatening and all
around him the estate carried the mantle of winter. To his left
the fields that led down to the lake were shrouded by a low
mist that hugged their snow-covered surface. Here and there
the top of the hedgerow could just be seen as the mist swirled

and parted, tormented as it was by the now slightest of winds. Beneath the great oaks that stood within the fencing of the winter paddock the deer herd fed from fodder. He watched a stag as it moved majestically amid the herd, great clouds of steam issuing forth from the animal's nostrils and rising up into the crystallised branches of the trees. The pine forest that lay to the east of the house and stretched up into the hill for as far as the eye could see had also taken on the same crystallised appearance and branches strained under the weight of a snowy burden. Winter's stark beauty held all in her magical grip. Only the blind or the sour of heart could fail to appreciate it. Otto was not such a man; he had an eye for beauty in any form and to him each season brought its own special beauty to the estate. But there was something about winter that somehow always stirred a mixture of emotions within him. There were bad memories hidden deep in his mind: memories of another time, of war-torn Berlin, of ground frozen so hard that they could not bury the dead. Bodies blackened by the frost, swollen fingers, bloated arms, staring dead eyes. How hard they had struggled just to survive, and yet, so many had died. At the very end, in the madness of it all, they had died.

Otto was sixty-three years old and tired. His large frame and authoritative way served well to disguise what was within the man, but for him, the last twenty or so years had taken their toll. Grief is never easy to come to terms with but for some it lingers with intolerable pain. Each day it is there, eating into pleasure and destroying life. Just when you think it has slipped into the mist that is time, it will reach out with spiny fingers and tug at a nerve end, renewing its agony in an instant. For Otto that was the way of things. Grieving had become a never-ending chapter of his life, surpassed only by the anguish of guilt. Today would be no different, just another turmoil of emotions that, in time, would again leave him drained of feeling and more than tired. Horst Urban would not help. His meeting with him would tax his brain. It would be an endless fencing match of accusation and retaliation. A conflict between capitalist and communist ideals, with no quarter spared. There would also be questions about her. There always were, and he did not relish the thought of it.

'Please mind the steps, Herr Mannerheim, they are still very slippery.'

Carl Kahler's words shook Otto's thoughts back to the present.

'Thank you, Carl, I will be careful.'

As the Mercedes pulled away from the house Otto could not resist the temptation to look back at the imposing granite structure of the building, which now stood bedecked in winter's snow. His wife had always loved it. She had been brought up there, in better times.

I promise you, when this crazy war is over, I will buy you that house and we will live in it.

They were words from the past that echoed in his head. He had kept his promise, he had bought it, but without her. It was just a dream, a dream that could never be. She was gone, killed in the tragedy that was war. Taken from him, as was his daughter, her young life full of hope, full of promise. Both lost in a second, a pointless second. Anger cut deep in his soul.

*

'She has stood up well to the operation, Otto, but I don't know how much more she can take.'

Wilhelm Meile had changed little in the fourteen years Otto had known him. As Wilhelm lit the Camel cigarette, Otto could not help but notice the Zippo lighter was still on active duty.

'Well, Wilhelm, you're the doctor, if you don't know, who does?'

'God perhaps, Otto; you see, cancer is a complicated thing we know little about it and she has a really quite advanced cancer of the cervix.'

'Do not blind me with medical terms, Wilhelm, just do what you can, will you?'

Wilhelm had never questioned Otto about his relationship with the woman. When Otto had offered him the job as director of his Berlin Clinic it had been too good an opportunity to turn down. But she had always been part of the deal. Nothing had ever been said, nothing was in writing, but she had always been there. Wilhelm had watched her mental state improve while the frailty of her body had steadily increased. She was still even now suffering from the years of abuse she had received in the camps, and in time the long arm of Nazi Germany would murder yet another Jew. For her, time was running out.

'She has been asking for you, Otto, she wants to see you.'

In the quiet of the room, Otto looked down on her as she slept, the crisp white sheet folded about her. The once dark hair, now almost completely grey and cut much shorter, still felt soft to his touch. She had been a beautiful woman, with a fine bone structure and the most wonderful eyes full of life and excitement. For a moment Otto allowed himself the luxury of memory and the magic that it held.

Then she stirred, her face turned slightly, and he saw again the large star-like scar that covered most of her right cheek.

The agony of regret returned to him. It always did return, and always would. The burden of guilt would never leave him.

'Otto, my dear Otto, I knew you would come to see me soon; how are you?' She pulled one thin arm from beneath the sheet and took his hand. The coldness of her touch surprising him.

'It is I who should be asking you that,' he smiled warmly at her.

'I am a little tired, Otto, and sore, but they say it will pass. Wilhelm fusses around me every day, he tells me I am a good patient.' A slight smile crossed her lips, lingering only for a second. 'No more Otto, no more,' she squeezed his hand gently. 'There will be no more operations now, we must both accept the inevitable.'

He looked away. 'If you mean the inevitable is death, then I can't argue with that,' he replied. 'Death will come to us all. But for you there will be many more good times. I promised you another holiday with my sister this summer and if Otto Mannerheim makes a promise, he keeps a promise.' He looked at her again and smiled.

'I will enjoy that, Otto.'

He sat with her for almost an hour as she drifted in and out of sleep. It was reassuring for her each time she awoke to find him still there, still holding her hand. It was not love that bonded them together, but then again it was. It was a special kind of love. The kind of love that two people learn to feel for each other when they have suffered life together and all the cruelties it can throw at them. She had loved him once with a passion, many years ago, in another time. But that had been the love that youth brings. Now it was different; they were kindred spirits both ravaged by time, by grief and by guilt.

*

'Otto! Otto!' Wilhelm quickened his step and caught up with the large man just before he reached the main doors.

'She is not too bad, Otto, do you think? In two or three weeks she will be back on her feet.'

'She says no more operations, Wilhelm. She has had enough.' Otto stopped and the two men faced each other.

'Well, that is her prerogative, Otto.'

'Then you must talk to her, it is a waste to come this far and then to give in to it. Talk to her, Wilhelm.'

'I said it is her prerogative, Otto, and who can blame her? She has gone through a lot.'

'Yes, so why die now? After all she has been through, why die now?'

'Perhaps, Otto, she just feels that life is not worth it. Not worth all the suffering, after all, she has been lucky to get this far. She has seen her family murdered, survived her own execution, suffered God knows what indignities, and now she is fighting cancer. If it had not been for you, Otto, who knows what would have happened to her?'

'Don't ever tell me she has been lucky,' Otto snapped back. 'And if it had not been for me, my dear Wilhelm, things may have been very different for her.'

Wilhelm knew the conversation was over. He stood and watched as Otto walked out of the building.

*

The thick lenses of Horst Urban's spectacles magnified his small dark eyes making their stare even more menacing. His thin nose and even thinner lips gave the man an almost weasel-like appearance that was not helped by his tendency to slick back his hair with large amounts of hair cream. He was a dangerous man who revelled in the power of position and, as the local Communist Workers Party representative, that power was far-reaching.

'It still continues, Herr Mannerheim!' His fist hammered on the desk as he spoke. 'Even after our last meeting, you have still done nothing!' The eyes narrowed as he waited for Otto to reply.

'And I shall continue to do nothing,' Otto replied calmly, refusing as usual to be intimidated by a little man for whom he had nothing but contempt.

'But you have read the papers. You know what Herr Ulbricht is saying, it must stop!' Again, his fist banged down.

'Frankly, Urban, I don't give a damn what the chairman says.'

Otto watched the weasel's face turn scarlet with anger.

'How dare you speak of our leader in such away? I shall report it, have no fear of that. You people are parasites. Capitalist parasites.'

'We may well be,' Otto replied. 'But answer me this, Urban, why do over 50,000 Grenzgaenger go over every day?' He did not allow Urban his chance to reply. 'Because we give them work, work and West German marks that are worth having. That's why they cross. What have they got here in the East? Nothing! Nothing but communist ideals and money that is worth next to nothing.'

'I will not listen to this capitalist bullshit!' Urban stood up. 'Over three million of our skilled workers have been stolen from us by lies and capitalist propaganda and you wonder why the East suffers!' He marched menacingly around his desk and threw a copy of *Neues Deutschland* onto Otto's lap, who ignored the gesture and let it fall to the floor.

'It's in there, all in there! The figures, everything. Read it!'

'I'm not going to read your stupid paper, Urban.' Otto's calm, unruffled tone goaded Urban to almost breaking point. He was used to intimidating and bullying lesser mortals, but this man refused to comply.

'As far as I'm concerned, Urban, my factory is in West Berlin and will remain in West Berlin. I will continue to offer work to East German workers as I have done since '47. Nothing is going to change.'

Urban smiled, it was a sickly sneering smile the art of which he had perfected better than any. 'Oh, things will change, Herr Mannerheim, have no fear of that. I, Horst Urban, have said it. Things will change.' He became quieter, returning to his seat. When he spoke again it was with the same sick smile. 'Tell me, is the Jew still alive?' It was a deliberate attempt to provoke, but like some seed, it fell on stony ground.

'She is well.' Otto's reply was casual.

'Shame! I was rather hoping she would be dead by now.'

It was Otto's turn to smile. 'Not while I've got her, Urban. Not while she's in the West.'

*

The day had lasted for ever, or at least it felt that way. His meeting with Urban had been as brutal as any, with neither giving any quarter.

Otto took a certain amount of pleasure from goading Urban, but he was playing a dangerous game and he knew it. The little man despised him and if he could find a way to harm him, he would. By now there must be countless reports on him floating around various government offices. Urban was working on the principle that if he wrote enough of them, someone somewhere would take notice. Otto stretched in his favourite chair and sipped at his cognac. What was the worst they could do anyway? Take his home, take his land? It was unlikely; there were many in higher places that liked the taxes his companies paid. They would not want to lose that. No, Urban was not that important, not yet anyway. But if he got his hands on her... the thought brought a chill to his spine... he would kill her. There was little doubt of that.

Otto picked up the pile of mail that lay on the small table beside him and thumbed through the letters with little interest, that is until he turned over the airmail letter from England. A smile came to the tired face. He had been waiting for it and his fingers tore with enthusiasm at the envelope. It was overdue.

Dear Father

I trust you are well. Progress here is slow but steady. Orders are increasing since the shake-up in marketing, I think the sales director now understands what we want! I will soon be in the position to make the other changes we discussed. I have the report now and the young woman I mentioned has done a good job. She has shown a keen interest and may be of further use to us when we bring in new blood. Her name is Ruth Valsac, she's about my age, we work well together.

I have written to Aunt Helen as you asked and will try to get things sorted so that I can come home for Christmas. Don't work too hard and avoid Urban; he will

only put your blood pressure up. So will cognac!
See you soon,
Love, F

Otto replenished his drink and then read the letter again. He was proud of his son and knew that Friedrich would soon shake the cobwebs from their stagnating investment. But he missed him. He was spending more and more time in England and Otto wasn't too sure that it was because the boy enjoyed it. After all, he had a completely free hand over there. With little else of interest in the mail, Otto finished his drink and went to his bed.

*

Her name is Ruth Valsac.

It started as just a glimmer that encroached into the darkest corner of his sleeping mind.

Her name is Ruth Valsac.

The words echoed around his dream bringing with it a light that turned all at once to flashing pictures. Pictures of a dark-eyed little girl from another time.

Her name is Ruth Valsac.

He remembered the face. Even in the dream he remembered it. Her name was Ruth. His mind tussled with the desire to sleep and the will to wake.

Her name is Ruth Valsac.

Otto woke. He sat up in an instant, his mind alert, the clarity of the dream hanging in his thoughts like a Picasso. Getting up, he put on his dressing gown and glanced at the small clock by his bed. It was 3.20am. He made his way downstairs through the dark hall and into the lounge where the smouldering remains of the fire glowed in the darkness. In the half-light of the room, he retrieved his son's letter from the table and taking it to his desk turned on the small brass table lamp. The first few lines of the letter flashed before his eyes with little significance; it was not until he reached the words of her name that he stopped.

'Ruth Valsac.'

What was it about the name? He took his pen and wrote the word on the back of the envelope. VALSAC. He wrote it in large letters.

VALSAC. Suddenly, the truth struck him. It struck him with such clarity that he cursed his stupidity for not seeing it before. He took the pen again only this time he wrote another name, CASLAV.

'I know it is late, but it is urgent that I send a telegram to England,' Otto told the international operator. 'It is for the attention of Friedrich Mannerheim, managing director of Bingham Ltd.'

EIGHT

CHRISTMAS, LONDON

THEY HAD ASKED QUESTIONS, SOMETIMES PROBING and persistent, other times casual and matter-of-fact, but nevertheless there had been questions. Ruth had fielded them like a seasoned player in the slips. It was the deception that she hated most of all, but it was necessary. There was no other way. She had told them that it was the added responsibility of her new post that kept her late at work most nights and also encroached into her weekends. That's what she had said and they had accepted it. Or at least they gave her the impression that they had. With Joseph you could never be quite sure what he was thinking. He was a wily old fox with a brain as sharp as a razor. Of course, in truth they were spending every spare minute together. Life had not been the same for either of them since that night in Trafalgar Square. Every evening he would meet her on the corner of Brewer and Glasshouse Street. It was their place, a quiet hidden place out of the way of prying eyes and office staff. She told him only that her uncle and aunt were of strict Jewish faith and would not approve of her meeting him. The truth of their fear and racial hatred she had dared not mention. But she had told him of her fear that the girls in the office might see them together, or even worse of Mr Brooks finding out. It could spoil everything for her. So, it had developed into a clandestine relationship. A relationship of stolen moments and fleeting kisses, of dinners together in quiet restaurants, or his hotel. But to both of them, their time together had become as precious as life itself. The focus of everything that was important.

'I will meet you tomorrow night,' Friedrich had declared, 'and we will have dinner at my hotel, then after, I have a surprise for you.'

She had questioned him long and hard and even threatened, with a smile, that she might not meet him, but still he would not tell her what the surprise was.

'You just wait and see,' he had laughed. 'If I tell you now, it will no longer be a surprise.'

That was last night and the memory of it probed at her mind and made it difficult for her to concentrate on anything other than their next meeting. It was Christmas Eve, and the girls were full of high spirits with much nattering and banter. At first, Ruth tried hard to keep them at their work, but in the end decided on this occasion to admit defeat. She allowed them to hang a few paperchains around the place and there was much laughter and giggling as Mary, skirt hitched up well above her knees, wobbled from desktop to desktop with paperchain in one hand and drawing pin in the other. Christmas cards were given and received and by mid-morning the place was awash with them.

Brooks paid his annual visit to all departments that afternoon and when he arrived at Ruth's she found him particularly agreeable.

'How are you, Miss Valsac?' he enquired, smiling broadly. 'I trust all is going well?'

The glow of alcohol was about the man, it lingered on his breath and reddened his face. *How different he was now*, she thought, *to when they had met the morning Mr Stones had died.* Then, he had looked drained and anxious, almost frightened. Now, he was relaxed and positively oozing confidence and obviously enjoying the after-effects of a good lunch. The jungle drums of office communications had warned her he was on his way and they had been prepared.

'Everything is fine, thank you, Mr Brooks,' Ruth replied, standing up from her desk.

'Good, good,' he looked around the room. 'Ladies all doing their bit, are they?'

'Yes, sir, they are all working very well.' Ruth smiled to herself; to think that, only minutes before, paperchain-hanging had been the order of the day. Now, despite their apparent enthusiasm for their work, 'the ladies' would be listening to every word of her conversation.

Brooks coughed as if to clear his throat, it had the desired effect; all eyes were suddenly fixed on him.

'Well done, ladies,' he began, his deep voice echoing around the office. 'It's not been an easy year what with, err, well you know, poor Mr Stone, we'll all miss him. But nevertheless, life goes on and Miss Valsac here has done a fine job so far, so keep it up, all of you. I'll be sending down something later to help you all celebrate. Merry Christmas all of you!' He was halfway to the door before they could return his festive good wishes. '4.30pm, Miss Valsac,' he said over his shoulder. 'No celebrations before then.' And with that he was gone, the door shutting behind him.

At 4.30pm exactly a large bottle of Harveys Bristol Cream was delivered, compliments of Mr Brooks. It was now official: Christmas festivities could begin. Ruth opened the bottle while Anne collected some cups, sherry glasses not being readily available at Brooks and Sons. It was a cheerful group that stood around Ruth's desk and laughed and joked as she poured the drink.

'Right, ladies,' she proclaimed, handing out the cups, 'a toast!'

There was a moment of controlled silence as order returned. 'I know it's Christmas,' there was a new serious tone to her voice, 'but it's at times like this we should spare a thought for others.' She lifted her cup. 'To Mr Stone.'

'The miserable old bugger,' Mary announced, ignoring the glares and downing the sherry.

Ruth sipped her drink then lifted her cup again. 'And to all of you. I couldn't have done it without your help and support so thank you all. Thank you all very much.' But before Ruth could drink, Ann interrupted her.

'Just a minute, Miss Valsac,' she said a little nervously, 'We all just wanted to say, miss, that,' she hesitated for a second or two as she searched for the right words, 'it's, well, we just think you're doing a great job, miss, and that we think they would be mad not to make you the permanent Head of Department and we want you to have this.' She took a small parcel from behind her back and handed it to Ruth.

'Open it, miss,' Mary said, unable to restrain her enthusiasm. 'I helped Ann pick it.'

Ruth looked at the present and then at them.

'I, err... I don't know what to say.' She had not been expecting this; Ann's few words had taken her aback and she suddenly found herself struggling to contain her emotions.

'Don't say anything,' Mary chirped in again, 'just open the present.'

Ruth could actually feel her hands tremble as she pulled the wrapping paper from the box and opened it.

'We've had it engraved,' Ann said quietly.

Ruth took the silver letter opener from its box and read the words engraved on the blade.

To Miss Valsac, Head of Department, from all her ladies. Christmas 1960.

'Well do you like it, miss?' Mary questioned.

Ruth tried hard to swallow the lump in her throat and had to blink several times to clear her eyes.

'It's lovely and so thoughtful, I will treasure it always,' she looked at the smiling faces. 'Thank you all.'

By 5.30pm the sherry had gone and the festive spirit was entrenched beyond redemption. The back door was finally locked, and it was a merry band of workers that made their way along the back alley to the street. Mary started to sing 'Silent Night' but was stopped abruptly by popular demand, her voice not being one of her strongest attributes. At the corner of the alley they all said their farewells and passed final Christmas greetings before heading off on their own separate ways through the crowds of last-minute Christmas shoppers. Ruth headed for Brewer Street.

The Christmas tree that stood in the lounge of the hotel looked a picture adorned by all manner of lights, tinsel and a host of multicoloured glass balls. Ruth had been surprised to find the place so highly decorated with paperchains everywhere and even Christmas carols being played. It gave the whole place a different ambiance.

Their meal was delightful, and the hotel staff appeared to be even more attentive than usual with the restaurant manager fussing over them both as he directed them to what, by now, they had come to consider to be their table. Six Dublin Bay oysters each was the first course accompanied by a particularly good Chablis that was wonderfully crisp, dry and severely chilled. Ruth stared wide-eyed at the crustacean delicacy nestling on the bed of crushed ice before her. She had never eaten them before.

'It's easy, Ruth, watch, a little lemon, a little wine vinegar and then the secret,' he looked at her and winked 'You just pour it down in one go.'

Ruth watched in amazement.

'I'm not sure I can do this, Friedrich,' she said, swallowing hard at the very thought.

'Trust me, Ruth, they are superb.'

Much giggling and encouragement went on between them both before Ruth actually managed to swallow one, but when she did, she quite liked the taste. By the time the sixth one had slid down she considered herself an expert and told him so. The main course that followed was pheasant served in a rich port wine sauce, which was superb. With it came a change to red wine, which Ruth declined. She was already feeling a little light-headed. They took coffee in the lounge after dinner with both of them settling contentedly in front of the log fire in the only two armchairs in close proximity. They sat in silence for a while; both were content to enjoy the warmth of the fire and the festive goodwill that somehow seemed to ooze from every crack and crevice of the old building.

Ruth wanted time to stop. To stop and leave them both trapped forever in the magic of the moment. Just the two of them together, like this, by the fire. Sucked into some Dickensian novel where nothing mattered but them, and time stood still. Nobody to answer to but themselves, no family, no work mates, no past to hide from. Just them. She stared into the fire watching the flames and twists of smoke as they spiralled upward from the burning logs. If it was just them, only them.

'Ruth.' His voice shook her from her thoughts, and she turned to look at him, reality returned.

'I'm sorry, Friedrich, I was daydreaming.'

'We must not get too comfortable here, Ruth, I still have my surprise to show you.'

His surprise, of course. It had slipped her mind.

'Come,' he said finishing his coffee and getting to his feet. 'I'm not going to let you spend Christmas Eve warm and snug in front of this fire.'

Before she had time to argue he had pulled her to her feet. 'We must get our coats; it is just a few minutes' walk from here.'

The cold of the night air shook Ruth's senses and swept away any remaining thoughts of the lounge and the fire.

'Where are you taking me, Friedrich? What's going on?'

He laughed. 'Wait and see,' was all he would say. 'Wait and see.'

She didn't take much notice of where they were going, she was too busy hanging on to his arm as he hurried along. Huddling close to him, for added warmth and protection from the cold wind, she was whisked along streets she had never seen before. Then, after about fifteen minutes or so, by which time she had no idea where she was, he stopped.

'We are here,' he announced triumphantly. And with that, he marched her up half a dozen or so wide steps to a rather grand front door.

'Friedrich, what is this?' He did not reply.

'Come on,' he said excitedly, taking a key from his pocket and opening the door. 'Come, quick, out of the cold.'

Before she knew it, she was in a large entrance hall, and still hanging onto him as he strode on across the meticulously polished marble floor, on which her heels clattered fit to raise the dead. She very quickly found herself walking on tiptoes.

'This way.' Friedrich steered her towards what was obviously a lift at the far end of the hall. 'It's on the second floor, quickly, quickly!'

Once inside the lift he pressed the button marked '2' and Ruth watched in stunned silence as the lighted numbers indicated the lift's ascent; she knew there was little point in continuing the futile questions. Almost before the lift had stopped, she was pulled out into the passage and marching towards a door at the end of the hall. Again, and as if by magic, Friedrich produced a small bunch of keys with which he fiddled for a second or two before opening the door.

'Come!' he said smiling, 'I want to show you.' She followed him in.

It was a large room, pleasantly warm and brightly decorated with pale lemon walls that bore an impressive array of watercolours. Strategically placed wall lights lit the room well yet with a warm soft light that picked out the golds and browns of a thick carpet. The far end of the room was dominated by a huge bay window draped with full-length curtains, which were similar in colour to the walls, gathered back with gold rope ties. An occasional table nestled in the bosom of the window. Ruth looked around the room in disbelief. It was beautifully furnished with predominantly antique yew furniture. There was also much Dresden in evidence with several delicately flowered pieces on display including a fine candelabra which formed the centrepiece for the dining table. Everything was immaculately set as if ready for the editor of *Country Homes*.

'This is the lounge,' he said, beaming with delight. 'Take off your coat, Ruth, it's warm, there's central heating.' He pointed to one of the large radiators. 'It's fully furnished too, with a modern kitchen, a bathroom and two bedrooms.' By now he was busy walking around the place opening doors and disappearing into rooms. Then he appeared back in the doorway.

'Come on, Ruth,' he said impatiently, 'come and see.'

She hesitated; it was strange, but she felt uneasy. She was alone with him. For the first time they were really alone. It was as if alarm bells began to ring deep in some hidden corner of her mind. She could only just hear them, but they were ringing.

'Come on, Ruth,' he shouted again.

She took off her coat and followed him.

'This is the kitchen, what do you think?'

Ruth looked around her, it was nice, very nice. He opened cupboards and shut them again, moving around the room at a pace far too quick to allow her the opportunity to really take in all there was to see. His enthusiasm was running away with him.

'Plenty of storage space,' he said, shutting yet another door. 'And there is a new oven too.' He pointed to an elegant new stove but before she could pass comment Ruth was whisked away to survey the rest of the rooms.

After a full guided tour, they returned to the lounge where Friedrich opened the drinks cabinet and, despite Ruth's objections, poured them two cognacs.

'Well, what do you think of it?' he asked, handing her the drink, his obvious delight reflected in the boyish grin on his face. 'Do you like it?'

Ruth was still struggling with her alarm bells. He had not mentioned getting his own flat before and she could not help but wonder why he had done.

'It's a lovely flat, Friedrich,' she began, taking a sip of the cognac. 'But why did you get it? Don't you like that lovely hotel?'

'Of course, I like the hotel.' He took her hand and they sat down together on the settee. 'But I want to spend much more time here in England. In the New Year I will get the changes I want in the company. I will start the expansion programme and it makes sense to rent this place. The hotel is nice but it's expensive, and it's not home.' He pointed to a small Christmas tree in the corner of the room. 'I've bought a tree.' He turned back to her and took her hand. 'We can be together here Ruth, it can be our place, and later…' He moved closer to her, putting his arm around her. 'When…' Ruth pulled away in panic. It was her own fault, she told herself; she had said she loved him. All of those times they had kissed, never once had she held back. She had let him hold her close and had taken pleasure in it. No, she couldn't blame him, it was obvious he had got this place so they could be together. So, they could make love.

'So, this is your surprise?' She stood up, turning around and pretending to take in the room again. 'It is very nice. No, it's more than that, it's lovely.' She was desperately trying to hide her apprehension. Friedrich took her hand again.

'Please, Ruth, sit back down.' He gently tugged at her arm, and she slowly sank back into the seat next to him.

'Friedrich, I'm sorry.' She looked away from him and at the small tree he had so carefully decorated. 'I know it's difficult and I do love you so but I…' She was struggling to find the right words and could feel her face blushing. 'You see, I…'

'This is only half of my surprise, darling.' His words stopped her. 'This is the other half.' He pushed a small box into her hand. 'Please open it.' His voice carried a new seriousness, a new depth of feeling.

'What is it, Friedrich?' She looked up from her hands, lost in confusion.

'Open it and find out.' A hint of a smile had returned to his face.

The lid was small and her fingers trembled as she fumbled to pull it open. When the light of the room struck the clarity of the diamond it was reflected in a multitude of prismatic colours that sparkled beyond belief. Its magnificence simply took her breath away and she was compelled to just gaze at its beauty.

'I hope it fits, and I hope you will wear it.' He took her hand. 'It's my way of saying I love you and I want to be with you.'

She remained staring at the ring, her eyes held as if by some hypnotic force.

'Will you marry me, Ruth?'

His words entered her head and bounced around as if it were an empty vessel: it was unreal, not happening to her, and yet strangely she knew it was. Like the lines of a play that someone reads when you are standing in the wings. It was happening, but not in real life. She looked at him and as she did, the cold reality of it seized her. How could it be? How could they be together? The German and the Jew. There was too much between them, they were from different worlds. The hatred in her family would never allow such a thing. It had for a moment been her play, her dream, but now, cruelly, the harshness, the cold blunt harshness of reality washed it from her. The pain of that brought the tears to her eyes.

'Why are you crying?' he asked, when he saw the tears start to spill to her cheeks. 'I thought you would be happy. I thought it was what you wanted.'

She looked at him and at the fear of rejection etched deep into his face. It was the first time she had seen him look so unsure, and she wanted desperately to hold him, to reassure him. But she could not.

'I do love you, Friedrich,' she whispered. 'I love you so very much, surely you must know that. But it is not that easy, you don't understand. There is more to my life than you realise.' She paused for a moment and looked back down at the ring. The time had come, she knew it. He had to know the truth but would it drive a wedge between them forever?

'You know I am Jewish,' she began, 'but what I have not told you is that I am also German.' She paused, waiting his reaction, but he remained silent.

'My family were from Berlin.' Again, she paused. She had not lifted her eyes from the ring; this was even harder than she had imagined. 'They murdered my family, all of them. My mother and father my younger sister and brother, they were all gassed at Dachau.' Even now they were not easy words to say and her voice trembled as she whispered them. She looked at him; it was not easy but she forced her eyes to search his face in a vain attempt to detect some sign of emotion. But there was none, just a stunned look of disbelief. She continued.

'My uncle and aunt managed to get out of Berlin in 1938 bringing me with them to England. If it had not been for them, I would have died with the others.'

Taking the ring carefully from its box she held it between her fingers. 'I will always love you, Friedrich, but how can I marry you? How can I wear this? There is so much hate still with my uncle it could...' She was unable to find the words to continue. Friedrich put his arms around her and pulled her gently to him.

'Why didn't you tell me this before? You said nothing, I never had any idea you had suffered so. You must hate me! You must hate all of us!'

'Oh no, darling,' she touched his face, 'I love you. I really love you.'

For a long while they were silent, the pair of them just holding each other, saying nothing, but inside both toiling with the reality of the past. Then he spoke.

'I understand how hard it will be, I understand that your uncle and aunt must hate me but I will always be grateful to them for saving your life.' He brushed the hair back from her face as he spoke. 'Even if it takes forever, Ruth, I promise we will be together. It can happen, it will happen.' He took the ring from her hand. 'Just for now, perhaps it is better, you wear it like this.' His hand moved up to her neck and gently he removed the gold chain that held her Star of David. He slid the ring onto the chain and then replaced it, his hands gently brushing against the softness of her neck as he did so.

'I don't want to wait for ever, Friedrich.' The words just seemed to spill from her lips; gone was the concern at being alone with him, there was only the need to love him. Maybe they did have a chance for a life together, perhaps it was possible for them to overcome the fear and resentment that still remained within her family. She didn't know and suddenly she didn't care. They loved each other and that was all that mattered. Taking both his hands she held them to her face kissing his fingers. 'I love you so much,' she murmured, looking into his eyes, 'why wait?' She kissed him and still holding his hands moved them down to her breasts, feeling them against the thin material of her blouse. She trembled as he explored the softness of her, and she made no attempt to stop him as his fingers fumbled with the tiny buttons. There was no protest as she felt his touch against the nakedness of her skin, only a satisfying urge within her when finally, his fingers reached the tenderness of her breast. She should have felt embarrassed, awkward, shy, as slowly he slipped the blouse from her shoulders and struggled with the clasp of her bra. But she felt none of those things. She felt only a need, an overwhelming need to love him, to let him love her and she unashamedly rejoiced as his eyes looked down at her naked breasts. No man had ever seen her like this but she wanted him to look and to touch and to enjoy. Yes, to enjoy. She pulled him to her again, kissing him hard, her whole body tingling with excitement as she pushed his hand hard against her firm breast. Then suddenly, in one movement, he pulled her to her feet and as easily as a child carries a doll, he carried her to his bed.

She could only whisper, 'I love you,' as his hands gently explored every naked detail of her. She made no attempt to resist as they lay together in the darkness of the room, his touch sending the most delicious sensations through her whole body as his fingers slowly moved over her skin. Her own boldness amazed her as instinctively she reached out and touched him. Just touched him. Even the most secret intimate parts of him she touched and delighted at how just the softest, slightest caress of her fingers could arouse him. Then her eyes opened, staring into the darkness and she moaned softly as she felt his fingers push, gently, into the moist softness of her. The ache of her womanhood made her whole body arch and reach up uncontrollably as the need took her and her hand moved down to his, pushing it even harder against her. Then, through the mist of what seemed like a dream, she felt him. It was not hurried, not brutal, not even lustful. It was gentle, he was gentle as she felt him take her and she gave herself willingly and completely to him.

*

It was the early hours of Christmas morning when Friedrich finally arrived back at his hotel and the receptionist handed him the telegram. In his room he opened it and blinked as his tired eyes struggled to focus in the poor light of the bedside table lamp.

FRIEDRICH THE WOMAN RUTH VALSAC IS SHE JEWISH? STOP FIND OUT WHAT YOU CAN IT IS URGENT STOP WRITE VALSAC BACKWARDS AND YOU WILL SEE STOP SHE MUST NOT SUSPECT ANYTHING STOP
　　OTTO

Friedrich did not write the word; he did not need to. He had seen it in an instant. It had to be her, there could be no doubt about it. What a fool he had been!

NINE

JANUARY 1961

'MR KHRUSHCHEV HAS SENT NEW YEAR GREETINGS to Mr Kennedy, and the President Elect said at Palm Beach today that he hoped United States–Soviet relations in 1961 would be marked by "Good will and a common desire for peace". And Ruth Valsac made a New Year's resolution.

Ruth gave up, her arms ached and she missed Peanut's, the back-page cartoon strip of the *Sketch*. She had bought *The Times* newspaper for the first time ever, but now, as she sat on the bus and struggled with the large pages, she began to question the wisdom of her New Year's resolution. She had made up her mind that this year she would take more interest in the world about her and in particular Europe. *The Times* seemed a good way.

It was the unusually mild weather that had helped January slip into existence with an almost nonchalant ease, and before people had realised it, the New Year and its first day of work was upon them. For many, their work was a means to an end, a way of existing. For others, for the lucky ones, it was a joy. Ruth was one of the lucky ones, for her work did not carry with it the dread it held for others. It was the start of a fresh year, a new challenge and her mind positively buzzed with the excitement of it as she made her way to work on that Monday. She folded the paper neatly and rested it on her lap, her idle mind bouncing from subject to subject before finally it bounced from work and settled on the luxury of him. They had only managed to meet once since Christmas Eve, and then it had only been briefly. He had to return to Germany; it was urgent. That's all he had told her. Some important business his father wanted him for, but now he was back and she was looking forward to tonight, when they were to have dinner together. She smiled at the thought. Now things would be easier, she told herself. The regular evening rendezvous would return, life would return to that happy comfort that was the norm, and despite the fear of discovery, she relished the thought of it. The fact that she thought about him so much did not surprise her, but what did trouble her was how often she thought about that night in his flat, the night they made love. For her it had been the first time, and she just couldn't forget it. She didn't want to forget it. The memory of it would invade her mind constantly with little or no respect for how she was occupied. She would be in conversation with someone and suddenly it was there, the memory would return and she would be back in the darkness of that room, in his arms, making love. At the most absurd, embarrassing times it would invade and she was sure people had noticed her face blush for no apparent reason. It was embarrassing, yes, the thought of how intimate she had been, but they were her thoughts, her own private thoughts and secretly she loved them.

'I've nearly got it right, Ruth,' Friedrich said as he finished the last of what had been a particularly fine brandy. They were in Rimando's, a small Italian restaurant that lay in one of the quieter streets leading off the Strand. It was the second time they had used it and both times they had found the food to be excellent.

'Got what right?' she asked.

'Everything,' he replied, playing on her curiosity.

'Friedrich, you know only too well that you are dying to tell me something so just go ahead, put yourself out of your agony and tell me.'

'Well,' he said leaning closer to her. 'Next week I have meeting.' It was an uncharacteristic slip in Friedrich's normally perfect English and it caused Ruth to smile. 'Then I will get the shake-up in the board that I want. By the time I have read them your report and made it clear that we cannot tolerate such bad management, well at the very least, the financial director will have little option other than to resign!' A smile lit up his face. 'Then I will be able to bring in, how do you say it, some new blood.' He paused for a moment as if to ponder the future. 'All will be well, Ruth.' There was a new softness to his voice, a sudden seriousness seemed to have taken him. 'I promise you all will be well.' Ruth frowned; she did not have the same confidence in her report that he had. She knew it was important for him to get the changes he wanted, yet she had given him the report over a month ago and still he had not acted on it.

'You must always wait till the time is right,' he had replied when she asked him why he had not yet used it. 'And next week the time it is right.'

Friedrich paid the waiter and left a generous tip before the two of them made their way arm in arm from the restaurant. Neither of them noticed the young man sitting in the far corner of the room who had showed a particular interest in them. He was a tall, thin young man with a mop of dark hair that, despite the heavy application of hair cream, continually fell untidily around his eyes.

'What is it you keep looking at, Robert?' the young woman sitting opposite him enquired with more than a little aggravation.

'Just thought I recognised someone, darling, that's all. Just thought I recognised someone.'

*

'Well, what do you think then?' Brooks fired the question at the young man who sat across the desk from him.

'Difficult, father,' he replied brushing back the hair from his eyes as he spoke. 'After all, you did appoint her acting head of department.'

'I know that!' Brooks' temper was becoming a little frayed around the edges by his son's obstructive manner. 'And I would not have done so if the situation had not demanded immediate action.'

'They're not going to like it, father, you know, after all, head of department, even acting head appointments, should be made at board level nowadays.'

Robert was enjoying his father's dilemma; it wasn't every day that his opinion was sought, and he realised that his support was vital if the old man were to avoid humiliation. But it would serve him right if he did get egg on his face. The silly old bugger had been panicked into making her appointment by the death of Stone and now he was on the hook.

'Look, Robert, I need your support on this, of course the girl can't remain as head of that department but with some internal reorganisation we could make her head of C floor.'

Robert got to his feet and took a few paces towards the window. There was no love lost between father and son and both knew it. Ever since Robert's mother had died the rift between them had deepened. The son had watched his mother die, alone and in terrible pain. Every day she would ask about his father, and then make excuses for him not being there. She carried on the pretence to the very end. Robert still was not really sure if she ever did know about her husband's long and well-publicised affair with that bitch Jennifer Dawson.

'I don't know what you expect me to do, Father?' He turned back to face him, lifting his hands in a gesture of bewilderment. 'I mean, how can I help?'

'Just support her bloody appointment, that's what you do!'

*

It was 2.30pm exactly when the other five members of the board of Brooks and Son filed into the boardroom to join the two men already seated. There were the normal handshakes and greetings before Brooks as chairman opened the meeting by saying that he hoped all were well and apologising for calling a meeting so early in the New Year. This was followed by the appropriate murmurs when the Chair announced the sad demise of the long and trusted employee Mr Eric Stone. The show of hands around the table was unanimous when Robert Brooks quickly proposed that the sum of £500 be paid to his widow, a sum twice that which, if the chair had been given time, he would have proposed. It was to be a special payment by way of gratitude for Stone's long and dedicated service. Brooks himself was somewhat taken aback by the financial director's ready agreement to pay out such a sum. Normally, Brown was, to say the least, conservative in any payments. Brooks cleared his throat.

'Now, gentlemen, Stone's untimely passing did cause the company some considerable difficulty. It was necessary for me, in the light of some ongoing and particularly important company commitments to Mannerheim International, to appoint someone to take immediate charge of the situation and thereby enable work to continue. Most of you are aware of course that they have bought out Bingham Ltd and that we are acting on the instructions of Herr Friedrich Mannerheim himself.' Brooks felt some relief as the heads around the table nodded their approval, all that is except Robert who doodled annoyingly on the notepad in front of him.

'I therefore took the unprecedented step of appointing Stone's second-in-command to the position of acting head of department.'

He was treading carefully, leading them step by step, gaining their approval slowly before informing them fully about Stone's second-in-command.

'Mr Chairman, if I may?' Robert had stopped doodling and was now holding his pen aloft in a manner so as to gain his father's attention. The chair acknowledged him.

'Stone's second-in-command, Mr Chairman? You have no doubt the utmost confidence in his ability, but remind me, has he been with the company long?'

It was a clever move by Robert and his father knew it. He had in those few words disassociated himself from any previous knowledge of the appointment and of the fact that 'he' was indeed a 'she'. He had also spoiled his father's timing. Brooks cursed his son's lack of loyalty.

'Gentlemen,' he began again, determined to put his case as best he could, 'Robert is right of course, I do have the utmost confidence in this employee and my confidence, I am pleased to say, has been confirmed by a letter from Herr Mannerheim confirming his satisfaction with the handling of his company's accounts, and what's more stating that he would be placing all their future accountancy needs with Brooks and Sons.' The nods of approval were again evident. This time, Brooks' attention was drawn to the rather overweight frame of Brown, the financial director. Jeremy Brown was a shrewd man who had plagued Brooks ever since he had been appointed financial director some six years ago. They had clashed countless times over the years and Brooks had long since learned not to be fooled by his casual attitude and expressionless approach.

'Very commendable, Mr Chairman, I am glad that this employee has done so well for Brooks and Son.' Brown sat back in his chair letting the Parker fountain pen drop from his hand and roll across the notepad in front of him. 'However, some of you may be aware that I myself played a small part in acquiring the Bingham's account and have some considerable influence in that company.'

There were several knowing smiles around the table.

'Therefore, Mr Chairman, I was somewhat concerned to hear that the person dealing with this client as acting head of department was a Miss Ruth Valsac, a young Jewish girl who found herself suddenly thrust into events at the last moment.'

Again, murmurs broke out around the table. Brooks noticed his son was having some difficulty disguising his delight, having set his father up, Brown had been obliging enough to deliver the *coup de grâce*.

Brooks pressed on, 'Gentlemen, Miss Valsac has been with the company since she was fourteen; she is now, I believe twenty-seven and a very capable employee. She has done a first-class job at Bingham's and you will recall Herr Mannerheim has himself been very complimentary of her work.'

Brown's hand was waving again.

'Mr Chairman, with respect, the work was all but finalised before Stone died; all the girl had to do was deliver the final report. We must not underestimate Stone's work on this, Mr Chairman. Let's not go giving all the credit to a bit of a girl who just had to give over the report, smile and look pretty.'

Brown sat back in the chair, his large stomach dropping in several layers over his trouser belt, a look of self-satisfaction on his face.

Brooks had been somewhat taken aback; Brown knew that the girl had been handling the Bingham's account, but as he was also the financial director of Bingham's, Brooks had expected him to know. What did surprise him, however, was how much Brown knew. He himself had been unable to find a copy of Stone's final report. The girl had told him that it was all that was left to do and that she would do it. Now Brown was saying Stone had finished it. Brooks was puzzled; had the girl lied? 'I am interested to know, Mr Brown,' Brooks asked as he rose to his feet, 'how you knew Stone's report was finished?'

The look of self-satisfaction on Brown's face turned to a smirking grin.

'The man had the good sense to confer with me, Mr Chairman, throughout his writing of the report. After all, I have been the financial director of Bingham's for over ten years now and if I don't know how the company works then who does?'

Brooks said no more about the Bingham's account. He went on to tell the board about the careful consideration he had given to the restructuring of the various floors so that Stone's vacant position may be filled with the minimum of disruption.

'As you are aware, Stone was the head of A floor. It is now my intention to seek board approval for Mr Weston, the current head of B floor, to be promoted to head of A.' Brooks sensed a general agreement around the table and so continued. 'It is therefore logical that Mr Hooper, the present head of C floor, take on the mantle of responsibility for B floor. This would then leave a vacancy for head of department C floor.'

Robert's hand suddenly went up.

'Mr Chairman, I would like to second your proposals so far on these appointments; after all, they are really only a natural progression.'

A show of hands around the table quickly confirmed that all were in agreement and the appointments were approved.

'Gentlemen, we are left now with the position of head of C floor.' Before Brooks could deliver his practised line about a golden opportunity for the company to break with the bonds of tradition and appoint the position to a woman, Robert's waving hand again interrupted him.

'Sorry to interrupt, Mr Chairman, but Herr Mannerheim, is he not that tall, somewhat good-looking man you introduced me to last year at the Institute of Directors meeting?'

'Good God, Robert, we are in the middle of discussing our C floor appointment, why ask that now?' It was obvious to all present by the sharpness of Brooks' reply that he was becoming frustrated with his son's continuous interruptions.

'It is relevant, Mr Chairman, only I wouldn't like any reshuffle to involve the moving of Miss Valsac from her position on A floor. After all, we would not want anything to affect the excellent working relationship Miss Valsac has formed with Herr Mannerheim.' The smirk in Robert's voice made it clear to all that he was suggesting there may well be more to the working relationship.

Brown was on it like a ferret. 'Are you suggesting, Robert, that there is a personal relationship between our Miss Valsac and Herr Mannerheim?' Brown questioned.

'In answer to Mr Brown's question, Mr Chairman,' Robert replied, one eyebrow raised, 'I have seen them both together at Rimando's restaurant recently on two occasions and both times it would appear that they had eyes only for each other.'

Brooks was sunk; he knew they would never agree to Valsac's appointment to head of C floor now.

Brown chuckled; his whole mass seemed to wobble with amusement. 'Well, gentlemen, it would appear this young lady does her best work between the sheets, her dedication to the company is commendable.' The chuckle turned into a laugh. 'Well as long as she's keeping Mannerheim happy, no wonder he's written to say he's pleased with her services!' Brown could hardly contain himself; it was obviously appealing to his sense of humour. But then suddenly he stopped laughing and, leaning forward in his chair, picked up his pen. 'Mr Chairman,' he said, waving the pen, 'may I propose Johnson for head of C floor? After all, he has been with us many years now.'

*

As the two men left the building, Brown put a large hand on Robert's shoulder. 'We must have lunch soon, young Robert,' he said slapping him several times on the back. 'Thought for one moment that father of yours was going to suggest that silly young woman, what's her name, Valsac or something, be appointed Head of C!'

Robert stopped and looked at Brown, 'You know damn well he was; I think the old fool's beyond hope.' Robert's words did not surprise Brown; he knew the lad was ambitious and that there was no love lost between father and son.

'Lunch soon then,' Brown replied, 'I think we've got a lot to discuss, don't you, me lad?' A smile came to Brown's face and he laughed. 'Can't stop now, got a meeting with that damn silly German at Bingham's; I'll just make it if I hurry.'

Robert watched as Brown made his way to the main doors. 'Lunch soon!' he shouted back over his shoulder as the door closed behind him.

*

Strange how even the briefest span of time can change the destiny of a man. Mere hours in a winter's afternoon can turn smiles and triumph into disaster. So it was for Jeremy Brown, for it was a bitter and humiliated man who emerged from the board meeting of Bingham's later that evening. How had the German put it? 'A wind of change was needed at Bingham's.' Unfortunately, that wind had blown him and two other directors from the board. It would never have happened, Brown told himself, if that stupid little bitch had not rewritten Stone's report. All that wasted effort making sure Stone had said just the right things. Four thousand pounds a year salary down the drain; she would pay for this, he'd make damn sure of that.

*

Jennifer Dawson dialled 71 on her telephone and waited.

'Ruth, you had better get yourself up here straight away, Mr Brooks wants to see you.' The tone in Jennifer's voice was enough to start Ruth's heart racing. As she hurried up the stairs to the top floor, she was sure this must be it. It was common knowledge there had been a board meeting yesterday and her appointment as head of department would most certainly have been on the agenda. She looked at her watch; it was only 9.30am, no one else would have been seen before her, not this early. She scarcely noticed the climb up the twenty-three stairs such was her excitement. As she reached the top, she asked herself again the same question she had asked a thousand times. Why shouldn't she be the first woman head of department? Everything had gone well. Bingham's had gone well, the girls were working better than ever and there was Friedrich's letter. Ruth stopped outside the door that led to Jennifer's office. What more could she have done? They just had to appoint her.

'Go straight through, Ruth, would you please?' Jennifer did not look up from her typing.

'What the bloody hell do you think you've been playing at!'

The aggression in the voice shook the smile from Ruth's face before she could even shut the door.

'You bloody silly little cow, do you know what you've done?'

Ruth stared at the overweight man who was half standing, half sitting as he struggled to lift his bulk from the chair in front of Brooks' desk.

'Now just a minute, Brown, this is my office and I'll handle this.'

The authority in Brooks' voice seemed to check the large man and Ruth watched as he aborted his effort to rise and sank back into the chair.

Brooks turned to Ruth. 'Come in, Miss Valsac.'

The man's verbal onslaught had left Ruth stunned and she had to struggle to regain her composure. She closed her mouth and moved towards the desk.

'This is Mr Jeremy Brown, Miss Valsac, he is a director of Brooks and Son.'

'Too bloody right I am!' Brown snarled as he glared at her.

Ruth could not help but feel intimidated by the man and his aggressive manner, but despite this she made herself speak.

'I think I have seen Mr Brown before, sir, but I didn't know he…'

Brooks raised his hand stopping her in mid-sentence.

'Miss Valsac, when I asked you how your first meeting with Herr Mannerheim had gone you told me that it had been successful and that it only remained for you to complete the final report.'

'That's correct sir,' she forced a smile.

'It now appears, Miss Valsac, that Stone had in fact already written his final report, but you in your wisdom decided to rewrite the thing in a manner that suited you, is this right?'

Ruth hesitated. Taken aback by Brooks' question, she had not expected to be asked about the report.

'I asked you a question, Miss Valsac!' Brooks banged the table with the flat of his hand making Ruth jump with the noise.

'Sir, the report was inept; it did not clearly identify the entrenched problems at Bingham's, it glossed over what had been obvious bad management. Herr Mannerheim was not happy with it.'

Before Ruth could get the last of her words out, she found herself stepping backwards as Brown, with one huge effort, heaved his great mass from the chair, his purple face ending up just an inch or so from hers.

'That report, young lady, was the result of much hard work by myself and Stone, who incidentally had forgotten more about running that damn office than a silly bitch like you will ever know.'

Ruth's temper surged.

'Why are you being so rude to me, you horrible man?' The words just seemed to spring from her mouth and were as much of a surprise to her as they were to the two men.

'Mr Brown was the financial director of Bingham's.' The significance of Brooks' words took a second or two to strike home but when they did, the sickening reality of them left her cold.

'Oh,' was all she could manage to say, and for the second time that morning, her mouth fell open.

'Oh! Bloody oh!' Brown retorted, his voice now booming louder than ever. 'You and your bloody boyfriend have lost me my place on the board at Bingham's.'

'That's not my fault!' Ruth retaliated, 'I didn't vote you off the board.'

'No but that bloody report of yours did the trick.'

Ruth noticed that Brown's face had now reached a shade of purple which, if circumstances had been different, may well had led her to fear for his safety. As it was, she would have been quite happy for him to drop dead. She turned to Brooks.

'Look, sir, I'm sorry if my report has caused you embarrassment but I only did my best. Nobody told me that Mr Brown sat on both boards, I just did what was asked of me.'

Brown jumped on her words almost as she spoke them.

'In more ways than one it would appear, Miss Valsac.'

'What do you mean by that?' Ruth made no attempt to hide the contempt in her reply, she knew it had gone too far for that.

'Come off it, Miss Valsac!' Brown spoke with a new sarcasm in his voice. 'We all know why Mannerheim wrote such a glowing report on your performance, don't we?'

'He was pleased with my work, that's why.' Ruth had shouted her reply directly in Brown's face as he had moved in close to her again.

'From what I understand, it's more the work you've done in his bed that kept him happy.'

The full force of her hand struck Brown square on the side of his fat purple face before she herself could control the instinctiveness of her reactions. The blow knocked him momentarily off balance and he stumbled backwards before collapsing back into his chair. For a moment, a stunned silence reigned.

It was Brooks' voice that finally broke Ruth from the shock of what she had done.

'I am afraid, Miss Valsac, in the light of your conduct here today and in view of the embarrassment your handling of the Bingham's account has caused this company, and in particular one of its directors, I have no option other than to terminate your employment. Your cards will be sent on to you, please clear your desk and be off the premises in fifteen minutes.'

*

As she sat in the taxicab the events of the last half-hour or so went around and around in her head. In that short space of time her world had been turned upside down and she had tumbled headlong from it. *How could so much change in so short a time?* she asked herself. Everything she had worked for all these years, just gone. Snatched from her by narrow-minded manipulative men who cared only for their own well-being. What a fool she had been to think she would be promoted to head of department, how stupid to let her temper get the better of her and to strike Brown like that, however much he had deserved it. She wanted to cry but she couldn't, she felt too empty to cry, too hurt, too stupid, too humiliated. But there was something even worse, something that overshadowed everything: without a doubt, Friedrich he must have known. How he must have laughed at her naivety as she rushed in, eager to do his bidding. Now she realised, Stone was not so stupid after all, he had known. He had written the report in such a way that it couldn't be used to hurt Brown. Friedrich must have thought her a gift from heaven when she delivered him the weapon he wanted. And to think she had fallen in love with him, she had slept with him, given him everything because she thought he loved her; but he had used her! Just used her!

This man Mannerheim, you must be careful, very careful, do not trust him, he will use you. Uncle's words rang loud in her ears. Had he been right after all?

When the taxi stopped Ruth got out and pushed a ten-shilling note through the driver's window. 'Keep the change,' she said.

'What change?' the cabby shouted after her, as she pushed her way past the doorman and in through the entrance of Bingham's.

'I'm afraid Herr Mannerheim has people with him right now, Miss Valsac, but if you care to wait I'll...'

As the door burst open six heads turned in the direction of the petite dark-haired woman who now stood facing them. Friedrich got to his feet in an instant, his mouth gaping open.

'Miss Valsac, how nice to see you.' He moved away from the table and towards her. 'Gentlemen, may I introduce you to Miss Valsac, she is the one that...' Before he could finish his words a copy of Ruth's final report hit him in the chest, its paper spilling out in all directions as it did so.

'I thought you might like my copy to remind you of your success!' Ruth's temper spilled out into her words as she shouted at him.

Friedrich looked at the paper around his feet, the smile gone from his face.

'Ruth, what is this?'

'It's my copy of the report, I told you, something to remind you of your success. You see I won't need it now, Herr Mannerheim, not now that I've been sacked. Perhaps it will also remind you of Christmas Eve and all the other times working with me, or should I say on me. It must have given you such pleasure. I trust I did give you pleasure?'

'Ruth, I don't understand, why have you been sacked?'

'You knew damn well Jeremy Brown was on the board of Brooks and Son and yet you let me write that report, didn't you?'

Friedrich didn't answer.

'Do you know what really hurts?' Her emotions were starting to take control now and the tears in her eyes flooded over, running freely down her face. 'I thought you loved me, how bloody stupid could I be, I was just another Jew for you to use, wasn't I?'

'Ruth, that's not true, please listen to me.' He moved towards her.

'Go to hell, Herr Mannerheim.' She turned to the men who sat in dumb silence at the table. 'You know what they say, never trust a German.'

She had almost reached the door before Friedrich managed to grab her and turn her to face him, several well-placed blows hitting him in the chest as he did so.

'Get out, all of you! Please just get out!' Friedrich's words were enough to set the men hurrying from the room, each of them acting as if the weeping woman restrained in his grip did not even exist. By the time the last one had left, and the door was closed leaving them alone together, the anger in her had given way to complete despair. It was as if all the agony and disappointment now just flowed from her, leaving her powerless to fight against his strong grip. For a moment or two he just held her to him, her tears washing what little make-up she was wearing from her face and onto the crisp white of his Van Heusen shirt.

'How could you think I would hurt you so?' He stroked her hair as he spoke. 'I have told you a thousand times that I love you.'

Ruth listened to everything he said; she wanted to believe him and she had to admit his argument was convincing. Why would he have allowed Brooks and Son to do the audit and write the report if he had known Jeremy Brown would have a hand in it?

'You must believe me, Ruth,' Friedrich protested. 'What would be the point? I wanted to get rid of the man! You must trust me, Ruth, come with me now, I have something to tell you.'

He had wanted to get rid of Brown, that was true of course, but now sitting quietly next to him as the car moved through the London traffic, she could not help but ask herself if he had not already found out about Brown's involvement? He had told her at their first meeting that he was about to dismiss Stone. Had he seen a golden opportunity in the man's death and her appointment to let the whole thing just work for him? Her head hurt and she felt a mess. She wanted to just go home, get some rest and think things out; after all, what did the future hold for her now? She was certain of one thing, though: she desperately wanted to believe he had not known. She had lost her job, her life was a wreck, but yet she may still have something if she could hold onto her love for him.

When Edward stopped the car outside Friedrich's flat Ruth protested.

'Listen,' he said, 'you can't go home like you are, come up to the flat, get yourself sorted out then I will take you home and perhaps together we can work out what you can tell your uncle and aunt.'

Edward was instructed to return in two hours and before she could protest any further, Ruth found herself in the lift. Once inside the flat Friedrich went straight to the kitchen and returned carrying a bottle of champagne and two glasses.

'There is no better way to meet adversity,' he said as the cork bounced off the ceiling.

'I'm really not in the mood for this, Friedrich!'

'No perhaps not, but things will get better.' He poured the champagne. 'I have a proposition for you and this is a way of celebrating your acceptance.' Reluctantly she took the glass.

'I need a new financial director; I was going to ask you anyway, so what the hell? You know I went home at Christmas; well, I've discussed it with my father and we want you to be financial director of our UK operation.' He smiled. 'Please say yes, Ruth. Then I want to come back with you tonight to meet your uncle and aunt and I want to tell them that, to hell with everything, we are getting married next week. Then I want you to come to Germany with me without delay and meet my father. Well, what do you say to my proposition?'

'There's a lot of "I want" in your proposition, Friedrich,' Ruth replied as she fought furiously to clear her mind. It was a wonderful opportunity for her but was it only being offered to her as a bed mate?

'Yes, I suppose there is,' he replied.

'What about what I want?' she asked.

'Well, when I first asked you to marry me you said you wanted to. Have you changed your mind?'

'I don't know what I want after today; I don't know what to think, I'm confused.'

'Do you still love me?' he asked.'

'Of course, I do.'

'Then to hell with it, Ruth, let's just do it, let's get married.'

She smiled. 'We've been through this before!'

Friedrich took the glass from her and pulled her to him.

'There's another "I want" in my proposition Ruth and that's you. I just want you and I will make it happen. Now tell me you will marry me, tell me you will come to Germany with me, tell me Ruth, tell me.'

Ruth wondered how a day could start so bad and yet end so well. As she lay in his arms, she told herself that together they would make it work, together they would face them. He had just made love to her again only this time it had been even better than she could have ever dreamed. He had stolen away all her worries and disappointments and replaced them with hopes and dreams. She had given herself more fully than ever before and for the first time had experienced a fulfilment she had not even realised could exist. How could she have ever doubted him?

*

When Friedrich returned to the flat later that night, he had still not met her uncle and aunt. It had been too late by the time he had got her home and Ruth had insisted that the time was not right. He did, however, have a new financial director for Bingham's and she had agreed to go to Germany with him. He picked up the telephone.

'I would like to send a telegram to Herr Otto Mannerheim in Berlin, please, it is to read as follows:

'ALL GOES WELL STOP SHE HAS ACCEPTED JOB AND WILL COME TO GERMANY STOP I AM SURE SHE SUSPECTS NOTHING STOP SEE YOU IN BERLIN SOON

FRIEDRICH.'

TEN

THE NIGHTMARE RETURNS

ELIZABETH LOOKED PERPLEXED. SHE HAD LISTENED carefully to her, to every word she had said; nevertheless she was having difficulty coming to terms with what her niece was saying. Ruth had tried to explain, she had done nothing else for probably the last twenty minutes or so. The trouble was Elizabeth didn't really want to hear her. Everything Joseph had said, everything he had prophesied, was becoming reality. She had seen the pain and the anguish in his face when he had warned her that Ruth would fall in love with the man, and he had been close to tears and frantic with worry at the thought of him taking over her life.

'History repeats itself,' he had told her. 'Their parents fell in love once and so will they.' There could be no doubting his words now; their worst fears had been realised.

'If you help me explain to him, Auntie,' Ruth had pleaded. 'If I know I have you on my side.'

How could she be on her side? She knew only too well how they both felt, she knew the past. Joseph would never accept this, her working for the man, her going to Germany. The thought of telling him was enough to make her blood run cold. But inside Elizabeth, there was a deep love for her niece. No natural mother could feel more for her own daughter than she felt for her. She desperately wanted her to be happy, for her to fall in love and to have all the wonderful things that life can bring, should bring, to young people. And to see her now, so full of excitement, so beautiful. It was as if she was looking back through time, back into the eyes of her dear sister-in-law. The lovely young woman from whom the cruelty of war stole everything that was precious. No, she could not allow it. For Ruth it must be different, she must not get involved with another Mannerheim and especially Otto's son. It was time now and Elizabeth knew it. There would be no way to spare her, she had to be told.

Joseph said nothing at first, he just sat one arm resting on the kitchen table, palm upwards supporting his head.

'She is coming down at seven to tell you herself. What shall we do, Joseph?' Large tears were already beginning to form in his wife's eyes. 'She says she is going to Germany with him. If Otto sees her, he will be bound to recognise her, she's so much like her mother.' She took the handkerchief from her apron pocket and blew her nose. 'What are we going to do, Joseph?' she repeated her question.

Joseph had feared that this moment would come, it had been inevitable. If Ruth's mother could fall in love with Otto Mannerheim all those years ago in Berlin then it was more than probable Ruth would do the same with the son. She was, after all, the image of her mother in every way. The worry of what might be had weighed heavily on his mind since he had first realised who the young man was. But now it was strange. There was no questioning what had to be done and that in itself seemed to lift a burden from him.

'We have tried to hide the truth from her, Elizabeth, we can do no more now. We must tell her, you know that.'

Elizabeth did not reply.

*

Ruth was somewhat taken aback when she found them together in the kitchen. There was no wine on the table, no glasses, not even Uncle's after-dinner whisky. Just the two of them sitting next to each other, Uncle's large hand holding Elizabeth's. Ruth knew this would not be easy. She had been planning it for over a week now. While Friedrich had been making all the plans for their trip, she had been desperately searching for an easy way to tell them. She had not found it.

'Hello, both of you.' A nervous smiled forced its way to her lips. 'How are…?'

'Please sit down, Ruth.' He did not let her finish. The expression on his face and the tone in his voice left no doubt in her mind that her aunt had told him. She sat down but as she did so her uncle got up from the table and went to the sideboard. Ruth watched as he opened the top right-hand drawer and reached inside. He returned carrying what looked to her like a brown oily rag.

'Before you say anything, Uncle, I know Elizabeth has told you and I know what you think, but I love him, Uncle, I can't help it, I just love him.' She had blurted out the words like some lovesick schoolgirl and now blushed at the thought of it.

Joseph looked at her. She was every bit as beautiful as her mother had been and just as stubborn. His face softened for a moment.

'I know you love him, Ruth, and I know you can't help that.'

The understanding in his reply brought encouragement to her.

The brown rag fell to the table with an unexpected clunk. He sat back down and taking hold of the rag unravelled it, revealing a pistol. Ruth looked at the gun, then at her aunt and then back at the gun.

'It's a pistol,' he said, as if it was necessary for him to explain the obvious. 'It was stolen from a drunken SS officer outside a bar in Berlin in January 1938. Take it, Ruth, pick it up.' He waved his hand at it in a casual gesture.

She looked at him. 'Why are you showing me this? What is this all about?'

'Please, Ruth, pick it up.' He slid it towards her across the table.

'I shan't touch it!' She sat back in her chair in a gesture of defiance as her temper gained.

'We had been drinking too that night, your father, me and our friend. We were nearly as drunk as the SS officer when we stole it.'

'Why are you doing this, Uncle? Ruth pleaded. 'What can it possible achieve?'

He continued, her words lost to him. 'It was me, your father and Otto Mannerheim who stole that pistol, Ruth. Otto Mannerheim, the father of Friedrich Mannerheim.'

'Uncle we've been through this once,' she was indignant. 'So, you used to know a man called Mannerheim, it's not that uncommon a name for goodness' sake!'

'Listen to your uncle, he tells you the truth.' The unfamiliar sternness in Elizabeth's voice shook Ruth and she listened.

'I will always remember the first time I met Otto Mannerheim.' Uncle got up again from the table as he spoke, only this time he retrieved the whisky bottle and two glasses. Sitting down, he filled both glasses, taking one for himself and handing the other to Elizabeth. Ruth was surprised that she took it.

'It was the summer of 1906,' he paused, lost for a moment as he allowed his mind to travel back to a memory. 'I was eight years old, your father, well he was younger, maybe just six years old. At the time we lived in a small village about thirty kilometres to the east of Berlin. One morning they brought a new boy into the class. He was a little older than the rest of us, about nine years old. His name was Otto Mannerheim.' Uncle emptied the glass in one and stared for a moment into the bottom of it before pouring another.

'We became friends, the three of us. We went everywhere together; we were inseparable as children and even more so as we went through all the things together that young boys go through as they grow into men. Then, in the summer of 1915, Otto was called up to go to war. Oh, how I envied him, Ruth. There he stood in all his fine uniform, a man. And then there was I, a mere year younger and yet still a boy. When later it was my turn, I suppose you could say I was lucky. By the time I had finished my basic training and spent some time in the Transport Corps, the war was over, and I had never fired a bullet. But not Otto, he came back a sergeant with wonderful stories of death and honour. He was the pride of the village, a hero. After the war he went to the University of Berlin to study history and as for your father and me, well we went to work for your grandfather to train as printers. Between the wars, life was good for the young people of Berlin, it was a city of great culture and great fun.' Again, Uncle finished his drink and without hesitation recharged the glass. Ruth took the opportunity to smile at her aunt, but she did not smile back. Her eyes were red from the tears that now ran freely down her face, the untouched drink still gripped in one hand.

'The first time we met her I think we all fell in love with her.' He turned and smiled at Elizabeth. 'Yes, I suppose I fell in love with her too.'

His words drew Elizabeth back from her thoughts and she smiled at him as he patted her hand. 'She was a young Jewish girl studying at the university. That in itself was unheard of, but she was very clever at mathematics and somehow, she got accepted. Well, Otto met her there and he would bring her to meet us, and we would visit the cafes of Berlin together. They were in love, the pair of them, and we were envious.' Uncle looked at her. 'Yes, Ruth, Otto Mannerheim and your mother fell in love.'

Ruth had listened; she had done what she was asked and she had listened, but this was just too much. She had to speak.

'How can you be sure, Uncle? And so what if this is Friedrich's father, how does this change anything?'

He made no attempt to answer her question but continued with his story. 'Even then, Ruth, it was getting difficult. Otto was from what they liked to call "good German stock". There was a sudden cynicism in his voice that came with the sentence and almost at once then disappeared. 'His family did not like the idea of him dating a Jewish girl, his father was strongly against it. In the end Otto gave way to their wishes. He stopped seeing her. Poor Mary was heartbroken at first, she did not know what to do. Then without any warning, another blow: she was asked to leave the university. They told her that there was no longer a place for her but she could reapply next year. She was Jewish, of course, that was the real reason, we all knew that. The flames of anti-Semitism were being continually fanned.' Uncle looked up from his glass, his eyes meeting Ruth's with an unexplainable grip. 'I am afraid, Ruth, that what I am about to tell you will cause you much pain, but there is no other way now.'

Ruth remained silent.

'It was not long before the friendship between your father and Mary began to blossom. It was no surprise to me; after all, he had always loved her. Otto met Ingrid, a girl from our village, and they married and I, well, I met...' He turned and smiled again at Elizabeth.

'I will always remember the day Otto and Ingrid were married. It was a wonderful summer's day. The sun had shone all day and the warmth lingered well into the evening. There was much wine and much music, we were all there dancing and singing, everybody was having such fun.' A smile returned to his face and for a moment, in that instant, he looked happier than Ruth could ever remember. 'Your father that night, Ruth, he was so full of life. I said to him "Luke you are in good form tonight." "Why not my dear brother," he said, "I have asked Mary to marry me and she has said yes." It was a double celebration. But in all the excitement we had not noticed several of the men at the wedding had been watching us and they had been drinking heavily. Later I asked Ingrid for a dance, she said yes and we were dancing when one of the men grabbed my shoulder. "We don't like Jews dancing with our women," he said and he pushed me. Before I knew it, Otto was there telling the man that Ingrid was his wife and she would dance with who she damn well liked. Then before I could stop him your father came from nowhere and knocked the man to the floor.

That, Ruth was the start of it, fists flew and there was a brawl. At the end of it all, Otto argued with his parents and Ingrid argued with hers. They said that we were their friends and to hell with everybody. Otto, with the help of Ingrid, stood up to his parents.'

'After that, Ruth, Otto came to work at father's printing works with us. He and Ingrid moved to the village and they became almost part of our family. As for your dear father, well, he and Mary got married the next spring.'

Ruth watched as Uncle filled his glass yet again, his face now taking on a new heavy sadness. 'Times got worse for us all, Ruth,' he swallowed the first mouthful of what was now his third glass of whisky, the alcohol obviously serving to deaden the pain of the memory. 'People would no longer do business with Jews, so your grandfather put Otto in charge of the business hoping that people wouldn't realise it was a Jewish firm. Then friends started to disappear. There was talk of new settlements in Poland. We were made to wear the Star of David on our clothes, new restrictions were imposed on us. Things got so bad that one day your grandfather called a meeting with your father, Otto and me, and it was agreed that we would hand the company over to Otto completely and he would run it until, God willing, better times would return. Then, when it was right, we would all become partners again. We gave our hand on it!' There was a sudden anger in his tone, and he paused as he struggled to contain his temper. 'By 1937 I had married your aunt, Mary and Luke had you and your brother and there was another on the way. Then, Ruth, when we thought things were as bad as they could get for us Jews, they got even worse. They started to confiscate our houses, our businesses, everything we had. We had to live under a curfew, we were jeered at on the streets and for no reason people would beat us and kick us, some would spit in our faces. By the spring of '38, things were so bad we had no option, we had to go into hiding. We left our own houses, just locked them up and left them. Otto took the rent on the top flat of an apartment block in Berlin and the same night he sneaked us into the city in one of the delivery vans and into the flat. I will always remember it, Ruth.' Again, he paused, absorbed in memory. 'It was not a big attic but it was safe and it was comfortable, well, as comfortable as it could be for the seven of us. But the important thing was, Ruth,' he leant forward and fixed her with an intense stare, 'we were safe and a lot better off than many. By day, we dared not leave the flat but sometimes in the evening Otto would take your father and me to a place where we would meet what Jewish friends we had left. If we had been caught,' he shook his head, 'God knows what would have happened to us. The women did not like us going out like this and Ingrid was particularly worried. Well, she had young Friedrich to think about and if they were found to be keeping a family of Jews in their attic...' He shrugged. 'There was no mercy for Jew lovers.'

Ruth seized on his pause. 'Well, if Otto and his wife hid you, looked after you, then surely...?'

Uncle shook his head; again, her words just seemed to bounce off him. He simply disregarded them and went on.

'Otto told us he was worried, everyone in the village knew that he had been friends with us and that we had disappeared at the same time he had moved to Berlin. The SS were offering rewards for people turning over Jews; it would only be a matter of time before someone said something. He realised it would not be long before the police would question him and if they searched the place...! No, we all knew we had to find a safer house. Otto knew a doctor and his wife, a well-respected couple with a large house on Kaepernick Strasser. They agreed to take us in. They were good people, Ruth. They risked everything. Without them...' Again, he shrugged. 'Who knows?' He finished what whisky remained in his glass and continued. 'I often wonder if they survived it all.' He was quiet for a moment but this time Ruth resisted the urge to question.

'Your poor grandad died in that house; one night, quietly, in his sleep he just died.' Ruth saw the tears glisten as they filled his eyes. 'He gave up, Ruth, he just didn't want to live with it anymore.' Joseph's voice dropped to a whisper. 'We couldn't even bury him. Otto took his body that night, stripped him of his clothes so that he could not be identified and dumped his poor body in the River Spree. And that was that!' He looked at her. 'The end of a man, the end of our father. By the time winter had come we had been in hiding nearly seven months. It was getting too dangerous; the police were doing house-to-house searches. We had to get out or we'd get caught. The doctor and his wife protested, they said that it was their duty to help. But we could no longer allow it. Otto had a plan, he would get us out of Berlin, even out of Germany! But with all the talk of war we had to go straight away, without delay. Otto had already managed to get some families out. Now he said it was our turn. His plan was simple. Three or four times a week the company truck would make deliveries of print. It would be easy: one night we would make our way back to the village and into the factory. There we would hide in the back of the truck and Otto would load the pallets around us. The truck would then make a delivery to Brussels and from there we would to be transported by others to France. Yes, it would be easy.'

Uncle reached across the table and took Ruth's hand. 'You can't believe what it was like, Ruth. The waiting. Day in, day out, all of us hiding there like scared rats caught in a trap. Waiting for another chance to live, waiting for Otto to get us out. Our dear friend Otto, the man who could save us all,' the sudden mocking tone betrayed the hatred. 'At last the time came. We were to travel in two groups, your parents with your brother and sister and you with us. Otto had arranged it, there would be two cars. It would be less conspicuous this way. The first would collect your parents and the children at 9.30pm, they were to wait on the corner of the Strasser. Then at 10.00pm it would be our turn. We were to take you and slip out into the back garden and then through the alley where a second car was to meet us on the same corner.

I remember shaking my brother's hand and he kissed me. 'Take good care of my Ruthy,' he said. I promised him I would. We held our breath, Ruth, until the good doctor told us they were in the car and away. Next it was to be our turn. I tell you, I have never been so frightened. I remember watching the clock as the minutes ticked by, and I felt sick. I doubted our chances and I suppose, I doubted myself. Out on the streets, that late at night,' he shook his head, 'we would be easy prey. But we had to go, there was no other way, we had to take the chance. Before I knew it, the time had come. I remember I carried you, it was quicker. I had not been out of the house for weeks and the coldness of the night air surprised me. I swear to God I could hear every beat of my heart as we moved quickly into the shadows and along the alley that led to the main road. You were young, Ruth; you just can't imagine what it was like. If we had been seen, if we had been questioned, if they had realised we were Jews,' Joseph paused to take solitude for a moment with his thoughts and his whisky. 'We waited on that damn corner for an eternity; I told Elizabeth, five more minutes that's all, five more minutes. It was late, Ruth! The car was late! Then, just as I was about to go back,' he turned to her, 'I never did find out the driver's name, I never asked, and if I had he probably would not have told me. It was safer that way. We were dropped just outside the village; a car would draw too much attention in those tiny streets. From there we made our way on foot. Your father and I both knew the village like the back of our hand, and I knew each turn I took he had probably taken them just a little while before me. It was easy for us to slip through unnoticed, especially at that late hour. By now it was raining and again I carried you. We went as quickly as we could, taking the back alleys, keeping in the shadows and away from the main streets. After a while we reached the back garden of Graf Urban; he was the village electrician, and his house was opposite the back entrance to our factory yard. There was a small path that led up beside the garden. I knew it well as we had all played there when we were boys. The path ran between Graf's house and that of the widow Madam Hantzige. The rain had made the path sodden and the mud was thick, but it was a safe cut through and from between the two houses I could get a clear view of the factory gates. Just as we were about halfway up the path a dog started to bark from Madam Hantzige's house. Then the back door opened and a young woman, who I did not know, let the dog out into the garden. She did not notice us, but the dog did. We went back into the shadows as quickly as we could and hid beside Graf's tool shed. The rain had turned to sleet by now and we were all cold and wet, but you were a good girl, Ruth, you did not cry. It seemed like forever before the woman returned to the door and called in the dog. By now we were very late and I knew they could not wait forever. I covered you as best I could in my coat and your aunt and I went quickly up the path and into the shadows between the two houses.' He took Ruth's hand. 'I will always remember that night, Ruth.' Again his eyes glistened, only this time they were unable to contain the flood, the tears spilled over. She had never seen him cry before.

'Just when I begin to think I have laid the past to rest, the memory will return. It is like a dark blanket of grief and anger that blots out everything, it consumes me in bitterness, Ruth, and I know, I cannot forget!'

Ruth could only watch as he filled his glass yet again.

'You say to me sometimes, "Uncle, why do you drink so much?"' He stared at her. 'I tell you why, Ruth, shall I? Because it helps me forget, it helps me deal with what happened.' He turned to Elizabeth. 'God knows how you deal with it. From between the two houses I could see out onto the street and across to the factory gates. It was the first time I had seen them in months. I gave you to Elizabeth and then moved slowly out into the road. To cross the street would be the most dangerous of all, I needed to make sure it was clear. There was no yard light on in the factory but I could make out the dark shape of a truck. There were two men loading it. Box after box was being loaded. There was no sign of your parents, Ruth, but I didn't expect there to be. They would already be in the truck, I knew that. Apart from the two men in the yard, the road was empty. I couldn't see Otto anywhere. I made my way back to you and your aunt. Then just as we were about to cross the street a truck came around the corner, its lights shining through the rain, lighting all before it. Quickly, I pulled you both back into the alley. I was sure we had been seen, but no, we had been lucky.

The truck stopped, blocking the factory gates, and then a car appeared from nowhere. The tailgate of the truck fell open and within seconds there must have been fifteen or twenty soldiers and SS men running everywhere. The two men loading the truck tried to run but the soldiers opened fire on them. I saw them both fall. I don't know if they lived or died, the soldiers just left them where they had fallen. Then an officer dressed in the black uniform of the Secret Police got out of the back of the car, unbuckling the holster of his pistol as he did so.' Joseph hesitated for a moment, the perspiration showing clearly on his forehead. 'We were so close to them, Ruth, no more than twenty-five metres away. The soldiers started to pull the boxes from the truck, I swear they knew what they were looking for. There was nothing I could do. I just stood and watched as one by one they removed the boxes. I prayed to God that Otto had got wind of what was going to happen and had somehow got them away. But it was not to be. One of the soldiers turned on the yard light and the whole place was lit up as bright as day. There could have been no more than ten or twelve boxes left on the truck when the officer climbed up to check for himself. Even then, Ruth, I still had hope, but within seconds they had dragged them out. Your father first then Mary and the children. They threw them from the truck, all four of them falling onto the wet ground. The officer climbed down and, dragging your mother to her feet, turned her round to face the grinning soldiers. I will never forget his words. "Look Gentlemen!" he shouted. "Another Jewish whore." Your father tried to get to his feet to help her but as he did so one of the soldiers kicked him. But again, he got up, desperately trying to get to her, to somehow get her away from the officer. But this time another soldier struck him on the head with his rifle butt. I swear the noise of that blow would have woken the dead.' Joseph suddenly buried his head in his hands, the emotion breaking out into his voice as he continued. 'The soldier had split Luke's head wide open and even from where I was standing I knew it was bad. There was so much blood. Surely, I told myself, they must stop now. But they did not, the soldier hit him again and again. But he kept getting up, Ruth. I screamed inside myself. Stay down, Luke, stay down.' Joseph shook his head, his hands still clasped to his face. 'If only he had stayed down, Ruth, then perhaps?' He was silent for a moment before taking up his story again. 'The officer then grabbed your brother and sister and turned them round forcing them to watch as they beat your father. "This is how we treat the son of a Jewish whore," he shouted at them. Then they took your father and threw him into the back of the truck.' Joseph wiped the tears away from his face and looked again at her. 'Ruth, no man could have survived that beating. He never died in the camps as we let you think. He was beaten to death that night on the street, in front of his own wife and children.'

Ruth suddenly got to her feet. 'What's the point, Uncle?' she cried at him. 'Why make me live through this now? Do you think it will stop me loving Friedrich? Do you think it will stop me from going back to Germany?' Her voice trembled through her tears as she banged her hand against the table.

'There is more, Ruth,' Elizabeth's voice was calm, almost serene, amid the turmoil of emotion that surrounded them. 'You must sit back down, you will listen.' Ruth, shaken by her aunt's sudden intervention, obeyed and Joseph continued.

'The officer took hold of your mother again, and the soldiers dragged the children from her. He pulled off her coat and trod it into the mud. She was crying, Ruth, but she was a proud woman and defiance blazed in her eyes. The man grabbed her hair, jerking her head back and shouting, "It looks like we have a defiant Jewish whore here, gentlemen, and we all know there is only one way to deal with this kind of bitch, don't we?" As the soldiers laughed, he slapped your mother across the face, knocking her to the ground, then he dragged her up and knocked her down again. He started ripping at her clothes, tearing her blouse from her body as he pulled at her. He twisted her arms up behind her and held her, then laughing he paraded her half-naked in front of his men. "As I have often said, gentlemen, there is only one thing a Jewish bitch is good for." He sneered and then dropping down the canvas flap of the wagon he pulled your mother inside. She screamed, Ruth, God how she screamed. But not a light went on. No one came to help her. Not even me, Ruth. Not even her own brother-in-law.' Again, he stared at her, 'I had that gun in my pocket, Ruth.' His eyes moved to the crumpled oily rag and the weapon it contained. 'Oh yes, even then I had it. If I had been able to find the nerve I could have used it. Shot him! But I did nothing. I just stood and watched like a stupid, scared fool. Oh, I have told myself a thousand times that I did the right thing. I did what she would have wanted me to do. I got you away, Ruth. I got you and Elizabeth away. But her screams still haunt me. To this day they still haunt me.' He wiped his eyes with his fingers. 'That's what I have to live with, Ruth, that's the memory that haunts me. But there's even more than that. When the officer emerged again from the back of the truck he was straightening his uniform. Then, standing on the tailgate of the truck, he spoke again. "I don't really care gentlemen how long it takes you to get her back to headquarters, but just make sure that she is still alive."'

His words echoed around the silent street as he got down from the truck and a soldier quickly opened the car door for him. As the officer climbed into the car, a soldier climbed into the truck. I knew I had to get you away but still I was unable to move. I was frozen by the horror of it all, of what I had seen happen, of what was still happening in the back of that truck. Then the car reversed towards us and for the first time I could see inside it. In the back of the car there were three men. I could not believe what I was seeing, I did not want to believe what I was seeing, but there was no doubt. It was him. Between the two men in uniform, smoking a cigarette sat, Otto Mannerheim.' No longer able to contain his rage, it suddenly exploded out of him and he slammed both fists on the table. Bottle, glass and Ruth jumped. 'We had been betrayed, Ruth. Betrayed by the one man we all thought was our best friend, the man that was to help us. Of course, now I understand why he did it. With all of us out of the way, murdered in some Nazi concentration camp, it would be easy for him. The company was already in his name, he would get it all. Everything would be his. And that, Ruth, is exactly what did happen. Otto Mannerheim built himself an empire.' Joseph shook his head. 'There was just no stopping him. The company grew bigger and bigger until it became what it is today, a highly successful international company, but it was built with the blood of Jews, Ruth, it was built with the blood of your own family! But there is one thing that Otto Mannerheim would dearly love to know. Since the end of the war he has been trying desperately to prove that we all died in the camps. The records are not clear, he cannot be sure, it is untidy for him. He knows we escaped that night but he can't prove what happened to us. Don't you see, Ruth?' his cold stare held her eyes, 'if he found out we were alive, it would start again. We would be a threat to him. He would have to do something. If the world were to find out what he had done to us, it would destroy him. No, Ruth, you must not go to Germany. He must not find out we are alive; if he does then we will all be in danger. You must end this relationship with his son, you must not take his job.'

'There must be some mistake!' Ruth pushed back her chair and stood. 'Why did you not tell me this before?' Her mind was a tangle of emotions, her voice raising as she spoke. 'Why have you let this fester? You said that you knew that I loved him. Well, if you did, why did you not tell me all this before?'

Neither of them replied.

'You've got to be wrong!' she almost screamed the words before turning from them as if to walk to the door. But she stopped.

'He's asked me to marry him, for God's sake!' she cried, turning back to them. 'He's offered me a directorship of the company.'

Uncle spoke. 'It is possible, just possible that they do not yet realise who you are. The man may well love you, but when they do find out, and they will,' he shook his head, 'there is no mistaking the past, Ruth. I wish it were not so but it is.'

Ruth sat back down, struggling desperately within herself to keep control. 'Of course, he knows nothing about this. He loves me,' she stammered.

'He may well love you, Ruth,' Elizabeth answered getting up from her chair and moving round to hold her, 'but it could be something his father has planned just to get you to Germany.'

Ruth looked up at her. 'How could you say such a thing?'

'Because we know Otto Mannerheim, we know what he can do. For God's sake, Ruth, don't go to Germany with him. Finish with him.'

Ruth turned to her uncle.

'You said that you had no option other than to tell me this. Well, I have no option now. You see, I must go to Germany; I must meet Herr Mannerheim. If Friedrich and I are to stand any hope of a life together I must meet him. Friedrich loves me, he will protect me I know it.'

'You must not take such a chance, Ruth! After everything we have told you. How can you take such a chance?' Sitting down next to her, Elizabeth took her hand.

'Because I am a month late,' Ruth replied quietly. 'I'm carrying Friedrich's baby.'

ELEVEN

BERLIN

'Business or pleasure?' The customs officer was busily scrutinising Ruth's passport and paid little attention to her as he spoke. Ruth looked vacant, she had not heard the question. Like the customs officer, her thoughts were on other things. 'Miss, is your trip business or pleasure?'

'Business,' Friedrich replied for her.

The man handed her back the document.

'Have a pleasant trip,' he mumbled.

Ruth had never flown before. She had been looking forward to it. That was, when everything was all right, that was before. Now the crushing weight of the past and all the implications that it carried bore down on her. Her hopes and dreams lay in the balance, dependant on one thing, who was Otto Mannerheim? She sat quietly looking out of the window watching the huge propellers as they picked up speed. The plane began to rock and the noise from the engines grew in crescendo until she thought they were about to explode. Then slowly, very slowly at first, the airport buildings began to slip one by one past her window.

As the aircraft left the runway and the small shops at Hillingdon Circus slipped from view, Ruth felt her stomach churn. There was some buffeting as they climbed through the clouds and then, as if by a magical power, the dull grey of the early morning was washed away by the bright blue of a new sky that was bathed in brilliant sunshine.

'Are you all right?'

Friedrich's voice was muffled by the buzzing in her ears. She swallowed hard.

'Yes, thank you, I'm OK.' It was hard for her to smile but she managed it. Something that only yesterday had been so easy to do was now so difficult.

'I didn't realise, Ruth, I'm sorry,' Friedrich said taking her hand.

'Didn't realise what?' The panic in her voice startled him.

'That you did not like flying.'

She smiled again then turned to look back out of the window without answering.

The huge wing, now airborne, had taken on a new supple form, and she watched as it flexed with every movement of the plane.

What about the baby? The thought returned to her again as it had done a hundred times since last night. If what they had told her was true… what about the baby? How stupid she had been? She had meant to tell him sooner but she had not been sure. It was too late now; she would have to wait until she was sure about his father. Occasionally, the clouds would break revealing what looked like model villages and towns, green fields and pencil-line roads. But she could not concentrate on them. She could not concentrate on anything. She had told herself at first that nothing would change. Nothing would be different between them. How wrong she had been. The dark shadow of doubt had slowly permeated even the most secret corners of her mind. Like a cancer, it had gradually spread within her, eroding away all that was most precious. Now she wondered if anything would ever be the same again; it was as if a metal shutter had fallen in her mind and no matter how hard she tried she could not move it. It was the shutter of doubt, doubt in him. Did he really love her? Or, as fantastic as it seemed, could he be part of some terrible sinister plot? Then there were her uncle and aunt. Was it fair to cause them so much worry? The question had tormented her. From the moment she had made up her mind to see it through, to challenge their memory, it had tormented her. She had left them the letter. At least she had done that. But if they realise what she's done. If they find that it's missing! The clouds broke again for a brief moment, only this time there were no villages, no roads. Just the greyness of the North Sea stared back at her and suddenly she felt alone and frightened, very frightened.

Friedrich gently shook her, 'You've been asleep for over an hour.'

It took her a moment to gather her senses.

'I'm sorry. I didn't sleep well last night.'

'We will be landing in about fifteen minutes. The pilot said it is snowing quite heavily in Berlin, but the runway is still open.'

Ruth could see he looked pleased.

'It must be nice to get back home after nearly three months, you must have missed your father.'

He smiled broadly.

'Yes, I have missed him. It will be good.'

She thought for a moment. 'Has he asked much about me, Friedrich?'

'Not much, no,' he laughed, 'he asked if you were good-looking and I told him not at all!'

She tried another question.

'Be serious, Friedrich, what have you told him about me?'

She looked at him, trying desperately to sense a reaction.

'I told him I loved you.'

The 'Fasten seat belts' sign came on.

'Better do as it says.' He reached for the buckle.

The turbulence became worse. Huge banks of swirling mist broke over the wing and flashed past the window. Ruth watched as the last of the blue sky slipped from view. Snow began to gather on the front edge of the wing and the cabin lights came on as the pilot steered the aircraft deeper into the heavily laden clouds. Ruth peered out into the murk. It was not clear at first. But then slowly she began to make out the shapes of trees and houses. The snow-covered shapes that were Germany. As the wheels met the runway of Tempelhof Airport with a heavy bump, Friedrich squeezed her hand.

'Welcome back to Germany, Ruth,' he said.

The airport bus took them quickly from the snow-covered tarmac to the warmth of the airport building. Once inside, Ruth could not help but marvel at the size of it. The building was busy. People were wandering around in all directions and she was surprised by the number of men in uniform.

'Do not lose me, Ruth, it is busy today.' Friedrich took her hand and, forcing his way past some French servicemen, made his way to the baggage reclaim area.

'Is this your suitcase?' The thin-faced man behind the customs desk was gesturing towards the small black case that was in front of him. It had happened all of a sudden. She had just been about to pick it up when the man had stepped forward and asked the question. She started to panic. If he opened and searched it, she was lost. Her mouth went dry and her head began to swim. She hadn't even tried to hide it. It was just there. Under her clothes, yes, but it was there. It would be obvious to any prying hands. For a moment she thought that she may faint as a clammy sweat took an instant grip on her whole body.

'Yes, it is mine.' It was almost as if someone had spoken for her and she surprised herself with the quality of her German.

'Are you here for business or pleasure?'

Friedrich leant towards the man. 'She is here to meet her future father-in-law.'

The man smiled. 'Then I hope your stay is a successful one, Fraulein.'

It was over as quickly as it had started. The danger had come and gone in just a few seconds. Yet it had brought with it a terror the likes of which she had never before experienced.

Friedrich tried to attract a porter.

'That was a close thing,' he spoke without looking at her as they made their way through the crowd.

'What do you mean?' She was almost running as she asked the question. It was difficult trying to keep up with Friedrich and the porter as they wasted no time in making for the doors.

'Well, you almost had your underwear out on parade back there.'

'I've nothing to hide!' The sharpness in her reply surprised him. He stopped, taking hold of her arm as he did so.

'You've been hiding something from me though, Ruth, haven't you?'

His face was serious. For the second time in just a few minutes Ruth felt panic.

'You never told me you could speak German as well as that.'

Before she could reply he was on the move again. Only now he kept hold of her arm.

*

The Mercedes made its way slowly out of the airport and onto the main *strasse*. The snow was thick and the driver was in no hurry as he negotiated the steep bridge that took them over the frozen waters of the Teltowkanal.

'This is the American section,' Friedrich spoke excitedly. 'Remember our bus ride, Ruth? The first day we spent together in London. Well now it's my turn to show you Berlin. We will go through the British section next, that's where we enter the Tiergarten. It's our Hyde Park, if you like. Then on to the Brandenburg Gate. We will cross into East Berlin there.'

The snow was still falling heavily as the car crossed at the British control point. There was just a momentary halt as a British corporal dressed in a heavy overcoat peered through the window and then waved them on without interest.

'It won't be so easy at the next crossing, I'm afraid.' Friedrich waved to the guard as the car moved away.

'What do you mean?' Ruth tried to sound nonchalant but again her mouth began to dry.

'Things are harder in East Berlin. There's a great deal of money to be made from certain commodities and a lot of people are making it. I'm afraid the communists don't approve. They are very strict about it and very hard on people taking things across that they shouldn't.'

Friedrich had not realised the impact his words would have on her. She had been in Germany less than an hour but already she had been made painfully aware of the tightrope she was walking. It was a stupid thing to do. She had not thought about it. Now her mind pondered the consequences. What would be the penalty in East Germany for being caught with it? Ruth was unable to concentrate on anything other than her pending fate.

Friedrich pointed to Victory Column as the car swung into Grosser Stern Square and turned left onto the Strasse Des 17 Juni.

'It's over 220 feet high.'

He was peering out of the window as he spoke but Ruth paid little heed. Something more important had taken her attention. Directly in front of them in the distance, through the snow, loomed the gigantic mass of the Brandenburg Gate, its five huge archways silhouetted against the grey of the afternoon sky. Friedrich noticed her attention was fixed on the Gate ahead of them.

'It has been rebuilt almost completely since the war. It was only finished in 1958.' He sat forward as he spoke, lowering his head to look through the windscreen. Ruth could feel the grip of fear tightening as they moved ever closer to the monument. The clammy sweat she had experienced in the airport returned and her mind began searching desperately for a way out. But she was as a fly caught in a web, and the spider approached ever closer by the second.

'Do they search every car, Friedrich?' she put the question as calmly as she could.

'Normally, yes.' He was busy looking out of the window again and the nonchalant tone of his reply infuriated her. The driver steered the car to the end of the shortest queue leading to one of the right-hand arches. Ruth counted seven cars in front of them, the first of which was surrounded by at least five soldiers.

'The ones in the darker uniforms are Vopos. They're the worst,' Friedrich pointed to three men who were standing back from the others, 'the "people's police".' The sarcasm in his voice was unmistakable.

The soldiers had removed most of the contents of the car and the occupants, a young couple, watched hopelessly as their baggage was removed for inspection.

'We could be here sometime,' Friedrich said as he sat back, accepting the inevitable.

She watched four more cars move up to the checkpoint and she watched all four being searched. Small beads of perspiration had formed on her forehead and the feeling of nausea grew with every suitcase and with every bag that she saw searched. Then before she knew it the car in front of them moved up to the barrier and within seconds the soldiers were on it, dissecting it as they had all the others. The realisation of the trouble she was in seized her brain and forced her to act.

'There's a pistol in my suitcase.' The calmness of her words betrayed no emotion.

Friedrich laughed. 'I hope not.'

She turned to face him.

'I'm not joking Friedrich, there's a pistol in my bag.'

The smile quickly drained from his face.

'For Christ's sake, Ruth, tell me you're joking!' The urgency in his voice was unmistakable.

'I'm not joking, Friedrich, it's in my bag.'

'God almighty, Ruth!'

The driver moved the car forward, blissfully ignorant of the significance of the English conversation going on behind him. The guard on the gate held up his arm and the car stopped.

Friedrich's words were sharp, in German and too quick for Ruth to understand.

Suddenly the car jerked backward, the driver wrestling with the controls as it did so. Friedrich wound down the window.

'Sit back! Sit back!' He shouted at her as he pushed her back into the seat. Again, Ruth could not translate what he shouted at the guard. His words were so quick. But whatever it was, it seemed to have the desired effect. They all moved back as the car managed to turn about in an almost impossible circle, and in seconds, they were speeding away from the Brandenburg Gate. Back down the Strasse Des 17 Juni.

*

It was several minutes before Friedrich spoke again and when he did it was to the driver not to her. They turned off left at Victory Column and onto the Klingerhofer Strasse. Ruth felt the car slide on the snow as they turned. They were travelling much faster than before. It was not long before they crossed into the American sector and as they turned right onto Schill Strasse it was only a matter of moments before they had disappeared into the maze of small streets that lay between Hohenstaufen and Grunewald Strasse.

'What the hell do you think you are playing at, Ruth?'

The driver had reversed the car into a small side street and on Friedrich's instructions had got out and was walking back to the main street. She could not help but feel sorry for the man as he stood in the snow, his collar turned up to shield against the elements.

'I'm talking to you, Ruth.'

'I'm sorry, Friedrich.'

'Sorry! Sorry! You nearly get us all arrested back there and then you tell me you're sorry.' He grabbed her by the shoulders and turned her to face him. 'For God's sake, why? Why bring a gun?'

Her mind searched desperately for an answer. What could she tell him? How much did he know? 'I was frightened, Friedrich, I wanted desperately to come and to meet your father. But I was scared. Everything I had heard, how it had been for us Jews in the past. I was afraid.'

She was telling the truth; she had definitely been afraid, but not for those reasons. She was more afraid of what she may find out and afraid of losing him. But even that had not been the reason for bringing the gun. There had been only one reason for that: revenge! If he ever found that out, it would be the end.

He was quiet for a moment. He was thinking.

'Is it locked?' he spoke more quietly now. 'Is the case locked, Ruth?'

'I'm so sorry, Friedrich, I didn't want it to begin like this.' She looked away fighting hard to hold back her tears. She had kept all the fear, all the emotion of the day trapped within her and now it yearned to break free.

'Ruth, just give me the keys.'

She heard the car boot slam and within seconds he was back beside her, the brown cloth bundle held in one hand. He unwrapped it.

'It's a Luger, a German Luger,' he examined it, turning it slowly in his hands. 'Where did you get this?'

She did not answer.

'Ruth, where did you get it?' his tone was sharper.

'It was my uncle's. From before the war.'

'Ruth, the safety catch isn't even on; did you know that?'
She looked blank.

'You're carrying a Luger around in your luggage and you
didn't even know that the safety catch wasn't on?'

'I don't know much about guns,' Ruth replied quietly. She
felt stupid. He removed the magazine.

'Ruth, where are the bullets?'

She looked at the metal object that he held outstretched in
the palm of his hand.

'Aren't they in it?' she replied.

*

An hour later they crossed into East Berlin, only not at the
Brandenburg Gate. They crossed at the American checkpoint
on the junction of Friedrich Strasse and Zimmer, the Luger
having long since settled into the soft mud at the bottom of the
river Spree.

'Ruth,' he had said, 'trust me I will look after you, I will
always look after you.'

She wanted to trust him. God knows she wanted to.
Especially now. Without him she was alone. Alone in East
Germany and she didn't even have the gun. With or without
bullets.

They had not spent long in West Berlin and for most of the
time Ruth had been preoccupied with her own dilemma.
But she had noticed something. The town had been full of
hustle and bustle. Busy streets, crowded shops and people

everywhere. Now as the car made its way along the east bank of the river Spree it was to her as if a curtain had been drawn. A curtain that appeared to veil life itself from this side of the river. There was little traffic and few shops compared with the West, and what shops there were had long queues outside of them.

Friedrich held her hand again. She was glad of that.

'There's not much here for them, Ruth.' He pointed to a long row of forlorn-looking people which stretched for almost the length of the street, men and women alike standing motionless in the snow.

'They're queuing for meat. If they're lucky they may get some.' There was a clear sadness in his words. 'It can't go on forever, Ruth. Thousands a day are walking away from it. Crossing the Spree to a better life. And who can blame them?'

Ruth thought it best just to listen.

'I have told him and told him: move over to the West, but he won't listen. Most of our business is there now anyway and so is the hospital but Father knows best! He won't leave the house; there are too many memories for him there.'

'Is he ill?'

Ruth's question surprised him.

'No. Why do you ask?'

'You said the hospital is there?'

Friedrich smiled. It was the first time he had smiled since Brandenburg. 'My father started the hospital just after the war. Its purpose originally was to help the Jewish. Many from the camps were treated there. It eased the conscience of Berliners. They gave thousands of Deutschmarks.' He looked at her. 'A small price to pay.'

'And your father, did it ease his conscience?'

She had not meant the question to come. It had been uncontrollable, almost instinctive. Friedrich didn't answer at first. Then he put his arm around her.

'I know this is not easy for you, darling, and yes I expect it did help ease his conscience a little. We must all bear some responsibility for what happened. But no one could have done more than he. Perhaps one day, Ruth, he will tell you of some of the things he has done. Some of the people he has helped. Even today there is one woman who will not leave the hospital, she lives there, he provides for her and cares for her as if he has known her all his life. He is like that; he is a good man.'

Ruth did not reply. She let her head rest on his shoulder and drew comfort from being close to him again. She prayed to God that he was right.

TWELVE

EAST BERLIN

CARL KAHLER PUSHED THE EMPTY PLATE TOWARDS the centre of the table and sat back in his chair; lunch had been good but then it usually was. Taking the Peer Export cigarettes from his shirt pocket he shook one free from the pack and lit it. The strong smoke stung his lungs as he inhaled, but they were cheap and they were East German. Gitta was making the coffee and Carl watched her, his eyes lingering on the soft curves of her body as she moved around the small kitchen. The thin material of the dress she wore had seen better days, yet still, even now, it looked good as it clung to every line of her firm body. She was a good-looking woman, quite tall and with a figure that would turn most men's heads. She normally wore her long fair hair tied back in a ponytail, but today she had not bothered and it fell softly and slightly unkempt about her shoulders. As he watched her, he felt the need in him rise. It had always been that way for him, he couldn't help it, he couldn't control it, he didn't want to control it. From the very first day he had met her he had wanted her. That's how it had been. He had fallen in love with her almost in an instant and even now, he could remember every detail of the first time they had made love. He would never forget it; for him it had been the first time. The desire for her had never left him, only the love had faded. At least he thought it had faded, he was not sure anymore. Eight years of marriage and two children later, he could not be sure.

She put the coffee in front of him and picked up the empty plate.

'Have you had enough?' she asked the question more out of habit than concern. He nodded.

'They say he's coming back today.' He watched for her reaction as he spoke.

'So why tell me?' She dropped the plate with a splash into the sink.

'Just thought you may be interested, that's all, what with you cleaning up there again now.' He picked up the coffee.

'Don't start, Carl, please don't start.' She leant wearily against the sink knowing there would be nothing she could say that could stop him now.

'I'm just saying, that's all. I mean there'll be more for you to do now, running and fetching after both of them.' The anger in his voice was beginning to show.

'We need the extra money, Carl, you know that. We need the money.'

Carl didn't answer. He finished his coffee, stood up and took his heavy leather jacket down from the door.

'Well, why not you as well?' he said, turning back to face her as he pulled on the coat. 'After all they had the pleasure of watching my father work himself to death for them, the pleasure of me working all these years for them and now...' He paused as he wrapped the thick scarf around his neck.

'And now they've had the pleasure of you. Tell me, Gitta, will Friedrich expect the same service he used to get? Is it meant to be part of the job?' Not waiting for her answer, he pulled open the door. He was halfway through it when he turned to speak again. 'Oh, by the way, did I tell you? The word is that he brings a woman with him. A woman from England. A lot of people are interested in her, very interested! They say that he plans to marry her. Perhaps you won't keep that job too long after all.' The door slammed and he was gone.

*

From the top of the hill Carl could see right down to the lake and beyond. It had always been his favourite place, ever since he was a boy and he and his father would stand together, on the very spot he was standing now, just the two of them surveying all about them. He would listen to his father's dreams of what he would do if it were all his. As a child Carl had never understood that. To him his father was the wisest, cleverest of men and yet he worked for others. But now it was his turn, he had done the same. Ever since his father had died, he had managed the estate and he loved every inch of it as if it were his own. He considered it his own, if not by law, it was his by love, by right. He watched the steady spiral of smoke that rose from behind the coppice that lay between the frozen water of the lake and their cottage and he thought of her. Why did he do it? Why did he have to hurt her? Every time he asked himself the same question and every time, he told himself no more, never again. But it would happen, he could not help himself. Ever since she had insisted on going back there to work, he had been unable to stop it. He had known about her and Friedrich long before they had married. She had told him herself. But she hadn't needed to, he had seen it with his own eyes. Most people on the estate knew. His father had told him. 'Carl, it can never be. The likes of him never marry housemaids.' His father's words had come true. But she had slept with him, she had confessed that, he had touched her, explored her body, had the one thing that was most precious to Carl and then tossed it aside as if it were of little significance. He loathed the man for that, even more than he loathed the thought of her sleeping with him. But why had she insisted on taking that job again? Was she still in love with him? Was it just the chance to be near him? They could manage on his money; they had done for eight years. It was this question that kindled the embers of jealousy that had for so long lain dormant in his mind. Now they had been fanned back to a flame that burnt with a new ferocity the likes of which he had never previously known. Carl shook his mind free from its torment and turned to walk down towards the woods but as he did so he stopped to look at the big house, the Mannerheim house. His father had been right as always: there was no doubt about it, no one family should have that much wealth, no one person should be able to dictate to others, control their lives. Hitler had taught them that. No, there was only one way forward now and that was the communist way. Reaching into his jacket pocket he pulled out the small worn photograph; it was yellowed with age and frayed but the image portrayed on it was still clear. It was that of a family, not his family but a family that could change his life, a Jewish family. He looked again at the woman in the picture. She was beautiful, even in that old-fashioned way she was beautiful. But would she look like that? Did the daughter have the mother's beauty? Would it be enough to satisfy Horst

Urban? He brushed a snowflake from the picture and returned it to the safety of his jacket. As he started on down the hill again the hate in him took hold and he cursed the capitalists and their greed-infested ways and he cursed the Mannerheims, especially the son. *Every dog*, he told himself, *will have its day.*

*

The journey from Berlin should have taken at the most an hour but it had taken almost three times as long. The last light of the day had long since been lost by the time the car finally inched its way between the imposing iron gates that guarded the entrance to the estate. Ruth was surprised by the amount of security present. The area around the gate was well lit by several bright floodlights that shone down on them as if suspended from heaven itself. Through the car window she watched with fascination as large snowflakes twisted and turned on their descent to Earth as if struggling in some vain attempt to escape their sudden illumination as they entered the artificial light. The guards were armed and she could see at least four of them. Friedrich wound down the window, the cold air entering the car as he did so. Ruth shivered.

'*Willkommen das Zuhause*, Herr Mannerheim.'

Ruth was pleased by her understanding of the young guard's words.

As the car passed the gate and started up the main drive to the house Ruth felt her heart start to quicken. She had come all this way. Taken the risk. And all because she loved the man. What would her mother have thought of this? What would her father have said of her returning to Germany? She would never know the answer to that. What she did know was that she was about to meet the man, about to face the past and discover the truth. She was scared.

It was some minutes later when the car, following a turn in the road, brought Ruth her first sight of the house. It must have still been over a mile from them and yet even at that distance it appeared huge. Like some fairy-tale castle, it dominated the valley below them, illuminated from the darkness by the orange glow of numerous floodlights. It was a building more suited to the magical tales of Liechtenstein than the forests of East Germany.

Ruth heard herself gasp, so taken aback was she by its beauty.

'Quite something, isn't it?' he said, his words prompted by her reaction.

Ruth could only nod, so enthralled was she with the house. She had already counted seventeen windows, in each of which a light was burning. Her Jewish nature turned her mind to ponder on the upkeep of such an establishment. But still it was a fantastic sight, all lit up, all sparkling in the darkness of the winter's night.

The car came to a halt at the foot of the massive stone steps that led up to the entrance and Friedrich turned to her.

'This is it, Ruth. This is where we live.'

'It's larger than I had expected,' was all she could manage to say as they got out of the car.

The huge oak doors swung open even before they reached them and a tall, thin, immaculately dressed man of about fifty years old greeted them.

'*Willkommen das Zuhause*, Herr Friedrich.' The man spoke slowly.

'*Danke*, Gottfried,' Friedrich replied and then turned to Ruth. 'This is Gottfried.' He handed the man his coat. 'Father would be lost without him, wouldn't he, Gottfried?' The man smiled. 'And he speaks perfect English. Gottfried, this is Ruth Valsac, from England.'

The man bowed smartly, 'Welcome to Germany, madam; may I please take your coat? Would you like me to show madam to her room, sir?'

'No thank you, Gottfried, if you would just arrange to get our bags taken up. It's been quite a harrowing journey one way or another.'

Ruth recognised the insinuation and looked away.

'Carl is seeing to it now Herr Friedrich.'

'*Willkommen das Zuhause*, Herr Mannerheim.' Ruth watched as a very broad, rather rugged man wearing a heavy leather jacket and carrying both their cases walked into the house behind them. Friedrich only nodded.

'Come, Ruth, I'll get us a drink.' He turned to Gottfried, 'Is he in?'

'Yes, sir, he has been looking forward to seeing you. He told me to tell you that dinner is at 7.00pm and he will meet the young lady then.'

Ruth felt intimidated as she looked around her. She had never been in such opulent surroundings before. The entrance hall alone was magnificent and was lit by what was the largest and by far the most spectacular chandelier she had ever seen. In front of her, a wide staircase, flanked by heavily carved banisters, seemed to go on up for an eternity before it split into two smaller sections each leading away at right angles to meet with a wonderful galleried landing. Fine works of art seemed to hang everywhere, and the most spectacular grandfather clock was in the act of striking 6.00pm, its chimes ringing out with the most beautiful clarity.

'Ruth! Come on, this way,' Friedrich beckoned, his enthusiasm to show her the house overflowing. She followed him into the room unaware that she was being scrutinised.

Carl had been close to her. She had even smiled at him when he had brought in the cases. It had been easy. He stood now in the half-light at the top of the stairs and watched as she walked into the library. Quickly he put down the cases and took out the photograph. He hadn't really needed to check, but he did. The likeness was unquestionable. The same eyes, the same high cheekbones, the same beauty. It must be her. He smiled; Horst Urban would be pleased, very pleased.

In this room, apart from the odd painting, books seemed to fill almost every space on every wall. Friedrich was standing by the drinks cabinet, a glass in each hand.

'A toast!' he proclaimed, handing her the glass. 'To your stay with us here, to our future.'

She took the drink and walked over to the fire. 'To us.' She raised the glass and took a sip. 'This painting?' she asked, looking up at the work of art. 'She is a beautiful woman.'

'Yes, she was,' he replied.

'Did you know her?'

*

Ruth's room was at the front of the house and overlooked the main drive. It was a warm, pleasant room with two large windows and its own bathroom. The bare stone walls were church-like but nicely decorated with paintings, nearly all of which were country scenes. A large vase of yellow roses stood on a table in the centre of the room. A card nestled between the blooms; she walked to the table, took the card and read it.

Welcome to Germany.
Regards
Otto Mannerheim.

She had not expected that!

Ruth had unpacked her things and now, as she sat on the bed brushing her hair, Friedrich's words echoed in her head. *To our future. But what would that future hold?* she asked herself. Did they have a future together? So much had happened in such a short time that when she thought about it, it made her head swim. Only that morning she had been in England, had left Hampstead. Now she was here, in his house. Thirty miles or so into the German Democratic Republic with nothing else but her love and trust in him to cling to. She would be meeting his father soon and that would be the real test. Did he know who she was? And if he did, had he orchestrated her visit? Would he guess when he met her? If he didn't guess, would she tell him anyway? Confront him with it, risk everything? So many questions; so many ifs! This morning, when she had set out it had been clear, she had known exactly what she would do. Now she questioned everything. She wanted desperately to believe it was all some mistake and that they were wrong. But inside her, deep inside her, she sensed there must be some truth in the story they had told. Surrounded now as she was by such splendour, her mind could not help but question how any one man could accumulate such wealth? Had it been bought with the blood of Jews? Had they, her very own parents, been a carefully planned sacrifice on Otto Mannerheim's road to wealth?

*

Ruth had felt embarrassingly underdressed when Friedrich had arrived to take her down for dinner. He had looked remarkably smart in an immaculate dinner suit and black tie. She had not expected such formality. Most of her wardrobe had suffered considerably from the rigours of travel. She had selected the black velvet and was grateful for that; at least the colour was in keeping with the occasion, if not the creases. It was one of three new dresses she had bought for the trip. They had all come from a small boutique near Bond Street and had cost her far more than she had really meant to pay. The black one was the smartest of the three and she thought the most appropriate for evening wear. It was plain with small cap sleeves that fitted just off the shoulder. She had decided to wear only two pieces of jewellery. One was her Star of David that hung from the thin gold chain around her neck. She had removed her engagement ring from the chain, she now wore that on her finger.

It had taken only a few short minutes for them to walk from her room, down the main staircase and across the hall to the dining room. But in those minutes Ruth experienced a turmoil of emotions, not the least of which was fear. It was too late now to change anything, there could be no turning back. She was going to meet the man; it was of her making that she was here, and she knew she had to see it through. Her mouth was dry.

'I am so nervous, Friedrich,' she confided in him as they reached the door to the dining room. 'You do love me, don't you?' she asked in a desperate last-minute attempt to seek assurance. Friedrich opened the door and smiled.

'Don't worry, just be yourself, Ruth. That's all, just be yourself.'

Otto Mannerheim had his back to them. He was standing staring into the fire apparently unaware that they had entered the room. Ruth had not expected such a big man. He was well over six foot, even taller than Friedrich and broader too.

'Father,' the man turned, 'this is Ruth, Father, Ruth Valsac.'

Otto Mannerheim stood there for a second or two, his eyes fixed on her. For a moment he said nothing, he just looked. Then suddenly he moved.

'Miss Valsac, I am so very pleased to meet you.' He walked towards her, covering the room in just a few large paces, his huge arm outstretched. Ruth took his hand. He was a good-looking man with neatly trimmed but receding silver grey hair and he had the same deep blue eyes as his son, but in his case they were heavily lined and looked tired. Ruth's first thought was that he must be older than sixty-three. She judged him to be well into his sixties, perhaps sixty-eight or sixty-nine. If what uncle had told her was right, he would be sixty-three or at the most sixty-four. But this man certainly looked older than that. It was the first light to appear at the end of the tunnel. It was just a glimmer, but she grasped at its beam. *He's too old, he must be too old*, she told herself.

'I hope the journey has not been too tiring for you. I am afraid the weather has not been kind. Come, I have opened a bottle of champagne specially to celebrate your arrival.' He was smiling broadly as if genuinely pleased to meet her. She relaxed a little.

'You speak very good English, Herr Mannerheim.' They were her first words to him, and she spoke them in German.

He laughed, 'And you, very good German.' He handed her a glass of champagne. 'But please, you must call me Otto.'

She smiled. 'And you must call me Ruth. Oh, thank you for the flowers, they are lovely.'

'My pleasure, Ruth, my pleasure.'

By the time Gottfried served them dinner, Ruth's nervousness had almost completely disappeared. Apart for some rather unappetising BOAC sandwiches, they had not eaten all day and the smell of the soup made Ruth's mouth positively water. She was not to be disappointed. The steaming broth contained the most wonderful array of vegetables and she enjoyed every spoonful. It was all she could do to resist the temptation to tip the bowl and forage for the few last remaining morsels, but she thought better of it. Venison steak grilled and served in a red wine and shallot sauce followed and, like the soup, it was superb. The wine that they had to accompany it was French, a Claret, and that surprised her. She tried to decline the sweet trolley but the look of utter disappointment on Gottfried's face persuaded her otherwise, but she had to struggle to finish the huge portion of gateau he had delighted in serving her. It was as she was finishing the gateau that the first probing question came.

'Tell me, Ruth, where did you learn to speak such good German?'

She had relaxed a little too much during the meal; the conversation had been interesting, but nothing more than the usual niceties exchanged at a first meeting. Now, Otto's question alarmed her.

'I was born in Germany,' she told him, 'I kept it up in England.' Almost before the words had left her lips, she regretted it. Her answer left the way open for him, but she could not lie, not in front of Friedrich.

'Yes of course, Friedrich did tell me.' He waited expectantly for her to continue. She obliged.

'Somewhere near here, I think, Otto.' Her reply was nonchalant.

He only smiled, apparently choosing not to pursue the subject. After dinner Otto took Ruth's arm and led her to the library where coffee, courtesy of Gottfried, was waiting for them.

'That was a wonderful dinner,' Ruth said as she took a cup from the tray.

'Good, I am glad you enjoyed it.' Otto chose a cigar from the silver box that stood on the mantelpiece. 'Do you mind?' He held the cigar up as if to seek her approval.

'Not at all,' she replied, as she sat down next to Friedrich.

'Tell me, Ruth,' Otto paused to strike a match, 'what do you think about this trip to Germany?' He turned the cigar in his fingers as he exhaled its smoke. 'It could not have been easy for you to return here.'

It was another probing question only this time she was better prepared and chose her answer with care.

'Being Jewish you learn to live with the past and things that are not easy,' she smiled at Friedrich, 'and you have to make certain of the future.'

Otto eased his large bulky frame into the armchair opposite them.

'I admire you, Ruth.' He puffed again on the cigar. 'I understand your family suffered terribly under the Nazis. Whatever you say, I know it must not have been easy for you to return here.' He looked away from her for a moment turning his gaze to the fire. 'Hitler's Germany has a lot to answer for.' For a moment he was silent then, as if filled with some new enthusiasm, he heaved himself up out of the chair.

'So rude of me,' he proclaimed, 'please forgive me, a cognac is in order. I have something very special for you.'

The cognac was good and as they drank the two men talked about England and how things were going with the takeover of Bingham's. Ruth was content to sit back and listen; it was easy, she was not under fire. Only occasionally did Friedrich draw her into the conversation, ask her opinion. Neither man mentioned her appointment as financial director.

It was during a momentary lull in Friedrich's prognostication that Otto suddenly leant forward in his chair and, looking straight at Ruth, asked the question.

'And what does our new financial director think of all these plans for expansion?'

'They are well thought out and provided there is no lack of commitment or adequacy of financial resources to underpin them, the expansion will provide you with a firm base to expand into Europe.'

She had replied without hesitation and with confidence, almost instinctively. Otto looked a little taken aback. He sat back in his chair as if pondering her comments. Suddenly he laughed.

'Then we can't go wrong! How can we with you two working together?' He laughed again. 'Now enough about work, let's talk about what really matters and that's you two,' he paused, his face taking on a more serious look. 'Are you really sure, Ruth, that you want to marry this son of mine? I mean, he can be a stubborn cuss, you know.'

She smiled at his mock concern. 'So can I, Otto,' she quipped, 'and I'm absolutely certain that I want to marry him.'

A smile lit up his face. 'Then you must tell me all about yourself; if we are to be in-laws, we must get to know each other better.'

*

It had been well after midnight by the time Friedrich had escorted her back to her room. She had half expected him to ask if he could stay, but he had not. He had simply kissed her gently on the cheek and like a perfect gentleman wished her goodnight. In a way she was pleased about that, she would not have slept with him, not here, not until everything was sorted out. She just couldn't have.

The evening had left her drained and her tired mind had craved the sanctuary of sleep but now, as she lay in the quiet darkness of the room, it steadfastly refused to give way to the temptation. Otto's questions continually replayed in her mind and she tortured herself with the inadequacy of her answers. Had they been probing questions designed to strip away any pretence? Or had they simply been the kind of questions people ask when trying to get to know each other? She could not be sure. But she had been guarded in her replies, and somehow, now she regretted that. What kind of impression had she given him? What must he think of her? There she had been, face to face for the first time with her future father-in-law, and she had spent the whole evening playing some stupid cat and mouse game. Friedrich must have noticed; perhaps that's why he didn't ask to stay? Perhaps he was angry with her. She tried hard to stop thinking and let sleep come but she could not. If their story was true, surely he would be younger, at the most sixty-four, but Otto looked nearer seventy than sixty. *No*, she told herself, *he must be too old*. She closed her eyes, taking comfort in the thought. But there was something else, something even more important: if Otto had been involved in betraying her family then Friedrich knew nothing about it, that was obvious now. If he had known he would never have still brought her here, not after he had found the gun. She closed her eyes again.

Downstairs in the library Friedrich had rejoined his father and the two men were finishing a final brandy. Otto was again staring into the fire, deep in thought, the concern showing clearly on his face. They had sat in silence for some while now. Suddenly Otto shook himself from his thoughts and turned to his son.

'We have to be careful, Friedrich, we can't be sure how much she knows, what her uncle has told her.' Friedrich did not reply but watched silently as Otto finished his drink. 'If this is not handled properly, Friedrich, you could lose everything.' He turned back to the fire. 'There is only one thing we can be sure of now: there can be no doubt, no doubt at all, she is Ruth Caslav.'

THIRTEEN

HORST URBAN

T HE EARLY MORNING SUNLIGHT FLOODED INTO THE room probing into her sleep until its invasion eventually forced her to open her eyes. It was nearly 7.30am and it was her first morning in the East. Despite everything, she had slept well; she felt refreshed and ready for the day. There was a new positive attitude within her and she wanted to grasp the day, shake it and extract the truth, whatever it may be. In one move she was up, out of bed and standing by the window looking out at a bright crisp winter's day. Gone were the drab, heavy snow-laden clouds of yesterday and now an almost blinding sun shone down from the bluest of skies, its rays bouncing and sparkling off the frozen snow. *Was it an omen?* she asked herself. *Would the future, like the weather, be so much brighter today?*

In minutes she had washed, dressed, applied the merest hint of make-up and hurriedly done her hair. Then like some lost schoolgirl she sat on the bed wondering what to do. She didn't know whether Friedrich would come for her or if she should go downstairs alone. After several minutes of indecision, she grew frustrated with herself; it was going to be a positive day and sitting around waiting for things to happen was just not on! Outside in the corridor she had to stop to think whether to turn right or left; it took her a second or two to remember. Finally, when she had found her way to the top of the stairs, she stopped and took a deep breath. *A positive day*, she reminded herself.

Gottfried looked surprised. 'Good morning, madam, I know not you awake so early.'

'It's far too nice a day to spend in bed, Gottfried, am I too early for coffee?'

Otto and Friedrich were already at breakfast and both men stood up as Gottfried ushered her into the room.

'Ruth!' Friedrich said with surprise. 'I wanted you to sleep in, it was such a long day yesterday.'

She smiled as he kissed her cheek. 'No, I'm fine Friedrich, I slept really well.'

Friedrich was enjoying eggs and bacon, a British tradition to which he had readily become accustomed. Ruth just took toast and coffee.

'How are you this morning, Otto?' she enquired.

'Fine, fine. I am glad you slept well and the weather is brighter for you today. Unfortunately, I need to go to Berlin and I must leave soon, you will forgive me?' He finished his coffee and got up from the table. 'I will look forward to us having dinner tonight.' Even before she could say goodbye, he was gone.

*

Immediately after breakfast Friedrich presented Ruth with a thick fur jacket, gloves, boots, some riding britches and a fur hat with ear flaps.

'I am going to show you the place,' he proclaimed, grinning from ear to ear. 'The trousers may be a little big. God only knows where Gottfried found them. Quick, go and get changed.'

The coldness of the air bit into her lungs and made her gasp.

'I told you that you would need the coat.' Friedrich had seen her reaction to the morning air. 'It's about ten degrees below freezing today.' He took her arm. 'Come on this way, it's best from the hill.'

It took them almost half an hour of steady climbing, step after step crunching into the frozen crust of the snow before they reached the summit of Friedrich's hill. Ruth's legs ached and her lungs felt fit to burst but finally, triumphantly, they had arrived.

'From here, Ruth, you can see nearly all the estate.' He swung his arm in a large arc as he turned around on the spot, churning up the snow as he did so.

Ruth looked about her. 'How far does it stretch?' she asked, lifting her hand to her eyes to shelter them from the harsh glare of the sunlight as it reflected off the snow. It had been a hard climb and she was still out of breath and feeling tired.

'It's about 600 acres in all, if you count the woods.' Friedrich was looking down towards the lake as he spoke, and Ruth noticed something had gained his attention.

'Oh yes, we mustn't forget the woods,' she mocked.

'Pardon?' Friedrich said turning back to her.

She pointed to the smoke that was coming from behind the trees, it had obviously been that which had attracted his attention.

'Somebody has a bonfire!' she proclaimed.

Friedrich put his arm around her. 'No, that's Gitta and Carl Kahler's house. It's behind the trees.'

*

'Do you think he likes me?' Ruth asked the question as they started on their way back down the hill. She was holding on to his arm tightly; it helped her cope with the snow.

'Of course he likes you. That's a silly question.'

Ruth protested. 'It's not a silly question at all and slow down a little, Friedrich, I'm not as fit as you! If it's so silly, why did he keep asking me all those questions? Perhaps he thinks I'm just a gold digger after the family wealth.' It was a calculated question and she had put it deliberately to gauge his response.

'Rubbish! He just wants to get to know you, that's all.'

'Well, I didn't ask him questions all night and I want to get to know him!' she tried to sound indignant.

Friedrich laughed.

'Don't laugh at me, Friedrich, it's true. I never asked him how old he was.'

'Sixty-four.' Fredrick's answer was instantaneous.

Ruth stopped walking. 'What was that?' she asked turning to face him.

'You wanted to know how old he was. He's sixty-four, looks older doesn't he!'

*

Ruth had never seen Friedrich so happy before and that pleased her. He seemed to talk and talk, telling her about the house, the estate and everybody on it. 'There's plenty of time for work tomorrow,' he told her as they sat down to lunch. 'When we have finished this I will take you on a guided tour of the house.'

He was true to his word for Ruth had barely finished her coffee before he had pulled her from the comfort of her chair and was leading her by the hand in and out of various rooms. 'I want you to learn all about me, Ruth, and all about my family as well,' he told her, as he steered her from door to door. It was a sentiment with which she readily agreed. He was speaking about his family more freely than he had ever spoken before and although it made her feel guilty, she used this to her advantage. She began asking as many questions as she could, gentle, probing questions, being ever mindful not to appear interrogating. But she needed to know, she needed to search for the truth and find it. A human jigsaw puzzle lay in front of her, and she desperately needed to build it into a picture that was the truth. She prayed to God it would be the truth, she wanted it not just for her but for the baby too. It had not started well: the revelation about Otto's age had shaken her. She had been certain he was older, but she had been wrong. It had made her realise that there were so many things she could be wrong about, and that frightened her. It was the first piece of the puzzle, a corner piece from which to build. But it had not been a good piece. Her positive day had taken its first setback earlier that morning on the hill. It needed to improve. Ruth's inquisitive eyes searched with desperation as he marched her proudly about the house. If there was anything to hide, Friedrich appeared totally unaware of it; that gave her hope. With an almost reckless abandon he pointed out everything he thought was of interest. But it was when they reached the study that suddenly, out of nowhere, a second piece of the puzzle appeared.

'What's that?' she asked, pointing to a framed scroll that hung on one of the walls.

'It's father's degree, I think.' He studied it more closely. 'Yes, it's his degree, he read history at the University of Berlin.' Friedrich moved on unaware of the significance of his words.

Joseph had told her that.

Later in the basement Friedrich showed her an old pre-war printing press. It was hidden behind the racks of wine and covered with a yellowing sheet; he made a rather grand gesture of unveiling it.

'Isn't it marvellous?' he proclaimed. 'And it still works. One day I would like to open a museum for old printing machinery.'

'Where did you get it?' she asked, pretending to be as interested as he with the intricacy of its cogs and pulleys.

'It's one of the original presses from before the war.'

Ruth seized the opportunity to probe. 'Has your family always been in printing?'

There was no hesitation in his reply.

'No, father was taken into the business by some friends of his.' The words just slipped from his lips and again he remained seemingly unaware of their significance. 'It was before the war, back in the thirties, I think. Father had known them since he was a child and when things got difficult here for them,' he looked apologetically at her, 'you see, they were Jewish, with all the anti-Semitism, well they asked him to run their business for them. He often says he owes them everything.'

Ruth could not believe what she had heard. There had been no pretence, no attempt to hide anything, he had just told her. It was another piece of the now ominous-looking puzzle that had slipped so easily into place. But he had simply no idea, that was obvious!

'Do the Jewish family still own a part of the business?' she asked, trying desperately to control the tremble in her voice.

'No, sadly they were all caught by the Nazis.' This time he turned away from her as he spoke. 'We believe they all perished in the camps.'

*

It had taken the whole day but slowly Ruth had put together the jigsaw; only fate could have honed the pieces to fit with such perfection. First the name, Otto Mannerheim, an unusual name, true, but on its own little proof. But then there was the rest: his age, the University of Berlin, the history degree, the story about the Jewish family. It was her family, it just had to be. It had all left her with little hope, and then as if jubilance in victory was not enough for fate, it dealt its final blow when Friedrich showed her the painting of his mother. She had stood in silence for some moments before summoning the will to comment.

'She was very beautiful,' she whispered. But her eyes had remained fixed on the small brass plate screwed to the base of the frame. It read, 'Ingrid Mannerheim'.

*

As she dressed for dinner, Ruth finally had to face the truth. She had tried not to. She had looked for all kinds of possible explanations, but there were none. Everything Joseph had told her was true, it had to be. It was the same man, there was no longer any question about it. She put her hand on her stomach and thought of the young life that rested there. It was a desperate situation and she had only herself to blame for being in it. If the baby was to stand any chance, if she was to have happiness, then she knew now, she would have to fight for it.

She would have to find out what had happened that night all those years ago. Had Otto betrayed them? Had he been responsible for the deaths of her family or had the facts become twisted with time? In the dark, in the rain, in the horror of it all, could Joseph have been mistaken? There was only one thing she could do: she had to face Otto with it. Confront him. The thought of that scared her to death, but the thought of not doing so scared her even more. No, she was more determined now than ever before to get to the truth. After all, if nothing else, Friedrich's openness had proved that he knew nothing. At least she could count on him.

Otto returned early from Berlin and took the opportunity to meet with Friedrich before dinner. He had gone to his son's room to talk.

'Has she said anything?' he asked, walking into the room.

'No but she has asked a lot of questions. I think she knows something. I did as you advised and told her only the truth. Everything she asked.'

'Good,' Otto replied. 'This will not be easy for any of us.'

'How is Mary, father?'

Otto did not reply immediately. 'She is nervous, frightened, unsure, but she believes. That is the main thing, Friedrich, she believes.'

*

Carl Kahler turned into the alley and stopped to check his watch. It was the second time in less than a week that he had made this trip and he was anxious, 6.25pm, he had five minutes to spare.

It took him less than a minute to reach the far end of the alley, it took him even less time to cross the street. He stopped only when he reached a small shabby door squeezed between two neglected shops. The red painted sign above it read 'Communist Workers' Party Headquarters'. He kicked the snow from his boots, took off his cap and opening the door, stepped quickly inside. The bare wooden stairs groaned under his weight as he climbed them. In the dimly lit hall, it was just possible to check his watch again. He was on time.

'Enter!'

The response to his knock had been instantaneous. Carl swallowed hard and opened the door.

Horst Urban did not look up. He was writing, his head bent over the page of a large book.

'Sit please, Kahler,' he gestured to the wooden chair in front of the desk. Carl did as he was instructed.

'I hope you have something of interest for me.' Urban blotted the page as he spoke.

'I think so, Herr Urban.'

Urban looked up from the book. 'Think so! Think so!' His voice was aggressive. 'I am a busy man, Kahler, I trust you are not wasting my time.'

Urban was a small man with sharp, pointed features and close-cropped black hair. He was thin as well, barely half the size of Carl, but despite that he dominated the larger man with ease, and he knew it. Urban was the local Communist Party leader. He was a man to be respected, even feared. Carl did both.

'She has arrived, Herr Urban.'

Urban sighed, his irritation obvious. 'She arrived yesterday, Kahler, they landed at Tempelhof Airport on the lunchtime flight. There was some kind of a fuss at Brandenburg, the car turned around, they crossed later at Charlie and did not arrive at the house till about 6.30pm.' Urban took a folder from his right-hand desk drawer and, tossing it towards Carl, sat back in his chair. 'Now tell me something I don't know.'

Carl was shaken. He had heard about the contacts that this man was meant to have, but his knowledge of her arrival surprised him. He reached into his pocket and took out the photograph. 'I have brought the photograph back, Herr Urban; I have seen her.'

Urban sat forward, 'How close were you?'

'Close enough, Herr Urban.'

'Well! What do you think?' Urban's agitation was clear.

'There can be no doubt about it, she is just like the woman in the picture. She has the same beauty, the same eyes, the same bone structure.' Carl leant forward and pushed the photograph across the table. 'I am certain she is the one.'

Urban picked it up, opened the file and clipped it to a copy of Otto Mannerheim's telegram to England.

He smiled. 'You have done well, Carl. I have already mentioned you to several of the party committee members. Your work has not gone unnoticed.' Carl smiled. 'I want to know everything that goes on.' Urban got to his feet and moved around the desk. 'Everything, do you understand?' Carl nodded. 'Find out why she is here, if it's true that they plan to marry. How much does she know?'

Urban paused. 'Do this job well, Carl, and who knows? There may even be a place for you on the committee.'

FOURTEEN

THE TRUTH

'DID YOU ENJOY YOUR DAY, RUTH?' OTTO ASKED handing her the coffee.

'Yes, thank you, it was very interesting.' She watched him with dubitation as he lowered himself into the large armchair opposite them. He had said little throughout dinner, appearing preoccupied, his mind so obviously engrossed in his thoughts that he had, several times, failed to respond to Friedrich's attempts to draw him into the conversation. But Ruth too had found it hard to concentrate. She knew what she had to do, and the thought of that made her more nervous, more scared than she could ever remember feeling. The knot in her stomach had made eating difficult and she had struggled with every mouthful.

But the revelations of the day had left her in no doubt that the charade could continue no longer. She had to confront him, get to the truth. It was the only thing left that she could do.

She had been going to say something at dinner, but finally decided not to. Several times she had made up her mind to grasp the nettle only to shrink back on the pretence of timing.

But now as the three of them sat together over coffee she knew the time had come; it could be put off no longer, she had to do it. The two men were talking, but she did not listen, her mind was too busy wrestling with her courage. She felt again the cold sweat, the dry throat, the same feeling of panic she had felt at the airport and at Brandenburg. It had to be now, or she knew she may never find the courage.

'We need to talk, Ruth.'

Otto's words pulled gently at her ears and slowly climbed into her mind. The implication of them shook her attention.

'Pardon?' she stammered.

He leant forward in the chair, one large hand resting on each knee.

'Why did you come here, Ruth? Why did you come back to Germany?'

The question was blunt and cutting and it threw her. Only seconds before, her mind had been enveloped in the confusion of what to say to him and how to say it. Now it was faced with the challenge of his question and she had to force her mind to respond with caution.

'I thought that was obvious, Otto; because Friedrich wanted me to meet you.' Her reply appeared to make little impression on him.

'Do you love my son, Ruth?' Otto's face gave nothing away; he asked the question as if it were of little meaning. That angered her.

'I am not in the habit of becoming engaged to men I do not love,' she replied indignantly. She turned to Friedrich who was sitting next to her on the settee.

'What is this about, Friedrich? Why do you let him interrogate me like this?'

'Be patient, Ruth, please be patient,' Friedrich replied taking her hand. 'There are things you need to know.'

'You have your mother's beauty, Ruth.'

Otto's words struck her with such force that for a second she was unable to reply. Her mind raced. It had been she who was going to attack him, ask him outright, get to the truth, but he had stolen her thunder, beaten her to the strike. He had taken control and it was not what she wanted.

'So I am told,' she replied as calmly as she could yet still allowing her indignation to show.

Otto was not to be stopped. 'I think you know more about us than you would have us believe, Ruth.'

He sat back in the chair, his eyes fixed on her with a questioning stare. He was waiting, like a man that throws a stone into a pool and then watches the ripples, he was waiting for the effect. She looked at Friedrich with anger. Anger that he was allowing this. Why didn't he jump to her defence? Protect her, tell his father to stop? But he did not, he just sat there and said nothing. He looked almost embarrassed, frightened to interfere.

'I am not sure what you mean, Otto, by, "know more than I would have you believe". What am I meant to know?' She was going to fight back even if Friedrich wouldn't.

'Ruth, you are the daughter of Mary and Luke Caslav. You know that and we know that.' Otto's tone was matter-of-fact. 'Now, we must discuss this.'

Ruth felt any pretence that was in her fall away with the stark truthfulness of his words. Suddenly, she felt terribly alone and humiliated. Like a schoolgirl who thought she had outsmarted the teacher only to find that he had been on to her from the start. But for her the consequences were far more dangerous. She turned to Friedrich.

'He said "we know"! What do you know, Friedrich?' The sudden realisation that Otto was speaking for his son as well made her realise how alone she really was. She had been convinced that Friedrich had known nothing about her past and the connection with his family. She had been wrong again, her trust in him had been suddenly and completely swept away with Otto's words. She felt betrayed and angry. She pulled her hand from his.

'I know that there must be many questions in your head. Questions that must be answered,' Friedrich replied as if to pacify.

'Then answer this one, Friedrich! What do you know?'

He said nothing.

'If you knew who my mother and father were, why did you not say something before? Why wait till now, till I'm here in Germany?'

'Because I asked him to say nothing,' Otto said firmly. Ruth turned to him as he spoke. She was quick to answer and did so with venom. Like a cornered animal, her fight back would be ferocious.

'And why was that, Otto? So, you could get me here. Trap me!'

Friedrich stood up. 'Ruth, it is not like that, you must understand. I did not realise who you were until a few weeks ago. When father contacted me and told me what he thought, I could not believe it. We have been looking for you for so long, Ruth. We had almost given up; we were certain you must be dead.'

'Well, I'm sorry to disappoint you both, but as you can see, I'm very much alive. The three of us are alive!' The anger in her voice had driven her to almost shout her reply at them.

'I am very pleased of that,' Otto replied quietly.

'Are you, Otto? Are you really pleased?' The sarcasm in her voice caused, for the first time, the expression on Otto's face to change. He frowned.

'We have spent years trying to trace the three of you. Then by some chance Friedrich finds you and falls in love with you, without even knowing who you are. Of course, we are pleased.' He leant forward again in the chair. 'Ruth, you do not realise what this means?'

'I think I do, Otto; I think I realise only too well.' She got up from the sofa and walked around it, away from both men. 'I know that I'm a threat to you. I know that you would never have had your company, your wealth, if it were not for my family.'

'Is that why you have come here, Ruth? To lay claim to what is yours? Or is it because you love me?' Friedrich asked angrily. 'Otto said we had to be sure, but I told him, no, Ruth loves me, I know she loves me. We are to be married; she knows nothing about what happened in the past. But you did know, Ruth.' He got up and, moving after her, grasped her arm. 'You did know about the past, didn't you? What do you know, and how long have you known it?'

'You question if I love you!' Ruth screamed bitterly. 'Do you think I would sleep with you just to stake a claim to my piece of the past? What sort of a person do you think I am? Perhaps you should be asking your own father about what happened in the past. About how my family were arrested about how they were betrayed!' She broke away from Friedrich's grip and turned to Otto, her fury now in full control. 'Tell him, Otto. Tell your son all about the past, tell him why my uncle and aunt were so fearful of me coming to Germany, tell him about the night we were betrayed.' Again, Friedrich grabbed her arm.

'My father only helped your family; he has always helped your family. Why are you acting like this? He knows nothing of that night and of who betrayed you. We have brought you here because there are things you need to know.' She pushed hard against his grip but it held firm.

'Just ask him, Friedrich. Ask him where he was that night, ask him!'

'My God!' he pulled her round to face him. 'You think it was him, don't you? You think my father betrayed you all.'

'Just ask him where he was that night,' she screamed again, 'ask him why he was in the car.'

'I'll ask him no such thing.' Friedrich shook her as he spoke, his strong hands biting into the soft flesh of her arms. 'I've told you, he did not betray you.' He pulled her closer to him, his grip now so tight that the pain was almost unbearable. 'But you betrayed me, Ruth! Didn't you? Didn't you?' he shouted the question at her. 'I was stupid. The gun, you didn't bring it because you were frightened of just being in Germany, you brought it to reap some kind of sick revenge. I don't know what your uncle has told you, but it's wrong.' He let her go, pushing her away from him as he did so. 'I was a fool, Ruth. I thought that between us we could overcome the past, be happy together.' There was a new coldness in his eyes. A coldness she had never seen before. 'Tell me, Ruth, when were we to marry, after we had buried my father or before?' He turned and started to walk away.

'It wasn't meant to be like that!' she cried. 'I do love you.'

He turned. 'You were right the first time, Ruth; do you remember when we first met and you said there was too much between us? Well, there is.'

He said no more but turned and despite Ruth's pleas left her and the room.

'He has always been a hot-headed boy.' Otto had not spoken for some time. He had watched the confrontation between them in silence. Now it was his turn.

'Please sit down, Ruth, we have a lot to talk about.' Ruth's eyes were still fixed on the door. 'He will not return now.' Otto sounded relaxed. It was almost as if he was pleased that his son had left. Ruth was having to fight hard to keep back the tears; she knew they would be a sign a feminine weakness, a sign she could ill afford. Friedrich's involvement and his reaction had cut her deeply, but strangely, with his leaving, her anger had subsided, left her almost completely. There was only a void left within her now. A feeling of emptiness, of hopelessness, loss and despair. He had walked away from her, left her alone. The one man she had ever really loved and depended on had walked away and she knew that she had probably lost him. Lost him for ever.

'As soon as I saw you, Ruth, I knew there could be absolutely no doubt. You see, you have the same beauty that your mother had when she was young.' Otto's words grasped her attention. 'I knew straight away who you were. The same eyes, the same hair. There was no longer any doubt in my mind, you had to be Mary Caslav's daughter.' Otto had left his chair and was pouring two cognacs as he spoke. He turned to her. 'When Friedrich sent me the telegrams and told me about you I could only hope, no, pray, that it was you. I dared not believe it. Here, drink this.' He handed her the glass. 'It was the name, you see.' He returned to the armchair. 'Please, sit down.' He waved his hand at the chair opposite him. Still stunned, she obeyed, dropping wearily into the chair. 'I did not see it at first. Valsac, Valsac. There was something about it. Then like a dream, in the middle of the night, it came to me.' He paused for a moment to sample the brandy. 'It was as if it was meant to happen; at last, luck had returned to us. I wrote the name over and over again but I could not be certain, not until I saw you.'

Ruth had heard his words but found it hard to concentrate. Her mind was still trapped in the tangle of her argument with Friedrich, but she forced herself to concentrate. It was just the two of them now. She had to face him alone, but she was not going to lie down and die, she was determined of that. If it meant a fight for the truth then fight she would. She looked at him, sitting there just a few feet from her, and their eyes met, but she did not look away; for the first time she held his stare. She looked right back at him with defiance.

'You were in the car that night, Otto, you were with that Nazi officer, Joseph saw you.' Ruth's spoke slowly, the coldness in her voice evidence of the conviction she held. She watched as he put his glass on the table next to him and then slowly, he rested his head in his hands. For the first time his control had faltered. It was there, a reaction, perhaps a weakness.

'Yes, Ruth, I was there. I saw everything and did nothing,' he answered almost in a whisper without looking at her. 'There was nothing I could do. You must believe me. It was a nightmare.' He picked up the glass again. 'I saw your father beaten and I saw what they did to your mother.' He finished the contents of the glass with one mouthful. 'Do you really think I wanted that, Ruth? Do you really think I wanted to be a part of that atrocity?' He looked up at her. 'I know now what Joseph saw, I knew he would be there somewhere, but I did not betray you, Ruth, as God is my witness, I did not betray you.' He got up and poured another drink, as he searched for some comfort in the alcohol. 'You think you know what it was like, Ruth? Do you think because Joseph and your aunt have told you, you really know what it was like? Can you remember?' She did not reply but watched him silently as he returned to his seat. 'It was hard for us, Ruth; it was hard for all of us. You are Jewish of course and you suffered. Your whole family suffered, but what about us too, us so called ordinary Germans? Some of us tried, Ruth, we really tried. We wanted to help. I've spent years trying to help. But it was not always possible.'

'You did nothing!' Ruth spat her words at him with a sudden renewed venom that surprised even her. 'You expect me to sit here and listen to you tell me how hard it was for you? Well, it was nothing compared with our loss, our sacrifice. My family died, for God's sake! All of them, my parents, my brother and sister, just children, small children, all of them and millions of others like them murdered in the Nazi concentration camps, and you tell me it was hard for you!' She got up from the chair. 'You were in the car, Otto, you knew what would happen. You betrayed them!' The anger had flown into her words again and her voice was raised; she struggled to regain some composure. She had to remain in control. 'It was your chance, Otto, wasn't it? You could see an easy way to gaining everything, with us all out of the way, murdered by the Nazis, it would be simple. Just a word in the right ear, that was all it needed. That's all you had to do!' She waited.

'I had been arrested that afternoon, Ruth. When I left the flat in Berlin, they were waiting for me.' He looked up at her; the cold blue eyes showed only control, a calm, calculated control. 'Please sit back down, Ruth, I have a lot to tell you and it will be better if you sit.' There was a new softness in his words and it surprised her. She had been expecting retaliation, a fight, but there was none. He was just waiting. She returned to the settee. 'I loved your family, Ruth.'

She made to speak.

'No please,' he lifted his hand, 'just hear me out. You want to know everything and you must know everything. Believe me, I loved them, I still do. They gave me everything. They befriended me when I was a boy, they gave me a job when I could not get work. I grew up with them. Your father and Joseph were my very best friends; no, more than that, we were like brothers, we did everything together. I could never have betrayed them. Don't you see that? I was trying desperately to get them out! I know these are just my words and I know what it must have looked like to Joseph. But if you really love Friedrich and you want to marry him then you must listen. Listen to the truth as it is. I can prove it, there are others you need to meet, others who can tell you.' He got up from the chair and walked over to the fireplace, turning to face her when he reached it. 'I had managed to get several families out of Germany. I know it was wrong but I sent others first. I had to be sure it was safe for all of you. We had run the same route six times. Every time it had worked well. A late-night delivery to Belgium. One, maybe two families hidden in the truck, a safe house waiting for them and then on to France and with any luck Switzerland. It was all planned, I was to drive the lorry myself that night. But that afternoon as I left the flat, they arrested me. I was taken to Gestapo headquarters for interrogation. Someone had been watching the factory and had reported us. I had been stupid. The Belgium run was always on a Thursday. A local Jewish family had been seen entering the factory late one Thursday night and the SS had been told.' Otto threw up his arms in despair. 'I thought I had been so careful. If I had sent you all on the first trip there would have been no problem.' He turned towards the fire. 'But I had not.' Sadness hung heavy in his words. 'You will never know, Ruth, how many times I have asked myself, why? Why, did I wait? But I did.' For a moment he was quiet but when he turned to speak again, the anger was evident. 'Of course, you were betrayed! We were all betrayed. At Gestapo headquarters they interrogated me. But they already knew. There were houses directly opposite the factory gates. In one of them lived a man called Graf Urban, the village electrician; he was also the local Nazi Party youth worker. It was an opportunity for him to shine, to gain favour with the party hierarchy. He had seen what was going on and reported it.' Ruth watched as Otto returned to the table and retrieved the half-filled glass of cognac. The anger had turned to despair when he spoke again.

'Everything that could go wrong went wrong that night, Ruth. The officer in charge at Gestapo headquarters was a particularly evil man named Kleister who took great delight in persecuting the Jews. He told me that they had enough evidence of my involvement to send me to trial. They would confiscate everything I had. Ingrid and Friedrich would be sent to workcamps. It was to be the end of us too. They beat me up, tried to make me confess. But I would not. Oh, make no mistake about it, Ruth, I wanted to tell them everything. I wanted the beating to stop. It was not bravery that made me hold my tongue, it was just the opposite. I knew that they couldn't connect me directly; it was my factory all right, my lorry certainly, but I denied all knowledge of it. It was my only chance, our only chance. When they realised I was not going to talk they made me go with them to the factory. I was to be made to witness the events. They were watching me, waiting to see how I would react. If I had shown just one tiny glimmer of concern, the pretence would have been over.' He turned to looked at her. 'So, you see Ruth, Joseph did see me, I was in the car, but my hands were handcuffed. I was their prisoner.'

She watched in silence as slowly he lowered himself back into the armchair. Her mind raced. Could it be true? Was it a straw to grasp at? She was determined not to be wrong again; up to now she had been wrong about everything.

'What is Friedrich's love worth to you, Ruth?'

His question surprised her; he was staring at her again, leaning forward in his chair with an expression on his face she had not seen before. For all the world it appeared to her to be a look of desperation.

'It means everything to me,' she replied with as much indigence as she could muster. Then suddenly, uncontrollably, 'I'm having his baby.' The words seemed to come from nowhere. Almost involuntarily, they sprang from her mouth and instantly she asked herself, why? Why had she told him? Otto of all people. The one man in all the world that she had the most reason to mistrust, to question. And she had told him. Just like that, she had told him. She suddenly felt very stupid and very vulnerable and had to bite her lip hard to stop herself from giving way. She would not let her emotion show. It seemed like an eternity before Otto spoke but when he did his voice was softer; he got to his feet, moving towards her.

'Then there is more to this than just you and Friedrich, there is another life to care for now.' He took her hand. 'Give me tomorrow, Ruth, just tomorrow. I will prove to you that I did not betray your family. I will show you the truth.'

FIFTEEN

THE TRUTH IN WEST BERLIN

THE BLACK MERCEDES SWEPT EFFORTLESSLY through the gates and out onto the main road to Berlin. Its two passengers travelled in silence, neither looking at the other, neither attempting to communicate. For both, the trip held uncertainties and doubts. For her, it was the uncertainty of what she was to encounter; she was now entirely in his hands. Friedrich had gone and she was left clinging to the remnants of their relationship and the slightest of hope that Otto could prove his innocence. He had told her they were going to Berlin, but who knows what he really had planned? Her uncle had told her the truth. He had always told her the truth. What reason was there for him to lie? After all, everything he had told her had come true so far. Otto was the man, he had not denied it, he had been there that night, he had not denied that either. But there was just a chance he was telling the truth. It was a gamble but she had to take it. If her relationship with Friedrich was to be saved there was no other way. Take the chance! She had no option.

For Otto too, the concerns were manifold. He had toiled long and hard with what would be the best way. How could everything be done without causing her too much distress, too much pain? There were others to think about too. She was there now, with him in the car. She had trusted in him so far, but he knew it was only the slenderest of trusts. If this was not handled right, then so many people could lose so much. The burden of what lay ahead weighed heavily on him.

It was not until the car started to wind its way between the drab buildings and dirty streets that formed the outskirts of East Berlin that Otto spoke.

'The Spree.' He pointed to the frozen river. 'We cross soon.'

At the border there was little formality and with just the minimum of checks a fair-haired young soldier waved them through. Otto returned his papers to his jacket pocket.

'First we visit Koepernicker Strasser.'

'Why?' she asked. He did not reply.

When the car stopped it was outside one of the many new apartment blocks that now formed the post-war face of West Berlin. Otto got out and the driver quickly opened the door for Ruth.

'Come.' Otto made his way quickly up the steps and pushed open the large white painted door. He was halfway down the corridor and had rang the doorbell of apartment number 3 before she had caught up with him.

He turned to her. 'I promised I would bring you here first.'

The door was opened by a thin, rather elegant woman who Ruth estimated was probably well into her seventies. She smiled warmly, 'Come in. Come in Otto.' Ruth followed him in. 'So, this is her?' The woman took Ruth's hands and before she could resist, kissed her warmly on both cheeks. 'I never thought I would see you again,' she said, squeezing her hands. 'When Otto told me that he had found you and that you

were alive I could not believe it. And your uncle and aunt too!'
She squeezed her hands again. 'I was so pleased, so very, very
pleased.' There was an awkward silence for a moment as the
old woman studied her. 'Just listen to me!' she began again, 'A
stupid old lady who has forgotten her manners. Come through,
please, come through.' She led them down the short passage
and into what was obviously the lounge. The room was tidy and
bright with a huge window that looked out over the *strasser*.
Several photographs adorned the windowsill. Ruth looked
at Otto who was taking off his coat; he made no attempt to
introduce her.

'I am sorry about the telephone call, but I thought you
would want to know. You are the first we have visited; she
knows only what I have told you.'

Ruth could contain herself no longer, 'I do not wish to be
rude, Fraulein but…'

'My name is Martha Vitnez,' she had not allowed Ruth to
finish. 'It was a long time ago and you were just a little girl, five
or maybe six years old, I cannot remember exactly.'

'She was six,' Otto said as he sat himself down.

'You were such a pretty, bright-eyed little thing. Full of
life and energy.' The woman hesitated for a moment and then
turned away from her. 'We thought they had got you too, all
of you,' she continued, still with her back to Ruth. 'We blamed
ourselves you see. Poor Herbert, it haunted him.' She picked up
one of the photographs and, turning back to face Ruth, pushed
it into her hand. 'I doubt if you remember him.' Ruth looked at
the faded photograph. It was obviously taken many years ago
and was of the woman and a man who Ruth assumed must
have been 'Poor Herbert'. She shook her head. 'That's all right,
dear, I did not expect you to remember.' The woman took the

photograph and returned it to the window, her disappointment obvious.

'How much do you remember about your time in Germany, Ruth?' Otto's question took her attention from the woman, who by now had sat herself on the edge of a small settee on the far side of the room. Ruth did not answer his question immediately but again turned to look at the woman. Was there something? Something hidden deep in the darkness of a child's lost past. She walked to the window and retrieved the photograph. This time she studied it more carefully.

'I was only six, what do you expect me to remember?' She was irritated and it showed in her voice. She had sensed the woman's disappointment and was sorry. But it was not her fault! 'There may be something, I don't know, I can't be sure, they look familiar. What do you expect!'

'Do you remember your time in Berlin? In the cellar where you all lived?' Otto's words carried a sense of urgency as if willing her to remember.

'Yes, I remember bits.'

'What bits, Ruth? Tell us, what bits?' Otto waited.

'We were taken to Berlin to hide, I remember, I think we were all there, my parents, my brother and sister, uncle and aunt.'

It was the first time in years that Ruth had forced her mind to stretch back so far and search for detail. It was difficult.

'It was a large house, a doctor's house, yes, that's what uncle said.' Ruth remained looking at the photograph as she spoke.

'Do you remember the doctor, Ruth? Do you remember him?'

'I must have seen him. They brought us food and cared for us.' Ruth looked again at the woman who smiled weakly at her.

There was something! Now she was sure, there was something familiar about her. Slowly, Fraulein Vitnez got to her feet.

'Do you remember, Ruth?' she spoke softly. 'Do you remember the doctor's wife who played with you every day? Who read to you and your brother and sister? Do you remember how she used to sneak you up into the house and you would help her make bread? Do you remember, Ruth? Do you remember?'

Ruth looked again at the photograph and then at the woman. Suddenly, it was as if some dark barrier had lifted and all at once her memory dragged her back across time, back to Berlin, to the house, to the kitchen where she had made the bread, and to the woman with whom she had made it. 'Her name was Martha.' Ruth whispered. 'Her name was Martha.' She looked at the old woman standing in front of her, who had started to cry, large tears running down her face. 'It was you?' Ruth had asked the question knowing the answer. The woman could only nod her head. As both of them took the other and embraced, Ruth remembered, she remembered the last time she had held the woman was when they had said goodbye that fatal night in 1938.

Otto handed Ruth the coffee he had made and sat down next to Martha.

'I brought you here first, Ruth, because it is important that you hear what Martha has to tell you.' He looked towards Martha who hesitated for just a moment then, without further prompting, began her story.

'I told you, Ruth, Herbert blamed himself.' She got up and put the untouched coffee on the small table beside Ruth. 'We thought we had been careless; someone must have seen you. Did we speak to the wrong people?' She shrugged her shoulders.

'All we could be sure of, Ruth, was that like so many Jews you had been betrayed. But we were scared, Ruth, petrified. It only needed one of you children to tell them about us and we too would be arrested. We had to get away, hide. Herbert had a brother in the south so we decided to go there. We would stay with them; Herbert would start a new practice.' As she spoke, she relived the time. The tension and the fear had for a moment returned and she paced up and down the small room as she spoke. 'So, we ran without thinking, like frightened rabbits we ran. It was not until we were stopped at the station that we realised we had no travel documents. They arrested us and we were taken to police headquarters for questioning.' Suddenly, Martha stopped pacing the room and knelt down by Ruth taking her hand. 'I was so frightened, Ruth, you cannot believe. It was only then, for the first time, I realised what it must have been like for the Jews, for your family. Anyway, Herbert argued, said he was a doctor on his way to visit his mother who was very ill and, in his rush, had not thought about travel permits. The officer in charge was angry with us and told him that in such troubled times everybody, even doctors, must have travel documents. Then all of a sudden, he changed, he offered to make out the documents there and then. But there was a condition of course. A simple favour. There had been some prisoners brought in the night before. A family of Jews, one close to death but that did not matter to him. However, there was another man arrested for trying to help them escape. He was not Jewish. One of the guards apparently had been over-zealous in his attempts to make the man confess and the officer was concerned that the man might die. "If a Jew dies, who cares?" the officer told us. But if the other man should die on his watch, there would have to be reports, an enquiry. He may well be held responsible. It was our chance, Ruth, our chance to get away. Herbert told the officer that as a doctor he would be pleased to do what he could but only if he was allowed to treat the Jews as well. The officer agreed but would only let Herbert see the Jewish man. He told us that the rest of the family was fine. I was not allowed down to the cell and I thank God for that. I will always remember Herbert's face when he came back. He told me that first, they took him to the man they had beaten.' Martha paused; she looked at Otto for a second and then continued, 'It was Otto, they had beaten him so badly that at first Herbert did not recognise him. As well as the blows to his face there were several deep burns on his back. Otto knew it was Herbert all right but he said nothing; the officer was with them all the time. There was bleeding from one of Otto's ears and Herbert told the officer that if he did not want the man to die the beatings must stop at once. He told him that the man had a bad concussion and should be transferred to hospital; there was also evidence of at least three broken ribs, any one of which may puncture a lung if the man was not treated carefully. Herbert did what he could for Otto, but it was precious little. Then he asked to see the Jew.'

Fraulein Vitnez looked at Otto. She was quiet and Ruth could sense her difficulty. After a moment she seemed to summon the courage she needed and continued. 'I will say only this: there was nothing Herbert could do for him, he was already dead, your poor father was dead. Otto has told me what you think, what your uncle saw, but don't you see, Ruth? It was not him who betrayed you. He nearly died trying to protect you. No, my sweetheart, it was not Otto.'

Ruth had found words difficult when she kissed Martha Vitnez goodbye. 'I will come back soon,' had been all she could say.

*

It took the driver less than ten minutes to negotiate the streets of the city before bringing the car to a halt outside the Bank of Berlin. Throughout that time Ruth had struggled. She had gone over and over in her mind what Martha Vitnez had told her. She wanted desperately to talk to Otto about it, but he sat in silence, his head turned away from her as if somehow fixed to the view from his window. She knew that if what Martha had said was true then Otto had told her the truth. But was the woman really who she claimed to be? Ruth could not be sure. In her heart she believed the woman, but her mind was not prepared to be fooled so easily. After all, how many more mistakes could she afford to make? She just prayed to God that, this time, her heart and her memory was right.

The Bank of Berlin was an impressive building that seemed to stretch up and up for ever. Huge marble steps led up to the entrance above which was mounted a magnificent bronze of the German eagle. Once inside Ruth followed Otto to the lift, which they took to the eighth floor. There they were quickly ushered into the office of Herr Langdoff, financial director. Both men shook hands. Ruth and Otto were soon seated facing Langdoff across a huge expanse of mahogany desk. Again, Otto did not introduce her.

'Thank you for seeing me at such short notice, Herr Langdoff, but this is a matter of some urgency.'

'It is my pleasure, Herr Mannerheim,' Langdoff smiled.

'This young lady is at present a houseguest of mine. I am anxious that she be advised of all my company's bank accounts, trusts and the contents of my will.'

The smile slipped from Langdoff's face.

'Pardon me, Herr Mannerheim.'

'I said, would you please advise this young lady of all my company's bank accounts, trusts and the contents of my will.'

Langdoff raised an eyebrow but without further comment pressed the button on his desk. Almost immediately a middle-aged, smartly dressed woman appeared. He fired some instructions to her and within minutes she had returned with several files and a younger woman who carried a tray which contained a pot of coffee and three cups.

'Where would you like me to begin, Herr Mannerheim?'

'With the coffee I think,' Otto replied.

*

The figure beside the word 'Balance' read 19,890,000 Deutsch Marks. Ruth had read it several times.

'That is the balance of the trust at this time, Fraulein; with projected profits expected to exceed last year's by some 7% we are confident the trust will have assets in excess of 21 million marks by the end of the year.'

Ruth read again the heading that was typed at the top of the page, which read 'The Caslav Memorial Trust.'

'Of course, all monies in this fund are strictly controlled by a board of six trustees, however, it has consistently been their policy to reinvest all profits to provide secure growth for the future.'

Langdoff paused for breath and as he did so he eyed the young woman with some contempt; he questioned her ability to fully grasp his fluency in financial matters.

'There are of course beneficiaries of the trust but as yet despite all attempts, they have not been found.'

'They are…?' Ruth's sudden question threw him.

'Pardon, Fraulein?'

'I asked who they were.'

Langdoff looked to Otto for guidance but the large man remained expressionless.

'Err,' Langdoff hesitated and looked again at Otto; still no guidance. He took the plunge.

'The beneficiaries are a Joseph Caslav, his wife and a young niece, name Ruth Caslav. Now, the accounts of Mannerheim International.'

*

Herr Langdoff was, if nothing else, a thorough man. He explained in detail the latest balance sheet of Mannerheim International and in particular the regular donations to the Jewish Israeli Organisation. Ruth tried hard to concentrate but her mind continually returned to the trust. Why had Otto set it up? The question would not go away. So much money. Surely, she told herself, this was not the action of a man who in the past had been motivated by greed. Or was it conscience money? Maybe even a calculated public gesture of compassion. After all, if Otto was confident the three of them were dead then what did it matter? No doubt the trust reverted back to the Mannerheim fortune in some way at some time in the future. Herr Langdoff closed the accounts file and put it with that of the trust.

'Now there are several smaller interests held by Herr Mannerheim and the Mannerheim Group, for instance there is the hospital and...'

'The trust?' Ruth asked, not allowing him to continue. 'If the beneficiaries are never found at what time does it revert back to the Mannerheim Group?'

Langdoff looked puzzled.

'Revert back?' he echoed her words.

'Yes, revert back,' she snapped.

'Well, never, Fraulein, it is a condition of the trust that when all trustees agree that there is absolutely no possibility of any of the beneficiaries being alive then the trust will be split between four designated Jewish Charities. Now about the hospital...'

'I think the young lady has possibly heard enough.' Otto's words stopped Langdoff instantly. Ruth nodded her confirmation.

'Well thank you, Herr Langdoff, you have been most helpful.' Otto got to his feet, extending his hand as he did so. 'I am sure the young lady found it most interesting.' Ruth smiled but said nothing. 'We will doubtless be in touch with you in the near future.' Otto started to put on his coat. 'Oh, incidentally, I never introduced you, how very remiss of me.' He paused for moment as he buttoned the coat. 'Herr Langdoff, may I introduce you to our financial director in charge of our new requisition in England.' Langdoff, instantly impressed, smiled warmly and made to shake Ruth's hand. 'Her name is Ruth Valsac.' They made to leave but just as they reached the door Otto stopped and turning back. 'Ask yourself, Herr Langdoff, what does Valsac spell written backwards?'

For the second time that morning, the smile slipped from Langdoff's face.

*

'Why did you do that?'

'Do what?' Otto asked as the lift doors closed. He pressed the button marked E.

'Not tell him who I was until after he had given me all the details on the trust.'

He smiled. 'You wanted to remember Martha, and you are probably reasonably convinced that she is who she says she is, but you can't be sure.' He turned to look at her. 'Can you? She could have been anybody, I know that, but an officer of the Bank of Berlin! Well, even I can't buy them. I wanted you to hear about the trust from him, an unbiased account.' Otto suddenly laughed.

'What are you laughing at?'

'Did you see his face when I told him who you were?'

The lift doors opened.

'I don't want your money, Otto.'

'And you shall not have my money, Ruth.' Otto walked out of the lift leaving her to follow. At the door he stopped and waited for her, opening it as she approached. 'But you shall have your money, Ruth, be in no doubt of that!'

She did not reply.

*

At a small cafe just off Gneisenau Strasse the car stopped again.

Ruth looked at him.

'Lunch.' He lifted both hands. 'That's all, I promise.'

Ruth got out and made her way around the car to where Otto was already waiting for her on the pavement.

'You promise?' she asked.

'Absolutely.' Otto lifted one hand in a gesture as if to swear to God.

'Then I believe you,' Ruth said and she took his arm. For Otto, it was a precious moment.

The manager made a great fuss of Otto when he saw him and they were quickly shown through the bar with its crowded tables of noisy Berliners to a quieter area towards the rear of the room. Lunch was a rare steak with boiled potatoes and cabbage.

'I hope the steak is to your liking.'

Ruth stopped eating and looked at him. 'It's fine, thank you.' She was about to attack the steak again but stopped. 'We must talk, Otto.'

He nodded, 'We have much to talk about.'

'When I came to Germany it was not to use that stupid gun.'

He smiled. 'I doubt if you knew how.'

'I came to find out the truth, to fight for what is important to me.'

'And what is important to you, Ruth?' He pushed the empty plate away from him, his bright blue eyes now fixed on hers.

'I think you know that, Otto. If Friedrich and I are to stand a chance of a future together, if the baby is to have a future, we have to lay the past to rest.' She hesitated, 'But maybe I have lost it all now. Perhaps there is just too much between us, perhaps I have hurt Friedrich too much. After this morning I don't know what to think. I want so desperately to go back to England and tell them they're wrong, tell them Otto is a wonderful man and it's all been a terrible mistake. But what can I tell them, Otto? I met a woman who said she was Martha Vitnez and she told me Otto did not betray us. I met a man called Langdoff who told me about the colossal trust that Otto Mannerheim has started for us. I don't know what to think myself, so how can I know what to tell them? It's still not enough, Otto, I'm sorry but it's not enough!' Her despair was obvious.

'I know that, Ruth, now finish your beer.'

She lifted her head and looked at him. He smiled. 'I have more,' he said. 'You cannot rush these things.'

*

Their next stop was at the West Berlin Police Headquarters. Again, the building was modern, but unlike the bank it was only three storeys high. Inside it was a warren of corridors with countless doors that no doubt led to countless offices. Otto, however, led the way to their destination with the confidence of a man more than familiar with his surroundings. She had to almost run to keep up with him.

'Ruth, may I introduce Herr Scholtze.'

The man stood up from behind his desk.

'Herr Scholtze is head of the West Berlin Police.' Otto shook the man's outstretched hand. 'He has something to tell you that may help.'

Herr Scholtze must have been at least six foot four inches tall, a giant of a man, even taller than Otto, with receding grey hair and dark eyes.

'I am so very pleased to meet you, Fraulein.' He took her hand gently. 'Please take a seat.'

Scholtze spoke in a deep, rather gruff manner. He came across to Ruth as a no-nonsense, plain-speaking man who did not suffer fools gladly. His manner gave him an air of authority that only the brave or foolish would question. But after all, he was Chief of Police.

'Otto has told me all about you, in fact I have known of you since I first met him in 1946. I can also tell you, Fraulein Caslav...'

Ruth interrupted, 'My name is Valsac.'

'Of course, I beg your pardon, Fraulein.' He continued unperturbed by her correction. 'I can tell you that Otto is a good friend of mine, we have done much together. He has worked hard to bring many Nazi criminals to justice. He has been a great help to me.' Otto shifted uncomfortably in his chair. 'Anyway,' Scholtze continued, 'after the war the Russians arrested a man called Graf Urban, the local electrician from the village where you had lived. He was arrested as a direct result of evidence given by several of the villagers, including Otto, and he was charged with crimes against the Jews. There had been several Jewish families arrested by the Nazis as a result of this man's activities. Some of the villagers were particularly outraged about what happened to you. They had known your family for years and many had been employed at the print works. Some had witnessed the events of that night but had been powerless to help. Two women in particular saw everything, they were Madam Hantzige and her niece. Apparently, the next day Urban asked Madam Hantzige's niece if she would like to go for a drink with him; while she was with him, he boasted of his membership of the Nazi Party and his connections within the SS. He told her that the officer who had been in charge of the events the previous night was a man called Kleister and that this man had a hatred for Jews second only to his own. He also told her that he had been watching the factory for weeks and it had been he who had told Kleister about the Jews. The woman was a prime witness at the trial. Urban was found guilty and was sentenced to twelve years imprisonment.' Scholtze pulled open his desk drawer and took out a green file.

'Here!' He slid it across the desk towards her. 'It is a copy of the transcript of the trial,' he smiled, 'of course it did not come from me.'

Ruth read the words on the cover: 'THE STATE AGAINST URBAN 1947'.

'After the war, Fraulein, a lot of people had scores to settle.' Scholtze looked for a moment at Otto, his face betraying some kind of hidden meaning.

'The man Kleister, in 1949 Otto found him living in Argentina. The German government took the necessary steps to extradite him for trial, but the Argentine government rejected the request on the grounds of insufficient evidence.' Scholtze was quiet for a moment. Again, the look to Otto, only this time it was just the merest of glances.

'Unfortunately, a little while after the German request was rejected Kleister was found dead, apparently someone had stuck a gun in his mouth and pulled the trigger.' He sat back in his chair.

*

When she left the building, Ruth carried beneath her coat the green file that Scholtze had given her. She remained silent until they were in the car.

'Why didn't you tell me?' she asked.

Otto looked at her. 'Would you have believed me?'

'And Kleister, did you have anything to do with what happened to him?'

Otto turned away from her. 'Some questions, Ruth, are best left unasked.'

She did not persist but took the file from beneath her coat and opened it.

'This is the proof I need, Otto,' she said flicking over the pages. 'With this, they have to believe.'

'I hope so, Ruth, I hope so.' Doubt showed on his face and the despair in his words brought home to her just how much it meant to him too. He desperately needed to clear his conscience of the guilt that he had harboured for all this time. He too needed her uncle and aunt to believe. For a moment she was silent as she remembered all the things she had said to him and to Friedrich and she realised how much it must have hurt.

'Otto, I'm so very sorry.'

'Sorry for what?' he asked.

'For not trusting you, not believing what you told me.'

He smiled briefly, 'I am sorry too, Ruth. Sorry I did not get you all out, sorry most of your family died because of my stupidity and sorry it has taken till now for me to tell you.'

She took his hand. 'Will Friedrich ever forgive me?'

Otto smiled. 'He loves you. He has nothing to forgive.'

'Then will you come back to England with me, Otto? See them with me. We can take this file, tell them about Martha. They have to believe us now. We're nearly there, Otto, we're nearly at the end of the past and all the hatred it holds.'

Again, the concern showed on his face.

'Ruth, the past is always just beginning, it can never end, and for you the past has still more to unfold, we are not at the end of it yet.'

'What do you mean?' she asked.

'We have one more stop to make, Ruth, I have left it till last because it will not be easy for you. It is a piece of the jigsaw puzzle that forms your past that is still to be put into place.'

'Otto, please just tell me,' she pleaded.

'Very soon, Ruth, very soon.'

SIXTEEN

THE MEETING

WILHELM MEILE PACED THE FLOOR OF HIS OFFICE. He was nervous; in fact he could not remember ever being so nervous. He had told himself it was foolish; he was a professional and as such should not allow himself to become personally involved in any case. But this was different, this was her. He stubbed out the half-smoked Camel cigarette cursing the habit as he did so. No matter how hard he tried he could not conquer his addiction. Sitting down behind his desk he picked up the file. She had been his patient for nearly fifteen years, how could he not be involved? He looked at the clock, it was a 3.45pm. They would be arriving soon, he knew that, but what he didn't know was how would this Ruth Valsac react. That's what frightened him most.

When the door opened and Ruth followed Otto into his office the effect on Wilhelm was one of stunned silence.

'Wilhelm, may I introduce Fraulein Valsac.' Otto had already started to take off his coat. 'Wilhelm, Fraulein Valsac.' Wilhelm's inability to react to Otto's first introduction had prompted the repeat. He shook his brain free from the grasp of surprise and rose to his feet.

'Fraulein, I'm so very pleased to meet you.' He looked at Otto who had quickly assessed Wilhelm's state of mind and was trying hard to help him cope.

'How are you Wilhelm?' He did not wait for an answer. 'I have told Dr Meile all about you Ruth, haven't I, Doctor?'

There was no reply. 'Haven't I, Doctor!'

'Absolutely!' the doctor was regaining control.

'Please take a seat, Fraulein.' Wilhelm moved quickly around the desk and positioned a chair for her. 'It's a pleasure to have you here.'

'I have told Fraulein Valsac that you have something of great importance to tell her,' Otto looked at Wilhelm as he spoke, 'and that it may well help her to understand better the past and my search for her.' Otto sat himself down and waited for the doctor to take his cue. There was silence.

'Wilhelm!' Otto's tone showed some impatience at the doctor's lack of response. 'We agreed!'

'Oh yes, yes I am sorry, I have been a little taken aback.' He turned to Ruth. 'Are you enjoying you stay here in Berlin, Fraulein?' He knew straight away it was a stupid question and was not surprised that the young woman did not answer and managed only the slightest of smiles in response. 'I am sorry, Fraulein; you have not come here for idle chatter.' He offered her a cigarette, she declined, he took one himself and lit it. 'It is difficult to know where to begin.'

'Try Belgium,' Otto retorted.

The doctor hesitated a moment. 'Towards the end of the war I was working in the Clinic de St Michel near Mons, my hometown in Belgium, I had been there since the liberation. One day the American military brought us some Jewish refugees. Apparently, there were so many sick and injured people that they were transporting them to any available hospital throughout Belgium and Northern France. These people were like none other I had ever seen before.' He paused inhaling deeply on the cigarette as he did so. 'Or ever want to see again! There were just twelve of them, all stretcher cases and all close to death, each one of them with terrible injuries. They were from Dachau.' Again he paused, only this time it was to study the young woman for a reaction. There was none. She was listening, there was no doubt of that, but Fraulein Valsac showed no emotion. 'Of the twelve we managed to save only four, one of whom was a woman. Apart from severe malnutrition, she weighed barely thirty kilos, she had been shot in the face.' Again, he paused to inhale deeply on the cigarette only now he toyed with it, moving it slowly between his figures as his mind searched for the words to continue. It was several seconds before he began again. 'On first inspection we found the wound was badly infected, she had lost several teeth and her jawbone was shattered. But those were just the obvious things. Further medical examination revealed she was suffering badly from a venereal disease that had been left untreated for God knows how long. It was painfully obvious that the woman had suffered terrible abuse at the hands of the Nazis.' He looked up from the cigarette. 'I am sorry, Fraulein, there is no easy way to tell you this.' He stood up from behind the desk and moved halfway around it perching himself on the corner nearest her. 'It was slow at first, painfully slow. She would not talk to anyone; her mind had closed itself down shutting out the horrors of what she had been through. She would sit for hours rocking, just staring at the wall. A friend of hers in the group told us that the woman had survived in one camp or another since 1938 and not only that but she had managed to keep her two children alive right up until the day before the Americans overran the camp. Towards the end of the war the Nazis were desperately trying to murder as many Jews as they could and then hide the evidence of their atrocities. Their group had been the last to be marched into a mass grave and then machine-gunned. Fortunately, the troops tasked with bulldozing over the grave fled from the advancing Allied forces before completing the job and she was found amongst the dead by the Americans the next day. Her two children had not survived.'

Ruth had felt sorry for the man when Otto had first introduced them. For some reason he obviously felt awkward, and she felt Otto had bullied him somewhat. His discomfort at telling her his story was plain to see and she understood that, after all, no one could really feel comfortable telling a Jew about how fellow Jews had suffered at the hands of the Nazis, albeit only one of a million such stories. She had wanted to say to him, 'Look, don't worry, I've heard all these type of stories before, don't be embarrassed.' But she had said nothing. She had listened to what he had said with an air of almost detachment. She was certain that somewhere along the line the story would hold even more overwhelming evidence that Otto was not involved in her family's betrayal and she had only now really started to wonder how this woman's story could have any bearing on things. She watched him as he dangled one leg over the corner of the desk. He was again struggling to find his words.

She smiled warmly at him. 'Perhaps it would help if you just told me, Herr Doctor, what this woman has to do with me.'

He lit a second cigarette from the first. 'I am trying to explain just that, Fraulein.' He moved off the desk and returned to his seat. 'Please forgive me, I am afraid I am not doing a very good job of it.' The doctor turned to Otto who was sitting, stony-faced, watching him.

'Ruth,' Otto got to his feet, 'perhaps I should continue.'

'Perhaps you should, Otto,' the doctor said, the obvious relief showing on his face.

'Ruth,' Otto began again, 'this woman had been in various concentration camps since 1938.'

It was the way Otto said it. It had not been just a statement but more of a question, as if inviting a response. She turned his words over in her head for a moment, conscious of the fact that both Otto and the doctor were waiting, waiting for her response.

'A good many Jews were in camps, Otto,' Ruth replied, unable to think of anything more profound.

He moved closer to her. 'She had two children with her.' Again, Otto's words were questioning.

'I understand that too,' Ruth nodded confirmation as she spoke. Her reply was almost matter-of-fact.

'Dachau, Ruth! A woman with two children, been in camps since 1938. Don't you see?'

Again, she turned his words over in her mind. A woman with two children, been in camps since 1938. What was she meant to see? Dachau. There had been hundreds of thousands of Jews in Dachau. Even her own family had died in Dachau.

Even her own family had died in Dachau! She allowed the thought to repeat in her mind. Surely Otto was not implying… it could not be! They had all died in the camp. Uncle had told her so; he had found out. It was a matter of record. What was Otto trying to say? The understanding between them was suddenly there. She looked up from the chair.

'Otto, you can't possibly be trying to tell me that this woman was—'

'Mary Elizabeth Caslav.' The doctor's sudden intervention surprised her. 'Yes, Fraulein, your mother was brought to my clinic in May 1945.' Wilhelm opened the file that was in front of him and took out a photograph. He smiled as he passed it to her.

It was the first time in her entire life that Ruth could remember ever seeing a photograph of her mother, other than the one that sat in her room at home in Hampstead. The photograph was her, she had no doubt of that, only she was thinner and looked much older than she remembered her. But there was something else different about her too. There was no smile, no life in the face. Just a face. Ruth felt the mist of tears cover her eyes as she looked at it. She blinked hard before taking her stare from the small piece of paper with its black and white image.

'I always believed she had died in the camp.' Her words were directed at the doctor but she turned to Otto as she spoke them. 'Uncle said that he had someone check and that her name was on the list.'

Otto nodded. 'It was on the list, Ruth,' he replied, 'but the list was made up of records taken from the camp commandant's office and it showed that Mary and your brother and sister were in the last group to be shot.' Otto crouched down by her and took her hand. 'I knew they had been in the camp, Ruth, so as soon as I could I got permission to go in. The Americans were uncovering hundreds of bodies and there were some still alive. I spoke to a man that had known your mother; he had been in the last group too but by some miracle he had not been shot. People had fallen on top of him and he had lain amongst them till it was dark before slipping away. The Americans found him hiding in the woods the next day and brought him back to the camp. He showed me the grave. The army were about to burn the bodies but I persuaded them to wait. Ruth, I found the bodies of Michael and Rachel, but not your mother. A young soldier told me that they had found some people alive and that they had been taken to a field hospital. I got permission to remove the bodies of the two children and I buried them in what was left of the Berlin Jewish Cemetery.'

Ruth had lost the battle to contain the tears and sat motionless as they gently ran down her face and fell into her lap. She had always known Rachel and Michael had died in the camp but to hear it again, like this, brought home the horridness of it. Their suffering. 'You must show me their graves, Otto,' she whispered.

He nodded.

Ruth turned again to the doctor, 'Thank you for helping my mother, Dr Meile, I am sure you did everything you could for her.'

'Ruth,' Otto squeezed her hand to gain her attention as he spoke. 'Ruth the doctor did a fine job with your mother. He worked very hard on her. It was not easy but after some time she began to respond to treatment. Then one day, suddenly, by some miracle, her troubled mind was released. It was as if a door unlocked and she was returned to us.' Otto smiled. 'It was a very special day for all of us.'

Ruth got up from the chair, gripped by a sudden anger at the thought of what she had lost. 'If they hadn't been so afraid of finding out, of coming back to Germany, I might have seen her again! Met her again, after all she had been through, I could have let her know that I was still alive, that I loved her.' She turned away from the two men. 'What little time I could have had with her was lost because they were afraid, and now it's too late.'

'Do not be bitter, Ruth, Joseph loves you, they both love you; they only did what they thought was right,' Otto spoke softly. 'Anyway, it is not yet too late.'

Ruth turned back to face them, 'What do you mean?'

Otto took her by the shoulders.

'Your mother, Ruth, she is still alive.'

For a moment, Otto's words seemed meaningless to her. They were just words that rattled around in her head with little effect. Then all at once it was as if she had stepped out of herself, she was watching a play, was watching others act their parts. Otto was speaking to her, but his words were little more than an echo, a distant noise that she was unable to comprehend. The reality of what was happening, of what had been said to her, was floundering in her own sea of disbelief. The more his words grasped at the part of her mind that was reality, the more it fought to reject them. A blackness seemed to rise up from within her, reaching out to take control of her mind. She felt herself slipping into its darkness. She tried to push it away, back into the depths from whence it had come, but she could not. She could not clear her head, it was taking control. Suddenly, despite all her efforts, her body succumbed as her mind conceded defeat.

Otto's strong hands held her as she stumbled and then he lowered her gently into the seat. 'Here, drink this.'

The actors had become people once again as Ruth felt the doctor put the glass into her hand. It was cognac.

'I am sorry, Ruth; this must have come as a tremendous shock to you.'

Otto was again crouched down beside the chair. 'Your mother is not well, Ruth, she has never really been well, not since the camp. The thought that you may still be alive was the only thing that has given her a purpose to live. A reason to carry on.' Otto's words were now reaching their target. Ruth's mind took them in and was again able to understand the implications of them. Although she did not reply, she understood. 'Ruth you must understand how important it has been for us to find you. For years your mother has thought of little else,' there was a sense of urgency in his voice. 'Even when others had given up on you, she would not. She always said that she knew you were alive.'

Ruth was staring at him, her eyes fixed on his. She could not believe; she would not believe!

'What kind of cruel joke is this, Otto?'

Ruth got to her feet letting the glass fall as she did so. 'My mother died in Dachau. It is documented, proven. I have lived with that all my life; I cannot just accept it to not be so.' She made to pick up her bag but was forced to steady herself against the chair.

'There is enough evidence in the file on Urban to make my uncle and aunt believe that you had nothing to do with our family's betrayal.' This time she succeeded in grasping the bag and retrieved it quickly. 'We have no need of more.'

She was halfway to the door before the doctor spoke. 'For God's sake, Fraulein, don't reject her now.' They were desperate words that cut into her as if they struck her very soul. She stopped; she could not help but stop. But she did not turn, she remained facing the door.

'She needs you. The memory of you is all she has clung to for the last fifteen years!' The doctor made no attempt to hide the emotion in his words. 'It has taken years to bring her back, to give her some kind of life, for pity's sake don't destroy it now. Don't reject the truth.'

Ruth stood for a moment without replying. She was trying desperately to control herself, to think logically, but her emotions were screaming inside her. Suddenly it was as if a dam had cracked within her; no longer able to contain herself she spun around.

'And what do you expect me to do? Go to this woman, take her hand, call her "Mother"! It's been a lifetime, for God's sake. We don't even know each other!'

Ruth had shouted the words, almost screamed them.

'Yes!' the doctor moved towards her. 'Yes, yes, yes, do just that, Fraulein. Go to her.'

Again, Ruth found herself fighting to contain the tears and her voice trembled as she spoke. 'And what do I tell her? Do I tell her I'm sorry I never bothered to find out if she were alive? Do I tell her I'm sorry, I just got on with my life and never gave a damn about her? What do I tell her, doctor? What do I say?' Ruth's head dropped as her emotions overtook her and she sobbed.

The doctor took her hand. 'Come, sit down.' He led her back to where Otto was standing and she sat back in the chair, hands held to her face. 'Ruth. May I call you Ruth?' The doctor did not wait for a reply. 'We knew today would be a gamble, we knew it would be hard for you. No one could have expected you to jump up and down in the air and just accept what we said. After all, for all these years you have believed her to be dead. But Ruth…' It was a deliberate pause, calculated to promote response. She lifted her head. 'You know that this is no lie, don't you? You know from the picture it is her. Why do you think I stumbled so badly when you walked in? Why do you think I sat there like some dumb idiot? You must remember that when I first saw your mother, she was about your age, maybe younger. The resemblance, Ruth, is remarkable.' He smiled. 'You have all her beauty.'

The coffee that Otto gave her was strong and sweet, it was difficult but she drank it and felt a little better for it. The doctor lit yet another cigarette and while he did so Otto took the opportunity to pour himself a large cognac.

'You said she was not well?' Her words prompted a concerned glance between the two men. It was the doctor that spoke.

'Your mother has undergone several operations in the last ten years or so, she is a brave woman. Unfortunately, the abuse she was forced to suffer in the camps is still taking its toll.' He picked up a file. 'These are her medical records.' He waved the thick brown file in her general direction before letting it drop back onto his desk. 'Ruth, I am afraid that your mother has cancer. However,' he continued quickly not allowing the gravity of his words time to take effect, 'she is receiving treatment from one of the best surgeons in Europe and we are hopeful that she may yet make progress.'

Ruth made no attempt to respond; she did not know how to. What was she meant to feel? What was she meant to say? She loved the memory of her mother; she had always loved the memory of her. But the woman herself, she was a stranger to her now. She knew she should feel sorrow, pain, even anger, but she could not. It was as if her emotions were unable to twist and turn any further, they had been numbed by events.

'She lives in the hospital, she prefers it. It has been difficult for her to come to terms with living an independent life so Otto has provided for her here.'

'Pardon?' Ruth's response took the doctor a little by surprise.

'I said she lives here,' he repeated.

Ruth looked at Otto. 'You mean she is here, in this building?'

'Yes, Ruth she is here.' Otto's reply was almost a whisper.

'My God!' She got to her feet as a sudden panic seized her. 'You can't expect me to see her? Not tonight, not now!' Neither of them replied.

'Oh no,' she shook her head, 'Not now. I won't, I can't!'

'Ruth, she knows you are coming today,' Otto pleaded, 'she wants to see you.'

'This is just not fair, Otto. What are you doing to me?' She slumped back down in the chair. 'Otto, remember the baby. I don't need this now.'

'No, Ruth, perhaps you don't,' Otto put his glass down, 'but she does. She needs it more than anything, more than life itself.'

*

In times of panic, desperation and even sheer terror, it is strange how a person's mind can somehow be distracted from events and start to focus on the slightest of trivialities. For Ruth it was the clip-clop of her shoe heels as she and Otto made their way along the clinically clean, highly polished floor of the seemingly endless hospital corridor.

'I won't know what to say to her.'

Otto did not reply.

'I said, I won't know what to say to her.'

'I heard you the first time,' Otto answered.

'Is it much further?'

'No.'

'Otto, for God's sake!'

He stopped, 'Ruth it will be all right, believe me.' He took her arm. 'Come on.'

The door said 'Private'. No name, no other distinguishing signs, just 'Private'. Ruth stood staring at it. To her it was the most imposing door that man had ever created. Otto went to knock.

'No, don't!'

He turned.

'Please, Otto, not yet.' Ruth struggled to open her bag. 'I must look a mess, let me tidy up.' She fumbled about amongst its contents.

'Ruth, you look fine.'

She looked up. 'Do I, Otto?'

He smiled and turned back towards the door.

'Don't knock, Otto!'

'Ruth!'

'No, Otto, please come away.'

He looked at her.

'I am all right now. I can do it.' Ruth knocked gently on the door, opened it and walked in, leaving Otto alone in the corridor.

It was a pleasant, bright room, not at all what she had expected. It was the large window at the far end of it that immediately took Ruth's attention. It was just a window, a large window, yes, but just a window. Looking out of it was a woman. She was standing with her back to her but even from across the room Ruth could see that she was painfully thin. Her hair was tied back neatly into a bun and she was wearing a simple black dress. Ruth took a few tentative steps towards her.

'I am sorry, it must have been a shock for you,' the woman spoke softly without turning to her. 'When Otto told me he had found you, I did not know what to do.'

Ruth said nothing but moved a little closer.

'Silly isn't it? All these years I've lived in hope of finding you alive and when they did, I didn't know what to do.' She had still not turned to look at Ruth and remained silent now for a moment. 'Of course, I knew you would have a life, a family, I did not want to turn it upside down.'

Again, Ruth moved closer.

'They tell me you are very pretty. But then you were always very pretty, such a lovely little girl. You were just five when I last saw you.'

'I am twenty-seven now.' Ruth was surprised how easily the words had come.

'You were always your daddy's favourite. Did you know that?'

Ruth did not answer this time. She had moved almost close enough to touch her.

'If I turn around and look at you, it may all disappear. Do you understand? My dream, it may just vanish.'

'I will not vanish, I promise,' Ruth replied quietly.

'I pray to God you will not. Tell me, are you Ruth Caslav?'

'I am.'

'Then I am truly sorry, Ruth Caslav, truly sorry I have not been there for you all these years. Will you try to forgive me?'

'Oh Mommer, it is me that should be asking to be forgiven. I never looked for you. I never searched. I never even questioned, I just accepted. What kind of a daughter is that?' Ruth's tired emotions spilled over again into tears.

'I love you, Mommer,' was all she could say.

Mary Caslav turned and for the first time in twenty-two years she held her daughter. The dream did not vanish, instead it became a reality. It was as if time, for a moment, moved backwards and all the love, all the care, all the tenderness stepped across the barrier that is time and returned to them both. After a lifetime they were together again.

SEVENTEEN

IT WILL BE A BOY

T HE JOURNEY BACK HAD BEEN VIRTUALLY SILENT. Despite the turmoil of the day's events, Ruth had slept. She had not wished to but had been unable to control the heaviness of her eyes. Even before they had reached the Brandenburg Gate, her head had dropped forward several times, jerking her back into wakefulness. Shortly after the crossing formalities, fatigue had eventually gained the upper hand and with her head resting against Otto's shoulder she had drifted into sleep. It was as if her mind needed to withdraw, step inside itself and take stock, such was the upheaval from which it had suffered. But it had been a restless sleep, almost a torturous one as her mind stepped from dream to dream and from image to image. It was not until the car was well into East Germany and nearing their destination that Ruth shook free from her tormented sleep. Her neck was stiff and she had a headache.

'Are you OK?' Otto asked.

She nodded. It was several minutes before Ruth spoke, and when she did it was in barely a whisper. 'I've lost him, Otto, haven't I?' Her large brown eyes were now wide open as she searched Otto's face for a reaction. 'I've lost Friedrich.'

'I doubt it.' The slightest of reassuring smiles was all she was able to detect.

'But he was right, Otto, wasn't he?'

Otto looked puzzled. 'What do you mean?'

She hesitated. 'I was so wrong about you, Otto. All these years you have looked after my mother, protected her. All the effort you have made to try and find us.'

Otto remained silent.

'The truth is, Otto; I did intend to shoot you. I had made up my mind that if I was certain that it had been you who had betrayed us, I would kill you.' Ruth waited for Otto's reaction.

He smiled. 'Good.'

'What do you mean, good?' Ruth was indignant.

'Good. That is what I mean. Good!'

'How can that be good?' Anger crept into her voice as she spoke. 'It has caused all this trouble between Friedrich and me, and you say it is good.'

Otto rubbed his tired eyes and thought for a moment before he spoke.

'Look, Ruth, Friedrich knew all about you, that is true, but as God is my witness, he had fallen in love with you long before he realised who you were. As for wanting to kill me,' he shrugged his shoulders, 'you are your father's daughter.'

'So that makes it all right does it? I'll just go to Friedrich and say I'm sorry I was going to kill your father, but I am my father's daughter. Perhaps then he'll forgive me.' The sarcasm in her voice was clear. It was a while before Otto replied, when he did, he spoke softly.

'I want to tell you something, Ruth.' The tone betrayed the importance of what he was about to say. 'I understand that you would have wanted to kill me. I loved your family too, Ruth, all of you and when they killed your father and took Mary and the children, I swore someone would pay.' Again, Otto was silent for a moment, his mind clearly pondering his next words. 'You asked about Kleister, remember?'

Ruth did not reply but merely nodded.

'I did go to Argentina, Ruth; I did search him out. At the time I was full of hate. I know only that if I were to finish this man then perhaps my conscience would be eased. I believed that I was putting right a thousand wrongs.' Again, he paused only this time he looked away from her. 'I am not proud of what I did, Ruth, because it solved nothing. It did not ease my conscience, in fact it only added to its burden. It did not put right a thousand wrongs it just added another.' He looked back at her, the anguish on his face undisguisable. 'You see, Ruth, it is easy for me to understand what you wanted to do; I did it.'

Ruth could only look at him, her eyes fixed on his.

'Do you think you could love a father-in-law who has done a thing like that?'

Instinctively she took hold of his arm and moved closer to him. In one day, she had learnt more about this man than she would learn about others in a lifetime. A special bond had grown between them and it was, all at once, very important to her. 'Otto, I would love you as a father-in-law,' she kissed his cheek. 'Unfortunately, Friedrich may now have other ideas. It looks as if I've found my mother and lost my future husband all in twenty-four hours.' She looked up at Otto. 'That must be a record, Otto. Even for me!'

*

Once inside the house, Otto arranged for some food. It was well past 10.00pm and neither of them had eaten since lunch.

'I must do something with myself, Otto, I'm a wreck. I'll only be a minute,' she said, disappearing to her room.

Ruth was not sure where Friedrich was. She had not asked Otto whether or not his son was in the house. But she hoped he might be. Apart from in the car on the way back Friedrich's name had hardly been mentioned all day.

Supper was some cold chicken with thick slices of brown buttered bread. Otto ate hungrily, but Ruth's appetite took second place to the events of the day.

'If he loved me, Otto, he would have been there today.'

Otto looked up from his food. 'He wanted to be,' he replied before taking another bite of the chicken.

'What do you mean, he wanted to be?' Ruth looked dismayed.

'He wanted to be there,' Otto repeated, 'but I told him it would probably only complicate things after last night. I wanted it to be a day just for you and your mother.'

'Otto, why didn't you tell me this before?'

'You never asked,' he replied amidst yet another mouthful of chicken.

Ruth got to her feet. 'But it's so important, Otto, I thought he never wanted to see me again after last night. Now you tell me he wanted to be with me today.'

Otto pushed away his plate and wiped his mouth. 'Ruth, was it so wrong of me to want today to be without the complications of an angry romance? Your mother had waited years to see you again; it needed to be handled correctly.'

'But the argument last night, when he said there was too much between us, when he walked away. Tell me, Otto, did you speak to him after that?'

'Of course I did.'

'Well, what did he say?' Ruth made no attempt to disguise the dire need in her voice.

'He said a lot of things.'

'Otto, are you being deliberately annoying?'

'Ruth, I am an old and tired man; I am going to my bed.' He got up and kissed her. 'Good night, Ruth.' He made his way to the door.

'But, Otto, please I need to know. It's the most important thing in the world to me.'

Otto turned. 'It has been quite a day, Ruth, quite a day.' Suddenly the door was closed and he was gone.

Ruth felt desperately confused and alone. She flopped down into her chair pushing the plate of food on the table next to her as far away as she could. It was more a gesture of despair than anything else.

'You should eat something, you know.'

The voice cracked the silence open like a nut cracks when squeezed between the jaws of a nutcracker. Her heart leapt. It was his voice, she had known it almost before the first syllable had been uttered. She jumped to her feet.

'Friedrich!' she said, turning towards him, praying that the voice had not been a figment of her imagination. 'Friedrich, it's you.'

He smiled, 'Were you expecting another lover?'

She did not respond to his jibe but stood silently as he moved towards her. It was not until he was standing barely inches from her that she spoke again and she did so without looking at him. 'I've messed everything up, Friedrich. I'm so sorry I doubted your father and even more sorry I doubted you. Can you ever forgive me? Is there really too much between us, too much hatred in the past for us to have a future together?' She looked up at him.

'Ruth, do you remember the first day we went out together in London and you showed me all your famous buildings?'

She forced a smiled.

'What is your most favourite place in all the world, Ruth?'

She thought for a second.

'Trafalgar Square.'

He laughed. 'You mean Trafalgar Square in the snow.'

She nodded.

'That first kiss, Ruth, in front of all the world,' he smiled. 'Even the Salvation Army! I knew then, Ruth, that I had fallen in love with you and that I wouldn't let anything come between us. I've never stopped loving you, Ruth, through all of this, believe me, I've never stopped.'

She reached for him. 'And I love you too, Friedrich, you'll never know how much I love you, but I've been so confused, everything that has happened…'

'I know, darling, I know,' he said, not letting her finish her words. He took her in his arms.

'I've met her today, Friedrich, did you know?'

'Yes, I know.'

'Oh, Friedrich, all these years she's been alive, and I didn't even know. All that lost time. I just don't know what to do, Friedrich,' she cried. 'How can I make up for all the years? How can I go back to England and just leave her?' She was quiet for a moment as she considered another thought. 'My God, how am I going to tell them?'

Friedrich held her tight. 'We'll work it all out, darling, don't worry. We'll do it together.'

*

Later in the quiet of the night she lay folded in his arms and again he could only marvel at her beauty. The moonlight that filtered through the bedroom window touched gently on the nakedness of her breasts as his fingers tenderly explored their softness. It was the first time they had made love since they had left England and both knew it was right, it needed to happen. His first touch served only to inflame their passion, as his hands travelled across the softness of her skin. Ruth sighed gently as her body, unable to resist the passion of his touch, moved slowly beneath it. She felt the ache inside her growing stronger as the desire for him grew. Reaching up she kissed him hard on the mouth pulling him onto her in an unashamed need to satisfy her want. 'I love you; I love you,' she repeated the words over and over again as she felt him take her and she was rejoicing at every move of his body, welcoming his hardness into her with an uncontrollable need. Arching her back she pushed herself against him as her body searched for satisfaction. The passion inside her grew stronger with every second, never before had she experienced such an overwhelming force. Suddenly she was lost to its control as the power of orgasm grasped her and shook her body; its delicious fingers played up and down her spine tugging at every tingling nerve end before bursting forth from her with an uncontainable cry. As the need left her, she could think only of his pleasure and she revelled in his enjoyment of her as she felt his body strain and she knew that he was experiencing the same wondrous fulfilment as she. Harder and harder he took her, one powerful hand beneath the small of her back lifting her body up to meet his, the other pushing hard against her breast as he searched for every last inch of pleasure. She wanted it to be as good for him as it had been for her and she pushed back hard against him as the sudden shudder of his body told her what was happening. His groan of ecstasy delighted her as she took the need from him.

They lay in silence for some time, neither of them wanting to move from the other. The perspiration from their bodies mingled as they held each other, both enjoying the contentment of the moment.

'That's never happened to me before,' Ruth whispered eventually as her hand gently played with his hair. 'It was nice before, it's always been nice, but never like that.' She felt him kiss her breast. 'We've not been very responsible, darling, have we?' she whispered.

He lifted himself slightly from her, until his face was close to hers and he kissed her. 'What does it matter? Soon we will be married and then we will have babies, lots of babies.'

'I'm glad you want that, darling,' Ruth replied as she felt him rise again within her, his desire returned. 'I have something to tell you.'

'What is it?' he asked as the movement of his body grew.

She smiled. 'It will wait,' she said, 'I'll tell you after.'

*

Friedrich was awake early. 'It'll be a boy!' he said excitedly, throwing back the sheets and jumping out of bed.

Ruth opened one eye. 'You know that, do you?'

'Yes, it will be a boy. I know.'

'What if it's a girl; will you be disappointed?'

He beamed at her. 'Of course not, she will be as beautiful as her mother and I will love her with all of my being.'

Ruth rolled over and retrieving the bedclothes covered herself up. 'Well, all I know is that it will be our baby and we will love it.' She closed her eyes.

'What are you doing, Ruth? You can't go back to sleep, we must tell Father, come on get up!'

She had not told Friedrich that Otto knew already, and she hoped he would keep her secret. 'I'm pregnant! So, I'm resting.' She looked as the smile slipped from his face. 'Oh OK,' she sighed, swinging her legs over the side of the bed, 'but be patient while I get ready.'

Friedrich wasn't patient, he hovered around her. 'You are sure, Ruth? When is he due? You are OK, I mean you are feeling well?'

'Friedrich please! Just let me get dressed.'

Otto acted both surprised and excited when Friedrich told him. Her secret was safe.

EIGHTEEN

HAMPSTEAD

THE YOUNG LAD RAPPED HARD ON THE DOOR AND when it opened thrust out his pad and pen without even looking up from the small bundle of papers grasped in his grimy hand. 'Valsac?' he asked.

'Pardon?' Joseph replied, rather taken aback by the abrupt manner.

The lad looked up, 'I've a telegram for a Mr or Mrs Valsac, are you 'im?'

'Joseph nodded.'

'Sign 'ere then, gov,' he pointed to a dotted line on the pad.

Joseph took the pen and signed.

'Ta very much.' He pushed a brown envelope into Joseph's hand and without further ado was gone. Joseph stood staring at the paper in his hand, somehow transfixed by its very existence.

'Who is it?' Elizabeth shouted from the kitchen. He did not reply. 'Joseph, who is it?' As there was still no answer, she made her way up the hall to where he was standing in the open doorway.

'A telegram.' He turned, holding it out for her to see.

'It must be from Ruth.' Even as she spoke Elizabeth felt

the sudden nausea of fear strike her. 'What's happened, Joseph? Open it, open it!'

Joseph closed the front door and without a word walked past her and into the kitchen. She quickly followed.

'In the name of God, man, what does it say?'

Joseph's hands trembled as he struggled to unfold the envelope and he fumbled for what seemed an eternity as he desperately tried to retrieve his glasses from the breast pocket of his waistcoat. He put them on. It was the first telegram Joseph had ever read and he was taken aback when he focused on the large letters that appeared to be pasted on the paper. He cleared his throat and read the words out loud.

DO NOT WORRY I AM FINE STOP WILL BE HOME ON FRIDAY STOP I HAVE SO MUCH TO TELL YOU STOP LOVE YOU BOTH STOP
    RUTH

Elizabeth breathed a sigh of relief and allowed her large frame to collapse into the nearest chair.

'She is all right, Joseph, and that is all that matters.'

Joseph removed his glasses, folded the paper and placed it on the kitchen table. He looked at her. 'Nothing will be the same, Elizabeth, you mark my words; nothing will be the same.'

She did not reply.

*

When the plane touched down at Northolt Aerodrome, Ruth changed her watch to read 7.20pm. The air that met them as they disembarked was cold, but the night was clear. Edward had parked the car in the same spot as always and in no time at all they were done with the formalities of custom control and were on their way down the A40 to London.

'Do you want to go straight there?' Friedrich asked.

She nodded.

The traffic had all but cleared for the night and it took Edward less than fifteen minutes to reach the North Circular Road at Hangar Lane. Ruth had turned things over and over in her head a thousand times and had decided on just as many different ways to tell them her story. But now, once again, she was not sure. It would be a shock for them, there could be no doubt about that, but she was worried that Joseph may still question the truth. She had been nervous about the meeting from the moment she knew that it had to happen, but now as the car cruised past the Welsh Harp reservoir, that nervousness had turned to almost terror.

'They're not going to believe it, I just know.' She blurted the words out almost involuntarily as the car turned right at the traffic lights and headed up the hill towards Hampstead.

Friedrich took her hand, 'Don't worry, everything will be all right, just stay calm.'

Ruth thought she saw the curtains move as the car pulled to a halt outside the house. Friedrich smiled confidently at her.

'Come on,' he said, 'they can only kill me.'

In all her life, Ruth had never felt such a way about entering her own house, their house. But this was no ordinary homecoming, no ordinary visit; she knew that what she had to tell them would, if they believed her, change their lives. At the door she instinctively reached for her key and then hesitated. She turned to Friedrich. 'Should we knock?' she asked.

He shrugged. 'What do you normally do?'

'I use my key.'

'Then use it now.'

Ruth put the key in the lock and pushed open the door. The light of the kitchen shone through the open door at the far end of the passage and Ruth could clearly see the two of them sitting at the kitchen table.

'It's me!' she shouted as she made her way towards the open door.

Elizabeth was first to greet her, throwing her large arms around her and almost lifting her from the ground as she hugged her.

'My Ruthy, my Ruthy,' was all she could manage to say. When Ruth did finally break free of her aunt's grip she reached for her uncle and, putting her arms about his neck, kissed him. 'Hello,' she whispered, 'I'm back, I did it.'

Elizabeth hurled a barrage of question at her that came so fast Ruth could barely answer one before another had started. Uncle remained silent.

'I've brought someone to meet you,' Ruth eventually managed to say.

She went back to the passage, took Friedrich's hand and led him through into the kitchen. 'Aunty, Uncle, I would like you to meet Friedrich, my fiancé.'

The smile of excitement on Elizabeth's face disappeared in an instant and instinctively she looked to her husband in an urgent need to seek his reaction.

Joseph's first thought was how much the young man looked like his father when he was young. The resemblance was such that for a moment it stunned him and he was unable to speak. He took his glasses from his pocket and putting them on stared at the man who held Ruth's hand.

'Uncle, I have found out so much, there is such a lot to tell you.'

He ignored her.

'I have nothing against you personally, young man, but I must ask you to leave my house.'

Uncle's words should not have come as a surprise to her, but they did.

'Uncle, please listen to what we have to say.'

Joseph turned his back on them. 'You have nothing to say that I want to hear!'

'Don't you want Ruth to be happy?' Friedrich's words shook Ruth and she knew instantly that they would provoke.

'Happy!' Joseph retorted turning as he spoke. 'What do you and your family care about happiness?'

'Uncle, please,' it had not started well and Ruth knew it, 'please give us a chance.'

'A chance! A chance for what? To tell us a pack of lies, a load of rubbish. Ruth, don't you realise they have lied to you? What chance did they give us?'

'We have not lied,' Friedrich replied calmly.

'Of course you have lied!' Joseph snarled angrily.

'Joseph, we must listen.' Elizabeth's words were simple, but they carried an authority the likes of which Ruth had never previously heard. 'We will give these young people a chance.' She took his hand. 'If we do not listen, Joseph, they will take her from us too.' She pulled out a chair for him. 'Sit down, Joseph, please do this for me.'

Ruth seized the opportunity with both hands and the story flowed from her lips with scarcely a pause for breath. Friedrich remained silent, he knew that they would only believe Ruth's words and until they did, anything he said would receive a hostile reception. The first part of her story about the bank and the trust made little impression on them. There was just the odd gesture of irritation from Uncle as he attempted to show his disregard for any financial recompenses that may have been instigated.

'Conscience money,' he muttered at one stage, but Ruth ignored him and continued. It was not until she mentioned the name Martha Vitnez that she sensed a positive reaction.

'I will never forget the good doctor and his wife,' Elizabeth said quietly. 'They were so kind to us.' She dabbed her eyes with her apron.

Ruth took heart.

'Then do you remember a Graf Urban?'

Elizabeth looked blank as she repeated Ruth's words. 'Graf Urban, Graf Urban. No, I don't know the name.' She looked at Joseph.

'He was an electrician in our village,' Joseph said slowly.

Ruth took the green file Herr Scholtze had given her from her bag and handed it to her uncle.

'You needn't read it all, I have underlined what is important.'

Joseph read the front of the file and then opened it. Clearly marked on page three was a subtitled section headed CASLAV. He read it.

'These are just words.' He dropped the file on to the table. 'Just words typed on a page that anyone could have done.'

Elizabeth retrieved the file and started to read.

'You can't just expect us to read and accept this,' Uncle continued.

'But Joseph, there is also a statement here from the Chief of Police,' Elizabeth said, pointing to a part of the text.

Joseph suddenly banged the table with his fist.

'Again words! Just words!'

'Yes, just words, Uncle, but true ones!' Ruth was finding her anger hard to contain. 'I've spoken to people, I've met them.'

'Do you really expect us to just believe?' Uncle retorted.

'No, Uncle, I knew you would never just believe.' Her anger forced the sarcasm in the reply and immediately she regretted it. She continued, only this time without the anger. 'There is more.' Opening the bag again, she took out the photograph of her mother, the one Dr Meile had given her. She looked at it for a moment and then at them. Both had their eyes fixed on her, watching her, waiting for what was to come. Ruth hesitated; she knew there was no easy way to tell them, but she knew they had to know. They had a right to know. She looked at Friedrich. He nodded.

'I have a picture.' She slid it carefully across the table.

Joseph took it and held it up to the light.

'It is Mary,' he said handing it to Elizabeth. She too held it up to the light and having looked at it held it to her chest.

'She was a lovely woman, your mother.'

'Look again, Elizabeth,' Ruth pleaded, 'look carefully.'

Elizabeth held the picture up again, straining her eyes to study every detail.

'Look at her face.'

Elizabeth looked hard. 'There is something on the picture,' she said wiping it gently on the arm of her blouse.

'There is nothing on the picture, Elizabeth, it is a scar.'

Joseph went to his drawer and returned with the magnifying glass that he used to read small print. 'Show me!' He took it from her without further request. Again, he studied the photograph only this time through the glass and he took much longer. When he had finished, he handed the glass and the picture to his wife. 'This picture is not right.' He looked at Ruth. 'She does have a scar and she looks older, different,' he paused. 'She looks as if the life has been taken from her.'

'I am going to tell you both something but before I do I want you to promise me, Uncle, you will not interrupt or say it's a lie.' She looked at him.

'He promises,' Elizabeth said.

As Ruth unfolded her mother's story to them their distress could not be disguised. She tried to avoid many of the graphic details that had been told to her but she was aware that the two of them knew only too well of the suffering in the camps under the Nazis. Almost immediately she had begun, her aunt had lapsed into quiet tears.

'So, you see, she did not die in the camps as we all thought,' Ruth said as she finished her story.

'Is that photograph the only evidence that you have of that?' Joseph's tone was different, the harshness had gone and he seemed for the first time to be searching positively for proof.

'No,' Ruth replied, again she opened her bag, 'I have another picture to show you.' The photograph she handed them this time was much larger than the other and newer. She pushed it face up to the centre of the table. Joseph picked it up and the pair of them studied it.

'It was taken just two days ago,' Ruth said, 'we had it done especially.' She watched as they both looked at the black and white image that Joseph held between his trembling fingers.

'I know this will come as a shock to you, God knows, I could not believe it, but my mother is still alive. That is her in the middle, you can see Friedrich and me with her. The man on the right, the one whose arm she is holding, is Friedrich's father, Otto Mannerheim.' Ruth waited. She knew the reaction would come but she was not sure what form it would take. Would they dismiss it as yet another lie? Or was there a chance, just a chance that they would believe? It seemed to her an eternity before Joseph took his eyes from the photograph and looked at her; when he did there was not an attempt to disguise his emotions. He was crying.

'You have met her?' It was a question to which he already knew the answer. She nodded.

'She is alive?'

Again, Ruth did not speak but only nodded.

Elizabeth took the photograph from his hand. 'It is her. I know it is her.' She looked at her husband. 'What have we done, Joseph? Why did we not look?' For a moment the two sat in stunned silence then suddenly Friedrich spoke.

'I have a letter for you.' He took an envelope from his jacket pocket. Ruth looked at him in surprise; she had not known about any letter.

'Mary asked me to read this to you.' He opened it. 'May I?' Not giving them time to answer, he began to read.

My dear Joseph and Elizabeth,

It is difficult for me to put into words my feelings at this time. I can only tell you that it is a dream come true for me. To see my Ruth again all grown up into a fine young woman has made my suffering worthwhile. I thank you and I know Luke thanks you for the life of our daughter. On the night we left her with you he told me she would be safe, you have served his memory well. War is a terrible thing; it takes the minds of men and distorts them beyond belief. Even the gentlest of men can become inhuman when gripped in its grasp. I have had to live through things the likes of which no human being should suffer, but through it all, even when I held my children in my arms and looked death in the face I took strength from the belief that Ruth at least would live. Only you made that possible.

After the war, Otto found me in a hospital in Belgium. I was close to death, my mind all but destroyed. But he helped me, he looked after me. He is a man of great conscience and in the fullness of time you will learn again how fine he is. Just for now believe me when I tell you that I know without any shadow of a doubt that it was not he who betrayed us that night. It is my dearest wish that before I pass from this world we may meet again. From the old days we have only the slightest glimpse of happy memories to hold onto; it would be nice to share them again. As for Ruth and Friedrich, well, they have a whole life in front of them. Help them live it.

I love you both.

Mary

Nobody spoke as Friedrich folder the letter and placed it on the table, such was the impact of its contents. For some time, they sat in silence, the four of them unable to do little else than stare at the paper. It was Elizabeth who eventually reached out and with a shaking hand retrieved the letter and opened it again. She turned to Joseph.

'We must believe now.' She waved the letter at him. 'We have been wrong.'

Joseph did not answer her; he remained silent, his eyes fixed on the table.

'Joseph,' Elizabeth spoke again, 'please!'

Slowly he raised his head and looked at her but still he did not speak. He turned to Friedrich.

'Herr Mannerheim, for over twenty years I have blamed your father for the betrayal of our family.' Joseph hesitated. 'Sir, when you see him again would you please tell him that I, Joseph Valsac,' he stopped, 'no, I Joseph Caslav, deeply regret the injustice I have done him.'

Friedrich stood up, but without response turned and left the room.

Joseph turned to Ruth. 'I am sorry.' The emotion within him choked the words as he spoke and he sank back to his chair. Ruth got up and moving round the table put her arms around them both. 'It will be all right,' she told them, 'I promise it will be all right.' She held them tightly.

'You asked me to give your apologies to my father,' Friedrich had returned to the room and now stood in the doorway. All three looked at him.

'I am sorry, sir, but I am unable to do that.'

Joseph stood. 'I understand how you feel,' he began, again his voice breaking as he spoke. Friedrich interrupted, 'If you wish to apologise to my father then you must do so yourself.' He moved towards them and away from the door.

'I do not believe apologies are necessary between old friends such as us.' Otto's voice jerked their attention back to the door as he moved from the shadow of the hall, his large frame all but filling the doorway. Ruth felt the weight of Elizabeth's body fall back against her as the shock of Otto's appearance all but stole the consciousness from her. Joseph could only sit and stare, mouth open. Eventually after some moments he managed to regain his composure and rose unsteadily to his feet.

'I never believed there would come a day that you would enter my house,' Joseph was choosing his words carefully.

He spoke softly, his eyes fixed on Otto. 'And that I would be pleased to welcome you.'

'I, too, despaired of there ever being such a day, of seeing you and Elizabeth again. Now that the time has come, I hope that the hatred of the past may be lost forever.' He moved towards them. 'It would appear that we owe these two young people a great deal for bringing us together again after all these years.' Otto had now reached the other side of the table and stood just inches from them both. 'I let you both down,' he said, with sudden anguish in his voice. 'I let you all down, Luke and the children paid with their lives and Mary had to suffer five years of hell. I have no excuse for what happened, Joseph, I got it wrong.' He was silent for a moment. 'Please forgive me.'

Joseph looked at Ruth and then at his wife. Their eyes said everything.

'I thank you, Otto, for all you have done for Mary and I thank you for the danger and the beatings you suffered trying to protect us.' Suddenly Joseph thrust out a trembling hand. As Otto grasped it, all the tension, all the embarrassment, all the awkwardness of their meeting seemed to evaporate, as did the years. Otto's large arms suddenly embraced them both and the three of them held each other and cried together.

*

Carl Kahler had been taken aback by Horst Urban's reactions when he told him the news. Carl had expected Urban to explode with temper and to shower him with abuse for not informing him sooner of their departure to England. Instead, the little man merely sat back in his chair and smiled.

249

'All of them have gone?' he asked. Carl nodded. 'Good, good,' he smiled again. 'If I give them enough rope...' he did not finish the parable. 'They will return. She will return, and who knows, perhaps she will bring them with her.' He laughed. 'Things are going to change, Carl, do you hear me? I, Horst Urban, said so. My day will come. They will cross the border once too often and I will have her. Then we will see.' He turned towards Carl, his eyes staring. 'Then she will have to leave that hospital, she will have to come back to the East.'

He paused, 'Then I will have what I want, I will have Mary Caslav.'

NINETEEN

THE WEDDING

OTTO WAS TO STAY IN ENGLAND FOR THE WEDDING, it was decided. Friedrich managed to get a special licence and hurriedly booked the registry office. The earliest date he could get gave them just two weeks and for Ruth they were the most hectic two weeks of her life. She and Elizabeth searched the shops frantically for new outfits and Otto and Uncle took themselves off to Savile Row. The suits they purchased were 'off the peg', they had to be for there was no time to have one tailored, but nevertheless up till then Joseph could have only dreamed of owning such finery.

Despite all the arrangements, and having to come to terms with depressingly bad bouts of early morning sickness, Ruth was determined to take up her new post as financial director. Friedrich and Otto both tried to dissuade her but she was resolute. Anyway, it helped. She had desperately wanted her mother to attend the wedding. Although it was discussed, Otto had argued that Mary was not up to the trip. She had not wanted to cause an argument for she knew he had only her mother's well-being at heart. But she did not agree. She telephoned Dr Meile several times from her new office to discuss it.

'Look, Ruth, I'm really not sure that she is up to the trip,' he told her one morning over a particularly cranky telephone line. 'Anyway, she could not manage it alone.'

'But have you asked her, Wilhelm? Does she want to come?'

Ruth heard her own voice echo back at her from down the line.

'Of course she wants to come,' Wilhelm replied.

'Then listen, Wilhelm, my mother deserves some happiness in her life, and I don't want her to miss this, she has already missed enough of my life. You bring her, I have arranged two tickets.'

'Ruth, that is ridiculous, I could not possibly leave the hospital.'

'Wilhelm,' Ruth replied, 'Otto told me to tell you he thinks you should come.' Wilhelm admitted defeat.

She told no one of the phone calls, or of her lie.

Two days before the wedding and the day before Mary and Wilhelm were due to arrive, Ruth decided she had no option other than to tell Friedrich.

'We will need the car tomorrow morning,' she said as nonchalantly as she could. It was the first time in days that they had been alone together. They were on their way to the Savoy Hotel to confirm arrangements for the wedding breakfast.

Friedrich looked puzzled. 'Will we?'

'Mm,' Ruth replied.

'Why?' His curiosity was obviously aroused.

'We have to pick up two people from Northolt.'

'Who?' he asked with surprise.

'Wilhelm and my mother.'

'But everyone agreed, Ruth, the trip would be too much for her,' he started to argue with her but almost immediately realised there was little point.

'Yes, Friedrich, everyone agreed,' she looked at him, 'except my mother, and nobody thought to ask her.'

Friedrich smiled. He knew the tone in her voice and the determination in that look and he loved both. 'We had better book two more for lunch then,' was all he said.

Ruth smiled.

At the airport the next morning Ruth felt almost as nervous as she had that day at the hospital. But the apprehension disappeared as soon as she saw Mary leave the customs hall. She was holding Wilhelm's arm and looked better than Ruth had dared hope. As they embraced, Ruth told her she looked wonderful.

'I hope so, dear,' Mary replied, 'I've got so much to live for.'

Ruth could sense Mary's apprehension as they arrived at the house; taking her mother's hand, she tried to help. 'It will be a shock for them, but even now they know the truth, I know they would never return to Germany.' Ruth smiled at her mother. 'Thank you for coming to them.'

Uncle and Otto were playing cards at the kitchen table when Ruth came in. Elizabeth as usual was fussing around the stove preparing lunch.

'Where have you two been?' Joseph asked casually looking up from his hand.

'Just to the airport,' she replied.

Otto looked; Joseph folded his cards.

'What for?' Otto asked.

'We have brought someone to meet you,' Friedrich said as he followed Ruth into the room. The conversation had by now attracted Elizabeth's attention; she stopped stirring the soup that was simmering on the stove and wiping her hands on her apron came over to them.

'I am afraid it is only me,' Mary said in a soft, emotional voice, as she stepped out from behind Friedrich, the look on her face clearly showing a mixture of pleasure and apprehension.

Otto jumped to his feet. 'Mary, are you all right? What are you doing here? Sit down.' He pulled a chair from the table.

'Stop fussing, Otto, I am fine,' she ignored the chair. 'I have come for Ruth's wedding and to see the rest of my family again.' She turned first to Elizabeth and then to Joseph. 'Thank you, thank you both for saving her life.'

Not many guests attended the wedding ceremony at the small Hampstead registry office two days later, but for Ruth and Friedrich that was not important. Those that mattered were there. In the front row sat four people for whom life had changed. The nightmare of the past had been laid to rest and despite its horrors, they had found each other again. Later, those that witnessed the celebrations at the Savoy Hotel would have seen just another family group enjoying just another family meal. They would never have known, could never have known, the significance of it all.

*

Ruth and Friedrich returned to Germany with the others shortly after the wedding. They spent a week with Mary before leaving for a two-week honeymoon in the Black Forest. Joseph and Elizabeth declined the invitation to visit Germany. Ruth had been right, there was no way they could face returning.

It was not until their return to Berlin that Friedrich and Ruth discussed their future with her mother and Otto. They wanted to continue to live in England and despite the difficulties, they promised they would spend as much time with them both in Germany as they could. Otto was disappointed, but Mary understood.

'I can't expect to step back into your life and turn it on its head,' she told them.

The day before they were due to return to England, Ruth felt the baby move. It was the first time and it felt strange. Friedrich lay with his hand on her stomach for ages but only grew frustrated when he could feel nothing. He sat up.

'Listen, Ruth, the baby will be due in September; I think it would be a good idea if we came back in June or at the latest July and then you could have the baby in Berlin, at the hospital. Your mother would be there and there is no better doctor than Wilhelm Meile.'

Ruth did not argue. 'I will do that, Friedrich,' she replied, 'if you don't keep on moaning about me working up to then.' A deal was struck.

On Ruth's return to work she immediately started to restructure the accounts department. She visited Joan, her number two at Brooks and Son, and offered her a job. Joan did not hesitate. She had missed Ruth, and things had gone from bad to worse since she had left. Ruth could not help but take some satisfaction from that. Having built her new team and ensuring that Joan could and would run the department while she was away having the baby, she then made an appointment at Brooks and Son. Ruth did not give her name to Mr Brooks' secretary but merely informed her that the new financial director of Mannerheim International would require a meeting at which it was particularly requested that Mr Jeremy Brown be present. At 2.30pm the following day Ruth took her pound of flesh. Both men had remained almost speechless as she swept into Brooks' office.

'Gentlemen,' she had begun, 'you will no doubt recall the last meeting the three of us attended in this office.' She had not waited for their reply. 'I am afraid I must inform you that Mannerheim International has now decided to handle all its own financial matters. We will no longer require your services.' Ruth had not lingered for comment but turned as she opened the door to leave. 'Oh, and as for my... how did you put it Mr Brown? Oh yes, my bloody boyfriend... well, my husband does not send his regards.'

The meeting had been short, but for Ruth, exceedingly sweet.

*

Their new home was in Harrow on the Hill. It was far enough from Park Royal to be pleasant but close enough to be convenient. It had been built at the turn of the century and stood in two acres of gardens on a small private road that was only a stone's throw from South Harrow Station. Friedrich said that the tube train would be handy, but they rarely, if ever, used it, as Edward and the Bentley were always at hand. Joseph and Elizabeth visited frequently, and Joseph would busy himself for hours in the garden cutting and tidying as he felt fit. It was a small part of their life in which he could share, and Ruth would not dare to interfere even if she had wanted to.

Ruth loved her work; it was demanding but gave her a wonderful feeling of satisfaction. She looked on it as if she had returned, returned to what had been her family's, and she was anxious to prove her ability. Friedrich for his part left her alone. He had made it clear that it was up to her how she ran the financial side of things and was happy to let her find her feet. Occasionally they would lock horns over some expenditure or other, but any differences were quickly resolved. As the summer approached Ruth found the demands of her job more taxing and by the time June had come, she was beginning to struggle. Summer came early that year and the first week of June brought with it a surprisingly blistering heat. Ruth was now six months pregnant and unbelievably large. By the middle of the month her ankles had become a general point for discussion as they had swollen to nearly twice their normal size. Friedrich could stand it no longer.

'Ruth, I have kept my part of the bargain, now you must keep yours.'

He dropped the ferry tickets on the table. 'I have arranged everything, next week we go to Berlin.'

She could not argue.

The first thing Ruth did on arrival in Berlin was to visit her mother, and she was pleased to see how well she looked.

'And how is my grandson?' Mary asked as she hugged her daughter.

'Mother, I don't know how you can be so sure it is a boy!'

Mary laughed, 'I know, I just know.'

Ruth told her that they would be staying at Otto's house until the baby was due and asked if she would join them. Mary refused.

'Otto would not like that, Ruth,' she told her, 'he does not want me to cross to the East.' Ruth looked puzzled. 'It's a long story, dear, but believe me, it's best I stay here.' Ruth realised from Mary's tone that she was adamant, so decided not to labour the point. She did, however, make a mental note to quiz Otto about what her mother had said.

'Then I'll have to visit you every day,' Ruth told her, as she kissed her goodbye. 'I'll see you tomorrow.'

It took them an eternity to cross at the Brandenburg Gate, such was the stream of people and traffic waiting to cross to the East. Friedrich told her that more and more East Berliners were crossing to the West for work. 'The wages are so much better here in the West,' he said as they waited. 'I can't see the authorities putting up with this daily workforce migration for much longer. The papers are saying that communist workers are voting with their feet. The Kremlin are far from happy with things.' There was concern in his voice. 'I think a ban on cross-border workers may be on the way.'

*

Horst Urban slammed his hand down on the large table in Otto's library.

'Why do you persist in enticing East Berliners to the West?'

The man's small dark eyes had narrowed to mere slits and the venom in his voice was unmistakable.

'I do no such thing,' Otto replied calmly.

'No such thing! No such thing!' Urban repeated, banging his hand a second time on the table. 'Then why do you have four factories in the West and only that old rundown print works here? How is it that your company employs some 300 East Berliners in the West, most of whom cross every day?'

Urban rested both hands on the table and leant partway across it to where Otto sat on the other side. 'Answer me that,

Herr Mannerheim!' The sarcasm hung heavily in his words. Otto waited in silence for a moment. He knew the little man liked people to jump to his every word, so full of his own importance was he. Otto had never played his game; he refused to be bullied or intimidated by some local Communist Worker's leader. Especially when that leader was Horst Urban.

'If this communist government allowed its workers to earn a decent wage, and if it were to encourage business and trade, then I would be only too happy to move my factories to the East. But until it does, they stay in the West.'

Otto's reply was not what Urban wanted to hear. He stood back from the table and straightened himself up to his full inadequate height. 'I have to tell you, Herr Mannerheim,' his words were laced with menace, 'I shall be reporting this conversation to a higher authority and I shall also have no option other than to report your derogatory remarks with regard to the communist way of life.'

Otto got to his feet and smiled. 'You can report me to God Almighty if you wish, Urban, but I won't be intimidated by you or your Kremlin puppet government. My factories and my hospital stay in the West because there you and your people can't get your hands on them and destroy them like you have everything else.'

'You have not heard the last of this!' Urban replied, his face red with anger. 'Things are changing, Mannerheim, and there will soon be no room for parasite capitalists like you. I will see to that; mark my words, I will see to it.' Urban turned and started to walk away.

'Oh, and by the way, Urban,' Otto called after him, 'she is well, very well.' Urban stopped momentarily but did not turn. 'I thought you may be interested, after all, that's really what this is about isn't it? Get at me and you get at her, that's it, Urban, isn't it? Still seeking revenge.' Urban did not retaliate but as he left the room the anger raged inside him.

*

Otto put his arm around his daughter-in-law and squeezed her ever so gently. 'I trust you have been taking good care of her, Friedrich.' His son did not bother with an answer. 'You look wonderful, my dear,' Otto continued as he led them both into the lounge. 'It's so good to have you here again. Have you seen Mary? How is the baby?'

Later that evening, after dinner, Ruth lowered herself gingerly into one of the large armchairs in the lounge to enjoy her coffee. 'Otto?' she began; he looked at her. 'Today I asked Mary if she would come here with us but she refused. She told me you would not like it, that you prefer her to stay in the West. Why is that, Otto?' Ruth waited. Otto filled another cup from the silver pot and handed it to Friedrich. Ruth was quick to identify the knowing look between the two men. It was the kind of look she had seen in the past and she knew it well.

'What's going on, you two? I don't want any more secrets.' Otto poured his coffee and joined his son who had moved to the settee.

'It goes back a long way, Ruth,' Friedrich began. 'It's safer for Mary in the West than it is here.'

'Yes, but why, Friedrich?' Ruth asked, her frustration showing.

'Because of Urban,' Otto said softly, as he stirred his coffee.

'Urban! The man that betrayed us?' Ruth directed her question to Otto, but Friedrich replied.

'Not Graf Urban, Ruth, we told you he is dead; it is his brother. Horst Urban. It is he who is the threat to Mary.'

Ruth looked puzzled. 'But I do not understand, Friedrich. Why is he a threat?'

'Ruth,' Otto took over from his son, 'in prison, Graf Urban had time to think and time to repent. He told everybody that he had found God and that he truly repented his past ways. He spent hours in church and with the prison chaplain. On his release from prison he returned to his village only to be shunned by all that lived there. Nobody would believe that a former Nazi collaborator and murderer of Jews was now a man of God. In desperation he went to the hospital and asked to see your mother. We would not allow it of course but he found out where her room was, and one day, he managed to get in to see her. As I understand it he fell at her feet and begged her to forgive him. He told her he was a different man now and that he wanted just to live his life and be forgiven for his sins of the past. Apparently when he got to his feet your mother spat in his face. She told him she would see him in Hell first. The next day he jumped from a railway bridge.

'Under a brick on top of the bridge the police found a letter to his brother. The letter was read out at the inquest. In it he said that he could no longer live with the sins of the past and that the Caslav woman's rejection had been the final straw.' Otto paused. 'I am afraid, Ruth, Horst Urban holds your mother responsible for his brother's death.'

Ruth sat silently for a moment. 'And Urban? Where is he now?'

'In the village,' Otto replied. 'He is the local Communist Party Leader and quite a little tyrant.'

'Does he know who I am?' she asked.

Friedrich was quick to reply, 'Not a chance, darling. There's no way he could possibly know you're Mary's daughter.'

TWENTY

AUGUST 1961
Altifascistischer Schutzwall

According to Ruth's dates, the baby was not due until the end of September. Dr Meile, however, was not so sure.

'This baby is a good size.' He pressed gently on Ruth's stomach. 'And the head is down.' He stood back and stroked his chin as he stared at her. 'It could come any time, you know.'

Ruth pulled down the gown and swung her legs round and off the examination couch, heaving herself into a sitting position as she did so. The exertion required was considerable.

'Not yet, Wilhelm, It's too soon.'

He helped her get down. 'Don't you be so sure, young lady, after all, I'm the doctor.' He laughed as he moved to his desk and retrieved his diary. 'I am a little concerned, Ruth; your blood pressure has been getting steadily higher over the last two weeks or so, and I think it would be for the best if you were to come into hospital a little earlier.' The concerned look on Ruth's face hastened him to continue. 'It's nothing to worry about, but all this travelling backwards and forwards between here and the

262

East is not good for you.' He opened the diary. 'As from next week I want you to come into the hospital.' Ruth opened her mouth to argue but he waved his hand at her. 'It's not open for debate, Ruth.' He looked down at the open diary. 'Monday will do fine, that's the... let me see...' he flicked over several pages, 'yes, 14th August, that will be fine, I'll arrange a room.'

Wilhelm's assertiveness left Ruth rather lost for words; it was a quality in him she had not as yet witnessed, and its impact robbed her of any desire to argue.

*

'Wilhelm says I must go into hospital on Monday.' Ruth's words seized both Friedrich's and his father's attention. They had been discussing the opening of a new factory in France over dinner and Ruth was a little annoyed that she had managed only the odd incision in their conversation. Now she had their attention!

'Nothing to worry about,' she continued nonchalantly, before stopping to devour another mouthful of lamb.

'What do you mean, nothing to worry about? It's much too early.' Friedrich was staring at her, his fork suspended midway between plate and mouth. Ruth ignored his question.

'I told Mother that there was little point in visiting tomorrow. Saturday is always hell to get over, the border points are always busy. Anyway, I'll be seeing her every day come Monday.'

'Ruth, you didn't answer my question. Why does Wilhelm want you to go in so early?' He put the fork down.

'I said it's nothing to worry about, my blood pressure is a little high, and he thinks all the travelling back and forth is too much for me.'

'Are you feeling well?' Friedrich persisted.

'Very, thank you.'

Despite the bravado Ruth had demonstrated during dinner, inwardly she was concerned. The visits to see her mother were becoming more tiring for her and she found the border formalities increasingly irksome. She had also started to suffer from headaches, and on her return today one had developed that refused to leave her. By the time dinner had finished she was tired and more than a little irritable, so she made her apologies and retired early.

*

'Women have been having babies for as long as I can remember.' Otto chuckled as he handed his son a cognac. 'Relax, drink this.'

Otto's flippancy was not appreciated.

'Look, Friedrich, she will be fine with me tomorrow, I promise you I will stay right with her, and the slightest sign of a problem she will be in the hospital before she can blink.' Otto sampled his cognac. 'Now take the opportunity, leave early tomorrow, visit Antwerp and tie up the French deal. Ruth said she didn't mind, you'll be back by Sunday, and you can take her to the hospital yourself on Monday morning.'

Friedrich swallowed the last of his drink. It was silly to worry and he knew it. The baby was not due until September, and Ruth wasn't worried about him making the trip. He put down the empty glass.

'Well, I'd better get an early night then too.' He got to his feet. 'If there's the slightest problem take her straight to the hospital.'

Otto smiled. 'I will.' He watched as his son made his way to the door. 'Friedrich,' he called after him, 'don't worry I'll will look after her, she'll be fine with me. I promise.'

*

Saturday the 11th August was hot. Ruth did not rush to rise from her bed; she had woken early with Friedrich, and had kissed him goodbye at a little after 5.30am. She had found sleep difficult after that and had lain on the bed drifting in and out of a variety of fleeting dreams until almost 9.30am. When she did get up it was with difficulty. She felt lethargic, her back ached, and it took ages for her to muster her clothes and dress. At the top of the stairs Otto intercepted her; she could not be sure, but it would not have surprised her if he had been waiting, on duty as it were, to ensure her safe passage down the huge stairway. They ate breakfast together and as they did so Otto handed her the newspaper.

'There's a lot of huffing and puffing about all the crossing still.' He pointed to the front page of the paper. 'It won't be a bad thing you going to the West on Monday. The border crossings are getting congested. They say the East Berlin guards are being told to make it more difficult for East Germans to cross, and that means it will make the wait longer for you.'

Ruth looked at him. 'They would never stop you crossing over, Otto, would they?' she asked with concern.

He laughed, 'No, I earn them too many West German marks, and I have too many important friends. They can't stop the crossing and they know it. There are houses half on the East and half on the West, there are entire streets bisected by the border.' He shook his head. 'Ruth, East Berlin is like a bucket full of holes, and those sick of communism are just pouring out. Sooner or later Berlin will be one city again.' He waggled his finger at her. 'And I wager it won't be a communist one.'

It was a little after 2.00pm when the telephone rang. Ruth had been dozing in her chair and its shrill ring made her jump. Otto picked up the receiver.

'Father, it's me!' Friedrich's voice was faint and, even by East German standards, the line was particularly poor. 'Father, I've only just managed to get over to the West. There are troop movements everywhere, thousands of them.' Otto detected a note of panic in his son's voice.

'Father, I don't like it; the roads are all but blocked with tanks heading towards the border. If Ruth needs to get to the hospital quickly it will be impossible. I'm coming back.'

'No don't do that!' Otto replied sternly, 'It will achieve nothing. I will bring her to you. Just go to the hospital and wait. If there really are that many troops on the move something may be about to happen. If it does, I want you both in the West.'

*

It had not taken Ruth many minutes to gather her things; the urgency in Otto's voice had prompted haste. And now, less than twenty minutes after Friedrich's telephone call, Otto swung the Mercedes out of the drive and onto the narrow road that led to the village.

'It's probably just Friedrich getting excited. No need to worry,' he smiled at her, 'I bet we'll sail through no problem at all.'

The village was quiet as usual and so was the road. It was not until they reached the junction with the main Berlin road that they saw any fellow travellers, but what they did see caused

Otto to curse. Tank after tank, lorry after lorry, all streaming towards Berlin in one long undulating convoy.

'What's going on, Otto?' Ruth asked as they sat motionless at the junction. 'Where are they all going?'

'God knows!' Otto replied. 'But I don't like it.' A small gap appeared between two lorries as he spoke, and he lurched the car forward to join the convey. 'We'll just have to be patient.'

For nearly an hour they trundled along sandwiched between the two trucks. In front of them the truck had its canvas flap tied up; the expressionless faces of the young men crammed inside stared back at them with little interest. On the outskirts of Berlin, the convoy ground to a halt and them with it. From then on it was stop-start, stop-start as they moved, barely a metre at a time towards the city. Eventually the truck in front moved away, but before Otto could get the car into gear and follow it, an army officer stepped into the road holding his arm up. Otto wound down the window.

'Where are you going?' The man did not bother with pleasantries.

'Berlin, of course,' Otto barked back.

'Not today, the road is closed to civilians. Turn your car round and return home.'

'I shall do no such thing,' Otto retaliated, 'can't you see that this young lady is about to have her baby? She must get to the hospital straight away.'

The officer leant in through the window and studied Ruth.

'What hospital?' he asked, his eyes fixed on her.

'The Caslav Memorial.' Otto's tone remained sharp.

'What's the matter with our hospitals?' the soldier sneered.

'The lady is from England she is here on holiday and is booked in for specialist treatment.'

'Papers!' He extended his arm in Ruth's direction. Ruth fumbled in her bag and produced her documents. 'You obviously speak German, Fraulein.' He examined the papers as he spoke.

'I studied it as a student in England.' It was an instinctive reaction and the first time in her life she had ever lied to hide her past. Otto looked at her.

'I congratulate you, Fraulein; you speak our language excellently.' He turned to Otto. 'And you?'

Otto handed him his papers. 'East German born and bred.'

'Wait here.' The man walked over to a small wooden hut that was still being hastily erected by two sombre-faced soldiers. Through the unglazed window Ruth and Otto watched as he spoke on the telephone. The conversation was brief.

'The lady is free to continue,' he said as he returned to the car. He turned to Otto. 'You, you will have to return tomorrow.'

'Will you escort her then? At least as far as Brandenburg?' Otto asked calmly. Ruth tugged at his coat.

'Not without you, Otto,' she whispered in English.

'Sorry, we are on manoeuvres.' The soldier's reply was sharp. 'Either let her continue on her own or get the car off the road.'

'This is outrageous!' Otto protested. 'Look at her, she's about to have a baby, how can she continue on her own?'

'I have my orders,' the soldier shouted, 'make up your mind.'

Ruth leant across Otto. 'Will it be clear tomorrow?'

The soldier looked at her. 'Tomorrow, Fraulein, the road will be empty.'

Ruth turned to Otto. 'Take me home, Otto, please, just take me back. We'll try again tomorrow.'

*

'But the road's blocked, Friedrich. Believe me we've only just got back. They say it's just manoeuvres and it will be clear tomorrow. Yes! We're going to try again first thing in the morning. No! No don't cross back, whatever you do, don't cross back. If they do close the border it will be easy for Ruth to cross, they may give you some trouble. Now just stay there, don't panic.' Otto handed the telephone to Ruth.

'Hello darling. Yes, I'm fine, don't worry. Just do as your father says, just stay in the West and I'll be there tomorrow. Yes, the soldiers told us it was just manoeuvres, the road will be empty tomorrow. Yes, I'll see you then. I love you too.' Ruth put down the phone and all but collapsed into the chair.

'Are you all right?' Otto asked, his face furrowed with concern.

'Just tired, Otto.' She looked at him. 'It will be all right, won't it?'

Otto smiled wearily. 'It will be all right, Ruth. I promise it will be all right.'

*

Ruth turned on the small lamp at the side of her bed. It was 3.00am. For a moment or two she was not sure where she was, or what was happening. There was only one thing of which she was certain and that was that the pain in her back was agonising. The bed was wet, she realised that it was soaked, and as she pulled back the sheets the realisation of what was happening suddenly terrified her. It must have been her first contraction that caused her waters to break and jerk her from sleep. She lay still for a moment to gather her thoughts. Then it came, and she could not help but cry out with pain as the contraction gripped her and contorted her body, creasing her in pain for what seemed an eternity. Then, as suddenly as it had come, it was gone and she fell back onto her pillow, the relief exquisite. It was several seconds before her mind began to function logically again. Otto, she must get Otto. Slowly she pulled herself from the bed and, turning on the main light, opened the bedroom door. She was halfway along the landing towards Otto's room when the next contraction came. Such was the strength of it that she was forced to bend double, gripping her stomach before finally dropping to her knees with a cry of pain. Even before the pain had left her, Otto was there. 'The baby is coming, Otto.' She gripped his hand. 'I'm sorry, but it's coming.'

*

'Who is it?' Carl Kahler shouted as he pulled on his shirt and started to unbolt the door.

'It's me, Carl,' Otto shouted through the door, 'I need Gitta. My daughter-in-law has gone into labour. Please, she must come and help!'

It took Otto less than fifteen minutes to return with Gitta. But to Ruth it seemed like a lifetime. The contractions were coming almost every three minutes or so and she realised that things were happening far quicker than they should. By the time Gitta arrived Ruth was drenched in sweat and in the throes of suffering another contraction, her face so contorted with the pain she could barely open her eyes. Through the midst of her suffering she heard Gitta giving Otto orders to fetch hot water and towels.

Gitta took her hand. 'I'm not a midwife but I've had two of my own, I'll help you. Carl, my husband, has gone to the village to fetch the doctor, he won't be long.'

Ruth took the woman's hand. 'It's so painful,' she groaned, as the contraction started to ease. 'This can't be right. What time is it?'

'Nearly 3.30am,' Gitta replied.

'I've only been in labour thirty minutes and already the contractions are coming every three minutes.' Ruth opened her eyes and for the first time looked at the pretty young woman holding her hand. 'That can't be right can it? And my waters have broken already.'

Gitta smiled reassuringly. 'Some babies take hours and hours to come, others, well, they just can't wait to get into the world. If you're lucky yours will come quick.' Gitta fetched a damp flannel from the basin and wiped Ruth's face. 'Now let's see if we can get you a little more comfortable.'

*

Otto, racked with anxiety, paced up and down the hall. He had been listening to Ruth's cries for nearly two hours now and things were getting no better. As yet Carl had not returned with the doctor and he cursed the two men for their neglect of duty. Several times he had considered taking the car and searching them out. But he had not. Instead, now he drew back the curtains to let in the first of the morning's light. He looked at his watch; it was 5.20am.

Carl and the doctor finally arrived a little after 6.00am.

'I'm sorry, Otto, I was with a patient who has had a heart attack.'

The doctor, a man well into his sixties, was an old friend of Otto's. He had treated his wife before her death and knew the family well. Making no attempt to explain further he made his way straight upstairs. Inside the room Gitta had been doing her best but it was obvious Ruth was in a great deal of distress. After a quick examination the doctor realised that the baby had turned into the breech position and was well on its way towards entering the world feet first. He also determined that the umbilical cord was firmly tangled about the baby's neck and that he had to act quickly to avoid a tragedy. He had arrived just in time.

At 7.07am on Sunday the 13th August 1961, Ruth was delivered of a seven-pound twelve-ounce baby boy. Fifty-three minutes later at 8.00am precisely it was announced on the National Wireless Station of the German Democratic Republic that to protect the interest of the East German people it had been decided to close the border with the West. A wall was being erected across Berlin; no longer would the East tolerate the evil capitalist influence of the West that had for so long been corrupting the East German people. The iron curtain was being drawn.

*

Otto had tried several times to telephone the hospital where he knew Friedrich would be staying. He was desperate to tell him of his son's arrival, but each time he dialled the West Berlin code the line went dead. He had not heard the radio announcement at 8.00am, he had been far too busy admiring his grandson. It was not until 9.00am that he turned on the wireless, which was as usual tuned to his favourite West German station. The first words he heard were those of the newsreader who, in a sombre tone, was reporting the latest developments with regard to the wall.

'What wall?' Otto asked himself as he sat down in his chair to listen to the man's rather mundane tones.

'For those of you just tuning in on this Sunday morning the 13th August 1961, I must repeat that during yesterday evening and the early hours of this morning East German troops have shut the border with the free West. The erection of barricades across the very heart of Berlin has begun. The West German government has lodged a formal complaint at what it interprets to be the infringement of rights of all Germans and in particularly the citizens of Berlin. The Mayor of West Berlin has requested that all Berliners remain calm and is confident that the blockade will only be temporary. The next news bulletin will follow at 10.00am.'

Otto could not believe what he had heard. A wall across Berlin! It was ridiculous, the people would never stand for it. How could they close off a city of that size? He reached over and twisted the dial on the wireless. The East German station was playing only sombre music, a definite indication that something was going on!

*

Wilhelm Meile had been watching Friedrich pace the floor of his office for the past thirty minutes.

'Look Friedrich, nobody really knows what's going on yet. It's far too early.' It was 9.30am and the doctor was about to light what was already his eleventh cigarette of the day. 'Anyway, they can't stop Ruth coming over, she's a British subject for God's sake!'

Friedrich stopped beside Wilhelm's chair and stared down at him. 'Who knows what they can do? And what about Father? No way will they let him cross now. What a bloody mess! I should have known yesterday when I came over. All those troops on the road. And still I didn't realise!' Fredrich banged his fist down on the doctor's desk. 'I'm going back for her, Wilhelm, I want her here when she has the baby, I'm going now!'

'Don't be a fool, Friedrich!' Wilhelm got up from his chair and grasped Friedrich's arm. 'If you go back now, that's it, you're stuck there. Oh, they'll let Ruth out all right, they can't hold her. But as for you?' He shrugged. 'You'll be stuck there for months, who knows, maybe even years. No, you must be patient. Otto will get her here today, he said he would. Anyway, while you're crossing back over there she might be on her way here. Now that would be stupid! Her here and you trapped back over there for no reason.' The doctor smiled at him. 'Just give your father time to work things out. Trust him.'

The English Sunday papers carried only the smallest of reports about troops massing on the East Germany border and the heightening of tension between both sides. The news of the closing of the border had come too late and the papers had gone to print without carrying it. Like most of the German public the British people heard the news either by wireless or on the television news. For most it was just another escalation of tension between East and West. Something that was happening too far away to be of any great consequence, and besides in many minds the Germans were still only paying the price for the war they started. But for others the news was sinister indeed.

Joseph and Elizabeth did not have a television set, so the latest developments were brought to them courtesy of the

BBC Home Service. For the pair of them it was the start of another nightmare, the kind which they believed had long since been left behind. Where was she, East or West? They could not even be sure about what side of the border she was. When they had last spoken to her, she had telephoned them from the West. But was she there now? And what about Friedrich and Otto? All day they listened to every news broadcast and waited expectantly for the new telephone Ruth had installed to ring. Finally, at 3.20pm, it rang. Joseph snatched the receiver up with such ferocity that Elizabeth had to grab the rest of the apparatus to stop it spinning from the table.

'Hello!' he shouted as he put the receiver to his ear.

'Joseph, it is me.'

'Thank God,' Joseph muttered as Friedrich's voice echoed down the line, 'are you all right, Friedrich? Where are you?' Joseph rolled both questions into one.

I'm at the hospital,' Friedrich answered, 'and I'm fine.'

'They're at the hospital,' Joseph relayed the message to his wife.

'No, no Joseph, Ruth is not with me,' Friedrich continued having heard Joseph's words to Elizabeth, 'she is in the East with Otto, but don't worry they can't keep her, she's a British Citizen, they have to let her through.'

It was not difficult for Joseph to detect the masked concern in Friedrich's voice. 'Have you heard from them?' he asked quickly.

Friedrich hesitated, 'No not yet, all the lines from here to the East have been cut, but I was with her yesterday and she was fine. I'm expecting her to arrive here today, as soon as she does, I'll contact you.'

'But what about your father? Will they let him come out with her?'

'I don't know,' Friedrich answered, 'but I doubt they can stop him.'

*

'How soon will she be able to travel?' Otto asked the doctor as he walked with him to his car.

'She will be all right in about a week,' the doctor replied as he opened the door of his battered old Citroen. 'But for now, she must rest.' He shook Otto's hand. 'Remember, Otto, the baby came quickly and was breech, it was not an easy time for her.'

'It's just that I will feel happier when she is back in the West.'

The doctor turned. 'And you, Otto, what about you?'

Otto shrugged, 'What can I do? There is no way open for me now, I will have to stay here until they open the border again.'

'Pray to God that will not be too long.' The doctor climbed into the car. 'They say thousands of families have been separated.' He shook his head. 'That can't be right.'

Otto watched as the old car turned the corner of the drive leaving behind it a trail of blue smoke. So much had happened in the last few hours that he had scarcely thought about what effect the wall would have on his life. But the doctor's question had prompted such thoughts. His first concern was to get Ruth back to the West as quickly as he could. But what about Friedrich? Would his son be patient enough to wait? What if he was not? Otto knew he must get word to him today. He must tell him about the birth of his son and beg him to wait in the West. The question was, how?

As he made his way back into the house Otto was surprised to hear the telephone ringing. He ran quickly into the lounge and picked it up. 'Hello?' he panted.

'Are you all right?' Otto recognised Joseph's voice at the other end of the line, it was faint but surprisingly clear.

'Joseph, thank God! Yes, we're fine. Now listen, this is very important,' Otto spoke quickly he knew that the line may be cut any minute and this was perhaps the only chance he would get. Have you spoken to Friedrich?'

'Yes, he says he can't get through to you so I thought I would try.'

'Listen, Joseph, you must contact him. Tell him no matter what, he must not return to the East. I will get Ruth out but I can't do it yet. Do you understand, Joseph? Tell him he must stay where he is.'

'I'll tell him,' Joseph replied. 'How is Ruth, is she all right?'

'Joseph, Ruth has had the baby, it's a boy and they are both well, but the doctor says she can't travel for about a week. Tell Friedrich about the baby but make him promise not to come back. I need a week, Joseph, that's all, a week and they will both be back in the West.'

Joseph did not reply. 'Joseph can you hear me?'

'I can hear you, Otto,' Joseph said, his voice heavy with anxiety. 'Bring her back to us, Otto.'

'I will, my friend, I promise I will. This time I will get it right.'

*

Horst Urban smiled. 'Finally, they have done it!' He got up from his desk and walked around it to where Kahler was sitting. 'They have actually closed the border. Do you realise that today, Carl, is the first day of a truly communist East Germany?' Kahler smiled but did not reply. He had never seen Urban in such a good mood and he was anxious not to say anything that may destroy that and leave him to reap the man's wrath. 'No more migration of East German labour, no more capitalist corruption.' He put a hand on Kahler's shoulder. 'People like you and me can start work now; we can build a stronger state with real power. We can squash capitalism, pluck out what's left of it, as you pluck a thorn from your finger.'

Kahler seized on a momentary lapse in Urban's pontifications. 'She's had her baby,' he blurted out. Urban turned.

'Do you mean the Jew?' His tone was suddenly sharp and aggressive.

'Yes,' Kahler replied, 'it came early, it was born this morning.'

Urban threw his head back and laughed. 'Then I have two of them now.' He turned to Kahler. 'Tomorrow I shall pay a visit to the Mannerheim house; after all, congratulations are in order, we have a new East German citizen!'

TWENTY-ONE

BID FOR FREEDOM

THE MONDAY MORNING NEWS REPORTS ON THE West German wireless told of ever-growing numbers of East German troops along the border and the continued construction of the Berlin Wall. The commentator reported that several cranes had been working all night lifting huge concrete blocks into position to seal roads and that several people had been arrested for attempting to cross to the West. Otto knew that Ruth would have to be told of the situation, there was no way he could keep it from her.

'What are we going to do, Otto?' she asked, her eyes wide open, fear fixed firmly in them. Otto sat at the end of her bed, his grandson nestled snugly in his arms.

'We are going to get you across as soon as you can travel.' He looked up from the infant. 'You know they will not stop you, Ruth, you carry British papers, it will be easy.' Otto tried to sound as nonchalant as he could.

'But what about you? If we leave you here it could be years before they open the border again.' Ruth could not control the tremble in her voice. 'You won't be able to see Friedrich or visit Mary.'

Otto got up from the bed. 'There are ways, Ruth, I will find a way. Right now that is not important, the most important thing is to get you to the West before my impetuous son takes things into his own hands and crosses back.' Otto passed the baby carefully back to her. 'Now today is Monday, with any luck you may feel up to making the trip by Saturday. It's a little earlier than the doctor recommends but then he has always been a cautious man.'

Ruth forced a smiled. 'I will be fine, Otto, it's just the thought of leaving you here alone that I don't like.'

*

It was almost lunchtime when Horst Urban arrived at the house; his unexpected visit concerned Otto. Both men exchanged only the smallest of pleasantries as Otto showed him through into the library. Urban, without waiting to be invited, lowered himself into the large armchair opposite Otto's desk.

'Well, Herr Mannerheim, I warned you things would change.' His tone was laced with his own particular brand of sarcasm. 'Now you will no longer be able to sap the cream of East German workers.'

Otto did not rise to the bait but merely sat down at his desk and readied himself for Urban's onslaught.

'The capitalist ways will no longer be able to corrupt our society. A good thing, don't you agree?'

'Oh absolutely,' Otto retorted, 'and in six months when there are no jobs, no money and very little food, perhaps we can reconsider the matter. But right now, Urban, I'm a busy man, what can I do for you?'

The grin of self-satisfaction that had played on Urban's lips since his arrival was all at once gone. Anger now shone clearly in his eyes. 'Do you think you can dismiss me just like that? You are a busy man! I think not, Herr Mannerheim. How can you be busy? After all, nearly all your business interests are in the West, and you? Well, you are here in the East and you have nowhere to go. Today is Monday, why are you not at work?' The grin returned.

Otto knew that he had no retaliation, how could he have? For as annoying as it was, the man was right.

'Anyway, enough of this nonsense.' Urban settled himself back into the chair as he spoke. 'Why waste time airing our differences about what has happened when we have no option other than to accept it?' He forced a smile. 'I have come not to argue but to congratulate: I understand you now have a grandson.' Urban had timed his thrust immaculately and Otto all but reeled from it. 'How is the baby?' Urban asked with mock concern.

'My grandson is well, thank you,' Otto replied.

'And your daughter-in-law?' Urban persisted.

'Thank you, she is fine too.' He had not fully recovered from the shock of Urban knowing about the baby and was trying desperately to hide that.

'Good, good.' Urban knew he had him and was not going to let go. 'And where is Friedrich?' he asked.

'Fortunately, he is in the West and Ruth and the child will join him shortly.' As soon as the words had left his lips Otto regretted them. His instincts told him it was a mistake to volunteer Urban any information.

'Oh really, and your daughter-in-law, what did you call her, Ruth, was it?' Otto nodded. 'They tell me she is very beautiful.'

Urban let his words hang in the air and in doing so prompted the response.

'Very,' was Otto's only reply.

The man leant forward in the chair. 'Tell me, is she as beautiful as her mother?' Again, the thrust was immaculate, only this time directed to the jugular. Otto found himself struggling desperately under what had been a completely unforeseen attack. It was obvious that Urban knew about Ruth, and who she was. His brain raced in an attempt to regroup its thoughts and repel the attack.

'How should I know?' was the best answer he could muster.

'Oh, come on, Herr Mannerheim, please, credit me with some intelligence.'

The forced smile had long since gone and Urban's cold eyes were now fixed on him. 'Did you think you could find her, bring her back here and parade her around West Berlin without me, Horst Urban, knowing! You made a mistake, Mannerheim.' Urban spoke with new aggression. 'You underestimated me.'

'I'm sorry, I don't understand what you are talking about.' Otto was not ready to concede.

'Really, then let me spell it out for you. You know and I know that your daughter-in-law is the daughter of the Jew Mary Caslav.' Urban's reference to Mary lit the touch paper that inflamed a rage in Otto and he made no attempt to hide it.

'I don't give a shit what you know or what you think you know! She is a British citizen and there is nothing you can do to her, and there is nothing you can do to stop her returning to the West when she is ready to do so.'

'If I were you, Herr Mannerheim, I would tread with caution; at this time she is still in the East.' Urban's words again struck home. 'She is no more a British citizen than you or I. The truth of the matter is that she is an East German Jew masquerading as a British citizen on false papers. Not only that,' Urban grinned, 'her child was born in the East and has an East German father. There would be those that would believe that the child has no right to return to the West, and that she should be detained and charged with travelling on false documents.' Again, Urban grinned. 'I warned you things would change, Mannerheim.'

Otto struggled desperately to regain his composure. He knew Urban had deliberately provoked him, and with this man a show of temper may well produce an unguarded word. A word upon which Urban may seize. But the truth was clear to him now, it had been laid naked at his feet by this communist jackal. He had to face it, for the second time in his life, he had allowed his own failure to assess the dangers to threaten Ruth and the ones he loved.

'You have no proof, Urban. These accusations are just the ranting of a vindictive little man. All the village knows that you hate Mary Caslav and why. Who will believe you? Who will want to believe you?' Otto had struck back as best he could. But he knew it was with very little venom.

'Again, you forget,' Urban replied calmly, 'things have changed, I represent the Communist Party and my masters are well pleased with me. Unfortunately, they see you as a capitalist infiltrator set to destroy the communist way. Oh! Do not fool yourself, my friend,' he shook his head as he spoke, 'these men, my masters, they would believe me, they would be only too happy to believe me. Nothing would give them greater pleasure than to send you to a labour camp for the next twenty or so years, and that little Jew with you. Of course, the child would be taken from her.'

Otto's immediate reaction was to choke the life from this miserable excuse for a human being that sat smirking at him. In fact, he felt himself start to get to his feet and the look in his eyes must have betrayed his thoughts.

'I would not recommend violence, my dear Herr Mannerheim.' Urban allowed his jacket to drop open as he spoke; it revealed a shoulder holster complete with automatic pistol. 'One feels so threatened these days, would you not agree?' Otto sank back into his chair.

'Now then, let us look at the situation. You are stuck here in the East and so are your daughter-in-law and your grandson, I would also wager that given a few days or so your son will return. Now then, you said I was a vindictive man; I shall prove to you that this is not the case.' Urban was silent for a moment. He was enjoying the control, the triumph over an old adversary. 'I have no interest in the girl or her baby and to be honest I have very little interest in you. Oh, I despise what you are and what you believe in, but it matters not to me if you go to the West; in fact I can think of no better place for you.'

Otto was taken aback by Urban's sudden change in approach but he knew the man too well to be fooled. 'What do you want, Urban?'

'I want a deal, my friend, I will sign the papers and you, the girl and your grandson will be able to travel to the West unhindered.'

'And in return?' Otto asked.

'Oh, in return,' the same sickly smirk returned, 'in return I want Mary Caslav. A very good deal, don't you think? Three for the price of one.'

Again, Otto felt almost unable to control his anger but the thought of Urban's shoulder holster forced his restraint. 'You're bloody mad. Do you really think that after protecting her from you for all these years, I am just going to hand her to you on a plate? You can go to hell!'

Urban stood up. 'Well, that of course is your decision, although somehow I wonder if the others would agree with you.' He tossed a typed document onto the desk in front of Otto. 'That is a pass for you to visit the West, it is dated for tomorrow; you may stay only four hours. If by then you have not returned, I will arrest the girl. Talk to them, arrange it. Remember: three for the price of one. Would the Jew want her daughter to live through the same hell as she did?' He buttoned his jacket. 'I think not, do you? Oh, and just in case you are thinking of trying to take the girl with you, I have to tell you that her picture has been posted at every checkpoint from here to Brandenburg. I wish you good evening, Herr Mannerheim. I can see myself out.'

*

'We'll just have to get you out, Ruth, and quickly.' Otto paced up and down the bedroom as he spoke. She had listened to him tell of Urban's visit and as the reality of the man's threats struck home, she had felt the nausea of fear grip at her stomach. 'Before they get too well organised,' Otto continued. 'Every day, every hour, the door is becoming more tightly closed. But we will play him at his own game. I will go to the West tomorrow, I will see Friedrich and I will visit Scholtze, you remember my friend the Police Chief.' He turned to her. 'Try not to worry Ruth, we will work something out, we will both get out.'

When Otto had gone Ruth laid her son in the cot that had once been Friedrich's and then sat herself in the armchair in the corner of the room. In her whole life she could not remember ever feeling so frightened. It was not just about what could happen to her, although that was bad enough. No, what was worse than that was what might happen to her son. As she sat there, alone in the quiet of the room, the full frightening reality of persecution reached out and touched her, and as it did it brought with it the light of understanding. For the first time since she had learnt of her mother's existence, and of what she had done to try and save her children, she understood. The determination to ensure her son's survival gave her a new strength from within. If her mother could endure all those years then, she told herself, she most certainly could survive the next few days. After all, she had Otto to help her.

She did not sleep well and as soon as the light of dawn reached into her room she slipped out of bed and, taking care not to wake the baby, closed the bedroom door quietly behind her. She found Otto was already up and dressed. He was drinking coffee in the lounge and she startled him as she entered the room.

'Are you all right?' he asked.

She could tell from his face that the strain of responsibility for their plight was resting heavily on him. 'I'm fine, Otto.' She handed him an envelope. 'When you see Friedrich give him this.' Otto took it. 'Don't worry, Otto, I've told him that whatever he does he must not cross back.' She tried to smile. 'Mainly it's about his son,' she hesitated, 'just in case…'

Otto stood up. 'There's no "just in case", Ruth! In two or three days I will get you across.'

'Then tell him that, Otto, and tell him I love him with every inch of my being.'

*

The Vopo at the checkpoint on Friedrich Strasse scrutinised the pass and then handed it to his colleague. 'I don't know about this,' he snorted, 'what do you think?' The other man examined it. 'I know one thing,' he replied after a few seconds, 'whatever happens we're in for a bollocking. If we let him through and it's a forgery, we'll get it, and if we check with command and it's not, we're in trouble for wasting their time.' The guard handed it back. 'It's up to you.' The first policeman took the paper reluctantly and picked up the telephone. He looked at Otto as he dialled. 'If this is a forgery, I wouldn't give a donkey's piss for your future.'

The walk from East to West was a solitary one and Otto was conscious of what he felt must have been hundreds of pairs of hidden eyes that were staring at him from surrounding buildings and streets. The guard that lifted the barrier mumbled something about friends in high places as he passed, and watched with a mixture of hatred and envy as Otto had started on his way across the 300 yards of barren concrete that was the frail umbilical cord between the divided city. The young American soldier watched nervously as Otto covered the last fifty yards or so towards the barrier that was the West. No one other than military personnel had passed his checkpoint that morning and this individual was plainly not military. At the barrier, Otto stopped and produced his papers.

'I need transport, young man, and I need it quickly.'

*

'The man's a maniac, Father!' Friedrich stammered. 'I'm going back. She is my wife; he is my son. I will go back.'

'Don't be a fool,' the deep authoritative voice of Herr Scholtze cut across the room. 'Your father is right; the only way we can beat this man is to play him at his own game.'

'For Christ's sake, you two,' Friedrich retaliated, 'this isn't '46, it's not some revenge campaign. It's happening, the whole bloody city's been cut in two. Half the Russian army has been positioned on the other side of that wall, and you say "play him at his own game"? Well, he's got Ruth and my son over there and I'll be dammed if I'm going to take chances with their lives!'

'Listen Friedrich,' Otto put his hand on his son's shoulder, 'if I do not go back, he will arrest her and he will arrest you too. Don't you see? I would have disobeyed him. We must make him think that we are dancing to his tune, that is the only way we can buy enough time to work out how we can get her across.'

Scholtze interrupted Otto, 'People are getting out, Friedrich. Already today seven have got over. They are dropping out of windows, swimming the river, tricking their way past the guards. We will find a way for them.'

'Look!' Friedrich pulled away from his father. 'I know you were something special back then, after the war. I know that between you, you righted a lot of wrongs, brought a lot of people to justice, but times have changed, this is different. For a start you are both older, a lot older, and secondly, we're up against the whole bloody Soviet army, oh and let's not forget a few thousand or so East German Vopos!' Friedrich threw his arms in the air in a gesture of despair before dropping into the armchair next to the up-until-now quiet Wilhelm Meile. 'Tell them, doctor! Tell them they're mad!'

Wilhelm removed the ever-present cigarette from his mouth. 'What do you suggest we do then, Friedrich?' the doctor asked in a quiet voice. 'Tell me, do we let you go back instead of your father? Wave you goodbye at the frontier and wish you, your wife and child a good and happy life in the East? Or perhaps the other alternative? We tell Mary. We take her to the frontier and we do the swap. She would not argue, she would do anything to save her daughter and her grandson, we know that.'

'For God's sake, man!' Friedrich, barely able to retain his temper, was back on his feet again. 'You know bloody well none of us would allow Mary to go back there.'

'Then we wave goodbye to you and Ruth, do we?' Wilhelm twisted the cigarette in his fingers, his eyes focused on it, not Friedrich. Friedrich sat back down. He had no answer, he knew he had no answer. All he did know was, he wanted to be with his wife, he wanted to hold his son and the thought of not being able to do either was driving him mad. He looked at his father. 'How did we let this happen?' he said in desperation. 'Why did we not see it coming?'

Otto shook his head. 'Because we believe what we want to believe. It is as simple as that.'

'Can we get them out?' Friedrich asked. It was a naked question, no pretence, a simple question, but its significance was beyond measure.

Scholtze's voice broke the silence. 'Together we can, the four of us. But we must start now. There is no time to lose.'

*

Otto crossed back with a little under fifteen minutes to spare and was not surprised to see the green uniformed police officer pick up the telephone as soon as he had passed the checkpoint.

He knew that within just a few seconds Urban would be aware of his return. It was not quite 2.00pm when he arrived back at the house. Ruth had been waiting for him and as soon as the car came into view around the bend in the drive she rushed to the front door.

'Did you see him? How is he?'

Otto took her hand. 'He is fine,' he smiled. 'It was difficult, but I have managed to get him to agree to wait. He wanted to come back instead of me, but we persuaded him it would do no good.' Otto took off his hat. 'How is my grandson?'

'Asleep.' Ruth's reply was curt. 'Did he have a message?'

Otto smiled. 'Yes, he said he will see you Saturday night.'

*

Otto was not surprised to see Urban's car pull up outside the house. What did surprise him was that two other cars, both of which carried four men, pulled up with it. Urban stepped out of his car and waited. As if complying with some prearranged plan, the men also got out but as they did so each of them went in different directions to strategic points about the house. It was another of Urban's game plans, it was a well-orchestrated show of strength. Otto looked at his watch. It was 3.15pm. He had been back just a little over an hour.

'A successful trip I hope?' It was more of a statement than a question and Urban did not linger for a reply but made his way straight into the library. Unlike his last visit, this time he sat himself down at Otto's desk. Another calculated show of strength. Otto ignored it.

'It depends what you mean by successful,' was Otto's belated reply.

Urban banged his fist on the desk. 'You know what I mean!' The aggression in his reply did not surprise Otto. 'Have you arranged it? Or do my men come in here and arrest you both? Be warned, Mannerheim, I am no longer in the mood for games.' Urban's cold, calculating eyes narrowed as he waited for Otto's reply.

'I have spoken to Mary, and to my son and we have agreed,' Otto paused in an attempt to embroider the agony in his words, 'we have agreed, we have no option. I would ask only, Herr Urban, that you remember, Mary Caslav is not a well woman and that...'

'Yes, yes, Mannerheim.' Urban waved his hand at what were, to him, tedious mumblings. 'When?'

'This Sunday, 10.00am.' Otto replied.

'Good, very good. I will of course escort you and your daughter-in-law to the checkpoint and there we will do the exchange.'

'I want to see papers for the child first.'

'My dear Herr Mannerheim,' Urban's tone had changed abruptly and now carried the old familiar sarcasm, 'do you not trust me?' Horst Urban did not wait for a reply but stood up and moved around the desk. 'I want to meet her.'

'Meet who?'

'The girl! The girl!' The aggression had returned. 'Get her!'

'I am afraid that is not possible, she is sleeping.'

'I don't give a damn what she's doing, bring her to me now, or shall I order my men to fetch her?'

Ruth did not feel fear. She thought she would, when Otto appeared at her door and told her, she thought she would. But she did not. In a way she wanted to meet him.

At the door Otto took her arm. 'Don't worry, it's not you he wants.'

Ruth stopped. 'I want to go in alone.' She turned to Otto. 'Don't you see, Otto? He wants to intimidate me, make me squirm. Well to hell with that.'

'Ruth please, do not provoke him.'

*

'So, you are the daughter of the Jew Mary Caslav?' Urban walked towards her. 'Tell me, Jew, what is it like to return to hell?'

Urban's lips curled as he spoke, contorted as they were by his sickly grin. Ruth made no attempt to reply. 'What's the matter, Jew, are you too frightened to speak?' Urban reached and gripped her face. 'Come on, Jew, you can talk.' He shook her head as he spoke.

Ruth pulled back. 'I'm not frightened to talk to you, in fact I want to talk to you.' Her words surprised him and the smirk vanished. 'You see, Herr Urban, for most of my life I have lived in a civilised country. I've never really met a true bastard before. Oh, and you can call me Jew all you like, you see I'm proud of my faith. Yes, I'm a Jew and I'm damned proud of it so you just keep calling me it you ignorant little man. Nazi Germany is dead!'

Urban's hand had been quick. In fact, so quick, Ruth had not even seen it coming but it struck her face with such force that the blow sent her backwards and she fell against the chair and then to the floor. 'I see, in your so-called civilised country they do not teach Jews their place.' Urban's eyes blazed hatred. 'You have that same arrogant way as that whore of a mother of yours.' He moved menacingly towards her. 'Well, she learnt what to do to survive and she's going to have to learn all over again when I get her back here.' He laughed. 'What do you think of that, high and mighty Jew?'

Ruth pulled herself to her feet. 'Is that all you are good for, Urban? Knocking women about?'

'No! But I do excel at it.' He moved closer again. 'Would you like me to demonstrate?'

'I don't think that would be a good idea, Urban.' Otto's voice stopped Urban almost in his tracks.

'Keep out of this!' he screamed.

'Do you want the mother, Urban, or the daughter?'

Ruth could almost see the man's mind working.

'This was a mistake, Jew,' Urban snarled, 'a mistake for which your mother will pay!'

*

Wilhelm recognised the young man dressed in the blue uniform of the East German Custom Guard and smiled. 'How are you, Jürgen?' he asked.

The young man looked concerned. 'Well, doctor, and you?' Before Wilhelm could answer, the man had taken his arm and had pulled him to one side.

'What are you doing crossing over, doctor? Are you sure your papers are in order?'

Wilhelm nodded. He had known Jürgen since he was a young boy and had treated most of his family, in particular his mother who suffered from a mild heart complaint. 'Don't worry, Jürgen,' Wilhelm replied quietly. 'Everything is in order.'

The young man looked relieved. 'My mother needs her prescription,' he whispered.

Wilhelm could detect the urgency in his voice. 'I will do what I can,' he replied.

'Reason for visit?' The Vopo at the desk obviously wore the green uniform of the East German People's Police with pride. He was immaculately turned out and his almost chiselled features showed no emotion whatsoever as he pursued his line of questioning.

'Medical!' Wilhelm replied abruptly.

'What do you mean?' the man asked.

'I would have thought that was obvious,' Wilhelm barked back, refusing to be intimidated. 'I am a doctor and I have patients on the East and I will not be deterred from doing my duty by them.'

'You have a twelve-hour pass. Do not exceed it.' The man handed Wilhelm back his papers. It was 7.45am on Thursday 17th August.

Having passed through the frontier formalities, Wilhelm made his way quickly across the street and into the drab coffee bar where Otto was waiting. Neither man acknowledged the other. Wilhelm ordered a coffee and drank it hastily. Within minutes both men had left and were on their way out of Berlin.

'Are they well?' Wilhelm asked as the car left the grey buildings of the metropolis in the distance.

'I think so,' Otto replied. 'The local doctor is an old friend; he has visited twice this week.' Otto shrugged. 'He seems happy enough.'

'Good, then if he is right it has been arranged for Saturday night.'

Otto swung the car off the main autoroute and on to the road to the village. 'Has Scholtze made all the arrangements?' he asked, as he steered the car along the narrow lane.

'Don't worry, Otto. We will have a team on our side and

the wire will be cut. All you have to do is be in the right place at the right time and run like hell.'

Otto braked hard to avoid a tractor that had emerged unannounced from a gap in the hedgerow. 'It would help if I knew the right place.'

Wilhelm took out a cigarette and lit it. 'Between Neukölln and Treptow.' He let the inhaled smoke drift from his mouth. 'The undergrowth is thick there and it is not so well guarded.'

'And the time?'

'At exactly 10.00pm, that's when the guards change.'

*

Ruth threw her arms around Wilhelm and hugged him. 'I have a letter for you,' he said pushing it into her hand. 'Now where is your son?'

Wilhelm spent only three hours at the house; he wanted to be back at the crossing with enough spare time to avert any suspicion. It was essential that the guards had no reason to believe he had been anywhere other than Berlin. During his stay he examined Ruth and the baby and was satisfied that both would be fit to make the crossing on Saturday. It was during the drive back to the city that Wilhelm mentioned Urban. 'Scholtze is concerned about Urban.' As Otto said nothing in reply Wilhelm continued. 'He asked me to tell you that in his opinion the South America treatment is recommended.' Wilhelm saw Otto frown. 'Look, Otto, I said I would help and I have. But I'm a doctor, for Christ's sake, I'm meant to save lives not pass on messages which I'm sure might result in the opposite.' Otto just drove on.

*

Ruth had opened Friedrich's letter as soon as the two men had left and now fumbled desperately with the flimsy paper in her attempt to read its contents. The familiar handwriting caused her to smile.

My darling Ruth,

Will you ever forgive me for leaving you alone? I wanted everything to be so right for you when the baby came. Instead you had to cope on your own.

How is my son? I love you both so much. Even though I have not seen him yet, already he is a part of me. We will get you both out, my darling, very soon. Do not worry I promise that everything is being arranged. The waiting must be agony for you, I'm so sorry. Just keep telling yourself that in a few days we will be together and back in England with our son.

I love you, my darling, kiss my son for me.
Friedrich

Ruth folded the paper carefully and returned it to the envelope. He had been careful with his words. No reference to how or when they would be together, just that they would be together. He was right. It was agony for her, but she knew it was just as bad, if not worse, for Friedrich. He was blaming himself for their predicament, that was obvious, and he must desperately want to see his son, but it was not only that, she knew he would be feeling utterly useless.

*

Friedrich spread the map out on Scholtze's desk. 'We will be here.' He banged his finger several times on the map.

'We will arrive from different directions at different times. We don't want to attract the attention of the Vopos. But whatever happens we must all be in position no later than 9.30pm.' He looked at Scholtze. 'Have you arranged the transport?'

'Yes, Wilhelm, and I will bring the Jeep.'

'And uniforms, do you have the uniforms?'

'They are here.' Scholtze removed three uniforms from the suitcase that had been lying beside him. 'I'm the sergeant,' he grinned.

Friedrich turned to Wilhelm. 'The ambulance?'

'All arranged, Friedrich. It will be waiting less than two streets away and we will be in radio contact. God willing it won't be needed.'

Friedrich sat down. It was late, well past 11.00pm and it was Friday 18th August. In twenty-four hours, if all went well, he would have her back.

*

For most East Germans, Saturday 19th August was just another day. True it was the start of a second weekend during which the frontier was closed. But for the millions who lived outside Berlin, that would not change their lives. For the Mannerheim family, however, it was to be the most important day of their lives. It would, God willing, bring them together again. The day would also prove to be significant for a young Vopo named Fritz Dike. He would carry the memory of it to his grave.

*

Ruth woke early that morning to find Otto was already up, dressed and busy organising things.

'I have much to do today, Ruth. We will leave at 7.30pm. Make sure you bring only the minimum and give the baby that powder Wilhelm gave you just before we leave.' Ruth nodded. She hated the idea of giving him the powder but knew it was necessary.

At 2.00pm Ruth heard the door slam and from the library she watched Otto make his way off across the fields towards Carl Kahler's cottage.

'Carl, I need your help,' Otto said as Kahler opened the heavy oak door, 'I am going to the West tomorrow.' Kahler looked surprised. 'I am leaving you in charge of the house and there are things you need to know. Please come with me.' As he waited for the man to put on his boots Otto asked after Gitta and was pleased to learn that she and the children had gone to visit her mother.

Ruth heard both men return to the house and from the top of the stairs watched as Otto led Kahler down to the cellar.

'I have hidden several works of art down here,' he said as the two men made their way down the stone steps. Otto opened a small heavy door at the end of the dimly lit room and turning on the light gestured to Kahler to lead the way. He did so but once inside Otto pulled a pistol from his pocket and waited for the man to turn. It took only seconds.

'It must have been you Carl,' he lifted the pistol, 'after all, it was only you and Gitta who knew about the baby. Why did you do it? Why did you tell Urban about Ruth and the baby?'

Kahler could not hide the fear in his eyes, but his hatred for Otto and his capitalist ways gave him the courage to reply.

'All this is not right! I have more right to this house, this land, than you,' he hissed. 'My father had more right to it! You worked him to death, that's what you did, and all for a stinking cottage and a pittance.'

'Your father drank himself to death, Carl, you can't blame me for that!' Otto backed towards the door. 'If you think you will get all this when I'm gone then you are a fool. This place will go to the hierarchy, to the evil-minded men in high places. You, my friend, well I pity you. There is water and food on the floor. I will make sure somebody knows where you are.' Otto moved through the door and slammed it shut. He knew that, as strong as Carl was, he would remain safely entombed until he sent word of where he was.

'What have you done with him?' Ruth asked.

'He's all right,' Otto replied as he locked the door in the hall that led to the cellar. 'I'll tell them where he is when we are safely in the West.' It was now 2.45pm.

Otto knew the next part of his plan had to be timed just right. It had to be left until the last possible minute. As the afternoon wore on, he became increasingly agitated and so did Ruth. Every minute seemed to take an hour as they waited. Finally, as the clock struck 6.00pm, Otto got up and slipped on his jacket.

'Are we leaving now?' Ruth asked.

'No. There is something I have to do. Be ready, we will leave as soon as I return.'

*

With just under half a mile to go until the village, Otto pulled the car off the road and onto a path that led into the woods. Slowly he steered the car along the track until he was satisfied that it was hidden from the road, then he reversed it into the trees, got out, locked it and started off towards the village on foot. He used the footpath and kept to the woods. At the outskirts of the village he checked his watch; it was 6.40pm. It had taken him longer than planned. Quickly he stepped out onto the road and started to make his way towards the village centre. The early evening air had retained much of the heat of the day and as he walked Otto felt the perspiration running down the side of his face. He had covered the best part of the distance now in less than twenty minutes and the physical exertion that had been required was beginning to take its toll. There was little life in the village and he passed only one man walking his dog before he reached the alley. He turned quickly into it and there he stopped. He stood for a moment or two with his back against the wall, breathing heavily. His mouth was dry and he could feel his heart pounding against his chest. 'You were right, Friedrich,' he mumbled, 'I'm too old for this.'

Otto did not hesitate when he reached the door, in one move he had pushed it open and stepped in off the deserted street. Urban was a creature of habit; he always worked late on a Saturday and Otto had been counting on tonight not being the exception. He was right. From the foot of the stairs he could hear a typewriter, it clicked on in a laborious one-finger pattern. Quietly he climbed the stairs until he reached the landing, there he stood motionless for a moment as he stared at the glass-panelled door that remained the last obstacle barring his way to Urban's office. Taking a deep breath, he gripped the handle and pushed open the door.

'Good evening, Herr Urban.'

The little man, obviously shaken by Otto's sudden appearance, reeled back in his chair.

'Mannerheim!' the word fell involuntarily from his mouth, 'What are you...?'

'Just a visit to say goodbye,' Otto replied, his eyes searching quickly about the room. Urban's shoulder holster hung on the coat stand. It was empty. Otto pushed the door shut with his foot and at the same time pulled the pistol complete with silencer from his pocket.

'Both hands on the desk now!' Otto snapped. 'Quick!'

Urban obliged.

'Where is the pass for the baby?'

Urban shrugged. 'In my drawer here.' He made to move.

'Keep your hands on the table!' Otto commanded. Again, Urban shrugged.

'What is all this about, Mannerheim? Tomorrow you will all be free. Why this?'

'I don't trust you, Urban; there is no pass for the baby is there? You won't be happy until you've got them all, will you?'

'I told you the pass is in my desk drawer.' Again, he made to move but again Otto rebuked him.

'Did you really think we would let Mary return to you and allow you to satisfy your sick lust for revenge? Your brother killed himself, Urban, it was the one decent thing that he did in his sorry life.' Otto watched the hate rise in Urban's eyes as his words sank home. 'They will never be free while you're alive. Even though you're in the East, you will always be a threat.'

Urban's face grew pale at the significance of Otto's words.

'Don't be a bloody fool, man. I can get you to the West tonight, all three of you. I have the passes here. Let me show you, for God's sake let me show you.' Urban's voice trembled. 'You'll get nowhere if you kill me.'

'If I kill you, Urban, surely I can just take the passes?'

'I have not signed them yet. I'll do it now!' In one move Urban took his right hand from the desk, pulling the drawer open as he did so.

He would never have heard the dull thud of the pistol for the bullet had done its work before the noise could reach his ears. A perfectly round hole appeared just above the man's right eye and Otto watched as a stream of thick red blood suddenly oozed from it. Urban slumped forward, his head hitting the desk. For a second or two Otto was unable to move; he stood looking at the body. Half of the back of Urban's head was now decorating the wall behind where he had been sitting, and the blood was slowly forming a sticky pool that covered most of the desk.

Death is seldom pretty.

Otto moved quickly. He pulled open the desk drawer and took out Urban's automatic pistol. There were no passes. He had not expected there to be. At the front door he waited for a moment then opened it slightly. The street was clear. He checked his watch: it was 7.10pm.

*

Otto was still short of breath and sweating heavily when he reached the house.

'You're late for God's sake! Where have you been?' Ruth looked at him. 'Christ, Otto, what have you done?' He ignored the question.

'Are you ready?' She nodded. 'Then fetch the baby; we must go now!'

At the bend in the drive Otto stopped the car and looked back. It would be the last time he would see his home and he knew it. Ruth saw his face and knew his pain but she said nothing. There was nothing to say. It was 7.55pm when, for the last time, Otto swung the car out between the gates at the entrance to the estate and onto the road.

*

'There are no road checks until we reach Berlin,' Otto said, 'but if stopped, our story is simple. You are a Professor of German from Oxford University. You are on holiday here and we are going to dinner with some friends at the Humboldt University. Germans are always impressed by academics.' He was speaking quickly, struggling to remain calm.

'What about the baby?' Ruth jerked her thumb over her shoulder at her son asleep on the back seat.

'Cover him with your coat and hope.'

It was 9.05pm when they reached the outskirts of Berlin and Otto grew increasingly concerned with every mile. There were armed troops everywhere and it seemed as if every one of them was looking at them.

'Sooner or later we are going to be stopped,' he said.

'I'm not sure, Otto,' Ruth replied, 'there can't be many Mercedes in the East, they may think we are important.'

Otto swung the car right towards the River Spree. 'Shit!'

Ruth ignored the curse; the large wooden barrier across the road had taken all her attention.

'Cover him up!' Otto shouted.

'Can't we turn around?'

'Not now, it's too late.' He stopped the car. Two Vopos, both heavily armed, sauntered over to them.

'Where are you going?' asked one in a broad Berlin accent.

'Humboldt University,' Otto snapped, 'and we're late.'

The young policeman looked taken aback.

'Why are you crossing the river here? You would do better if you crossed further up, at Gruner Strasse perhaps?'

Otto leant out of the window. 'Young man, I have been driving around Berlin all my life, I know exactly where I'm going. Now if you would like to explain to the principle of the university and the government dignitaries that their guest speaker is late because of your stupid roadblock then you may get in the back and accompany us the rest of the way.'

The policeman shrugged. 'Stay away from the frontier, the guards have orders to shoot on sight.' He moved over to the barrier and lifted it. Otto half-waved as they drove away. It was 9.20pm when they crossed the River Spree and turned right towards Treptow.

On this side of the river the area was more rural and the closer they got to Treptow, the fewer houses there were. Ruth noticed that Otto was driving faster now and that worried her.

'Otto, you are driving too fast, it will attract attention.'

He looked at his watch. 'Ruth! We have less than twenty minutes to make it to the crossing point. I have to drive fast.'

Less than five minutes later Otto pulled the car to a halt at a bend in the road and turned off the lights.

'This is it,' he said; he pointed to an old barn about fifty yards away. 'A hundred yards beyond that barn is the wire. Two hundred yards beyond that is the West.' Putting the car back in gear he drove it slowly off the road and into the trees. 'From now on, Ruth, say nothing. Just follow me and do what you are told.' He lifted the baby from the car and handed him to her, 'God bless you both.'

Ruth obeyed. At the edge of the treeline he stopped and looked up and down the road, then he looked at his watch: it was 9.47pm.

'Now, come on quickly.' Otto grabbed her arm and together they ran across the road and down into the ditch on the other side. Ruth felt her feet sink into water. 'From here to the barn we must crawl.' He pointed to a large observation post that stood less than 300 yards away to their right. 'Show me your face.' Ruth looked at him. Otto took a tin of boot polish from his pocket and quickly smeared it on her face and then his. 'Come on, we must go now.' It was 9.51pm.

Ruth's knees hurt like hell as she crawled across the hard earth and it was difficult trying to keep on her knees and hold the baby. Otto, following behind, soon realised her difficulty and took the baby from her. 'Quickly,' he whispered, 'keep going.'

Eventually they reached the barn and stopped at a large hole in its wooden structure. Otto pushed Ruth through it and into the darkness. The strong smell of cow's muck struck her as she stumbled to her feet.

*

Fritz Dike knew he shouldn't, but to hell with it. He took a cigarette from the pack and, shielding his lighter under his jacket, lit it. It was 9.55pm and normally he would have been off duty in five minutes. But he had drawn the short straw. A double shift. It was happening more and more nowadays with such an area to guard. It was commonplace to have to do a straight eight hours without a break. He cupped the cigarette in his hand and moved to the edge of the tower. From his perch forty feet up, he could easily see the lights and the people in the West. For the past three days he had watched them and often he had thought how easy it would be for him to cross. A routine inspection of the wire, that's all it would take. A stroll across to the second tripwire, one easy step over it. Inspect the barbed wire beyond. Cut it and then run like fuck. If you were lucky your mates would hesitate about shooting you and you would be free. He puffed hard on the cigarette. But then there was his mother. What would they do to her? Suddenly the light on top of the tower came on as did several mounted on poles along the fence. It was the first time they had worked all week.

Inside the barn Otto and Ruth suddenly found themselves silhouetted against the light that impregnated the old building in a multitude of areas.

'Jesus!' Otto instinctively pulled her down. 'What are they playing at? This place is not meant to be lit yet.'

Ruth looked at him. 'What are we going to do?' she whispered.

Otto moved over to the wall and through one of the slots in the timbers looked up at the tower. He checked his watch. It was 10.00pm.

Ruth followed him over, the baby still asleep in her arms.

'We have one chance when the guard changes, it will be any minute now, then we make a run for it. Do you see the fence post there?' He pointed through the crack. 'The one closest to that ditch. That's where the wire is cut. Come on.' Otto pushed her out of the hole in the barn wall and together they crawled around the building keeping it between them and the tower. At the far side of the barn he checked his watch again. Still no sign of the guard change. He looked at the hundred yards of open ground that lay between them and fence. Then he looked to the left. The next tower was nearly half a mile away; that would be no problem. His mind raced. They had to go, they had to try. 'Get down in the grass and stay low. If we are spotted before the fence, stand up and hold up your arms. If we make the fence and you are through before they see us, stop for no one, just run. We will get cover from the other side.' He pushed her forward.

Ruth found the grass easier going than the hard mud. In the barn she had tied the baby's shawl around her and the little one now hung strapped to her chest.

*

From their Jeep, less than twenty yards from the fence on the West side, Friedrich and Scholtze watched in horror. The lights had not been working up to now, it was a cruel twist of fate that had brought them into operation tonight. Through binoculars they could just make out the two shapes moving towards the fence.

'Surely he's not still going to try?' Friedrich said. 'For God's sake, Father, go back,' he whispered to himself.

'We must help them,' Scholtze said calmly. He took the bottle of Scotch he had been saving to drink with Otto from beneath his seat and opened it.

'Hey, Vopo,' Scholtz's gravel voice rang out across the silence. 'Why don't you come over and have a drink with us?' Scholtze held the bottle above his head and staggered towards the fence. 'Come on, I will meet you in the middle.'

Fritz Dike watched with some amusement as the soldier on the West paraded up and down the fence.

Otto had also heard the voice and had recognised it instantly. He wasted no time in taking advantage of his friend's diversion. Quickly he moved passed Ruth, telling her to stay down but keep moving, and he ran ahead almost bent double until he reached the wire. He had managed to pull most of it aside by the time Ruth reached him, and the pair of them lay together flat in the grass as they got their breath.

'There is a tripwire about fifty or so yards in and then more barbed wire,' he whispered. 'The barbed wire should be cut for us and I will pull it clear for you but you will have to stand up and step over the tripwire first. If you don't and you pull it, all hell will break loose.'

'Oh God, Otto, what are we doing?' Ruth looked at him, 'If we don't make…'

Otto put his finger to her lips. 'Crawl to the wire, go!'

Ruth did not argue; she went through the gap in the wire and started to crawl forward.

'Why don't you piss off to bed?' Dike shouted back, 'You will get yourself shot if you are not careful.'

'But who will shoot me?' Scholtze slurred. 'It is not me they will shoot, my friend, it is you. They will shoot you if you try to cross, not me!'

Dike did not bother to answer; he had heard a car pull up behind him and, seeing it was his sergeant and a Russian officer, quickly stubbed out what was left of his cigarette. Scholtze saw them too.

'What is going on here?' the officer shouted up. Dike snapped to attention. 'He's drunk, sir.'

'Get back from the wire!' the officer shouted.

'Go fuck yourself,' Scholtze shouted back.

Ruth was now in the full brightness of the searchlights and was moving as quickly as she could. She could hear Otto close behind her and she could see the tripwire no more than twenty yards in front of her. She could also hear the soldiers and Scholtze in the distance. When she reached the wire, she stopped and waited for Otto to move up beside her.

'When I tell you, get up step over the wire and run. Don't look back, just run. I will be behind you. When we get to the barbed wire, stand back, I will pull it to one side. When it's clear, stop for nothing, just run. You will have about a hundred yards of open ground and then the last fence. Someone else will pull that aside for us.' Otto rolled onto his back and pulled Urban's automatic pistol from his under his coat. 'Whatever happens, Ruth, don't stop.' He looked towards the tower, 'Go!'

Fritz Dike was the first to see the two figures in the middle of no-man's land and well towards the second wire. The Russian officer was second.

'Halt!' shouted the officer. 'Halt or we fire!' Neither stopped. 'Fire at them!' the officer shouted at Dike. 'Fire at them now!'

Otto was pulling back the barbed wire fence when the first of Dike's bullets kicked up dirt less than three yards from them.

'Go on!' he shouted as the wire parted and in a second Ruth was through and Otto behind her. Both now had a hundred yards in front of them to reach the last fence.

Scholtze took the machine gun from his shoulder and sent a hail of bullets in the direction of the tower before dropping to the ground for cover. Friedrich started the Jeep and swung it round, driving for all his worth towards the point where they would come through. Fritz Dike fell to the floor of the tower with a bullet in his leg and the Russian officer and Dike's sergeant made off towards the hole in the fence.

Otto and Ruth kept running.

Dike had never felt such pain before. Why did they shoot him, didn't they realise he could have hit the two runners anytime he wanted? He was missing them on purpose, for fuck's sake! He moaned in pain as he pulled himself to his feet. Well, if they wanted to shoot to kill, he would do the same. He peered over the edge of his tower and spotted Scholtze still belly down in the dirt and firing at the Russian. Dike took aim and squeezed. The bullet hit Scholtze square in the top of the head. Dike now looked at the runners; both were less than thirty yards from the second fence. He took aim again.

Ruth thought her lungs were going to burst. But she did not stop.

The fence was getting closer. She could hear Otto's heavy footsteps behind her.

'Go on, Ruth, keep going, you're nearly there!' he shouted.

For the first time her son started to cry.

Dike's second shot hit Otto high in the back. The bullet passed through his right lung before shattering a rib and blowing a huge hole in the front of his chest. Ruth heard him cry and fall. She stopped.

'Otto!' she screamed turning back, 'Otto!' She fell down beside him. 'Come on,' she cried pulling at his arm. 'We're nearly there, come on.'

He looked up and Ruth watched in horror as the blood ran from his mouth.

'Go on, Ruth,' he gasped, 'For God's sake, go on, don't let me fail her again.'

Ruth stood up and looked around her. She could see the two soldiers running towards her from the East. She looked to the West. The wire was still there, only a few yards from her but it was still there.

She was trapped.

Dike levelled his rifle for the third time and took aim. The second runner was making no attempt to move. Now, standing upright, and in the searchlights, he saw that the other runner was a woman. Through the telescopic lens of the rifle he saw her clearly; she was holding what looked like a baby! He waited. Surely, she must try now, she was nearly there. Dike had not enlisted for this! He had probably killed two German citizens, and for what? Was he now to kill a woman and her baby?

Friedrich drove the Jeep straight through the wire and round in front of Ruth, letting go a burst of automatic fire as he did so. The Russian officer fell.

'Get in!' he shouted, grabbing her and throwing her and his son into the Jeep. 'Get down in the back!'

Ruth got down and pushed the baby under the seat. Friedrich lifted his father up and dragged him to the Jeep, pushing him into the back with Ruth. Suddenly bullets flew around them as the sergeant opened fire.

Friedrich fired back. In less than twenty seconds he had killed two men, in less than thirty, he was back in the West. Dike had not fired a third time.

Ruth tried desperately to stem the flow of blood from Otto's chest, pushing her hand hard against the wound. But the blood oozed through her fingers as she cradled his head on her bloodstained lap.

'Just hold on, Otto,' she cried. 'We'll be at the hospital soon.'

Otto groaned.

'For Christ's sake, Friedrich, do something!' Ruth screamed at him from the back of the Jeep. 'He's dying, do something!' She looked down at the contorted face that lay in her arms. Suddenly Otto's eyes opened, the grimace of pain gone from his face.

'Tell them,' he whispered, 'tell them, this time Otto Mannerheim got you out.' She felt him grip her arm. 'Tell Mary,' he smiled as the life slipped from him.

Once in the ambulance, Wilhelm fought desperately to save his friend's life. But it was to no avail, the wound was terrible and Otto Mannerheim could not be revived.

Five men had died that night, three of them in the tangled mess that was to become the Berlin Wall. On a piece of wasteland that lay between Neukölln in the West and Treptow in the East, they played their part in a tragedy of life. The burden of responsibility for that and all the countless deaths that followed must be carried by many. But in real life, only those that lived through it will pick up the load.

The price of freedom will always come high.

EPILOGUE

Otto Mannerheim and Herr Scholtze were both buried at the Friedrichsfelde Cemetery in West Berlin. The funerals were attended by city dignitaries including the Chancellor and the Mayor of West Berlin and several Jewish leaders. Hundreds of West Berliners lined the streets.

Joseph and Elizabeth attended the funeral: their one and only visit to Germany. They stayed two nights at the hospital with Mary where they felt safe, before returning to England. They accepted only a small income from the trust, and despite their access to its huge wealth, spent their lives in their ground-floor flat in Hampstead. They both enjoyed their visits to Harrow and meeting Mary there. Joseph died from a heart attack on 12th October 1982. Elizabeth, unable to deal with her grief, died on Christmas Day the same year.

Fritz Dike, the young East German soldier manning the watchtower on that fateful night, struggled to come to terms with the fact that he had shot the two German citizens, Otto Mannerheim and Herr Scholtze. After weeks of turmoil he went AWOL from the army. He returned to his village and in a local wood placed his service revolver in his mouth and pulled the trigger.

Mary Caslav remained at the hospital and under Wilhelm's care. She lived to see all four of her grandchildren born. She would visit Ruth and Friedrich three times a year and they would often travel to Berlin to see her. She died in her sleep in May 1971.

After the fall of the Berlin Wall in November 1991, at the age of fifty-eight, Ruth returned with Friedrich and their children to file a claim on the Mannerheim estate. The claim was upheld by the German court and the property and its land was reinstated to them. With the help of Gitta Kahler they restored the property to its former glory. Gitta, now a widow, took on the role of head housekeeper. Otto Mannerheim Junior took on the role of estate manager of his late grandfather's estate. The whole family returned to live on the estate and run their business interests from there.

Ruth went on to be a prominent businesswoman, speaking at the Institute of Directors at the Albert Hall in 1981. She was decorated for her work for the Jewish Holocaust Movement and dedicated much of her time to fighting for the rights of others. She died on the 10th August 2017 at the age of eighty-four. Friedrich still lives with his family in Germany and celebrated his eighty-eighth birthday this year. He remains the owner of the house in Harrow and the flat in London where he had decorated their first Christmas tree, and they had first made love.